SERIAL KILLER

BY

JAMES NEWBURRY

PublishAmerica
Baltimore

First printing

ISBN: 1-59129-279-4
PUBLISHED BY PUBLISHAMERICA, LLLP
www.publishamerica.com
Baltimore

Printed in the United States of America

***

FOR MY FAMILY

***

CHAPTER ONE

Sitting across the street and down the block from the white, two-story home, he waited for his prey to return home. He was driving a Ford sedan instead of his usual BMW, Mercedes, Corvette or Jaguar. The sedan allowed him to blend in better with his surroundings, amongst what was a middle class section in the Los Angeles suburbs.

It was 5:35 p.m. They should be home soon. The Donaldsons. The occupants of the object of his stakeout. They were running late and it was a few hours past their usual arrival time. They probably had a flat tire or some other type of breakdown. But it made no difference. It was their house, they would have to show up sooner or later. It wasn't like they were expecting him and were staying away. No one ever expected him.

Watching and waiting, he reclined back into the soft driver's seat. It wasn't exactly first class, but it would do for now. Fussing about until he was comfortable, he watched the Donaldson's home with great anticipation. Soon he would be joining their life essences with his own, thus raising him one step closer toward his goal. An all mighty power, more powerful than the Lord himself. The time was coming, but there was still quite a ways to go. He knew that it was going to be a long night before this next step in his ascenion could begin.

***

A maroon mini van rounded the corner up ahead; it was them. He knew that mother Donaldson would not let him down. She was just running late. But here she was now, with her brood. Donaldson parked the van in the driveway of the house that he had been watching for weeks, now. Her two boys bolted from the sliding cargo door on the passenger side. They ran directly into the front yard and began tossing an old football around. Just as they had done yesterday, the day before that and the two weeks before that.

The Mrs. left the van and walked around to the passenger side, freeing her youngest child from her car seat harness. Then secured the van door, before heading for the house. She held the hand of her youngest. Three years old, or so, he guessed. She led her by the hand to the front door of the house. Letting her baby girl inside, she looked back at the boys in the front yard.

"You boys come inside and do your homework. Then, you can play ball."

He lipsynced her every word, as she uttered them. Again, they were so predictable and it had all gone to by the letter, thus far. Except of course for their late arrival. They seemed to hold a patent on monotony and this continued with the boys. The younger brother threw one more pass, before grabbing his backpack and heading inside, with his big brother right behind him.

He relaxed in his seat and waited for dad Donaldson to come home. The seat was warm and comfortable and he began to fade off into a half sleep, where memories of his own parents, began drifting through his semi-consciousness.

His mother, a former super model, had quit her dream job once she had become pregnant with him to give to him a stable home life, and had no regrets in doing so. She was the kindest, gentlest woman. Very caring and giving, devoted and loved him with all her heart. And was she ever so beautiful. A five foot-eight brunette with the deepest blue eyes, like the waters of the ocean itself. She was truly a vision.

A year and a half before she had become pregnant with him, she had fallen in love with, and married his father. A shipping tycoon, restauranteur, night club owner, hotel magnate, and owner of five other fortune five hundred companies. They lived in the lap of luxury in their gigantic Beverly Hills mansion. With security in mind, his father had a fifteen-foot high, brick privacy wall installed that completely surrounded the house and its grounds. It was topped off with razor wire all around and a solid iron gate, to keep out the world.

A brigade of servants lived within the walls as well. Servants to tend to his familys' every want and need. But it was his mother who was always there for him. Whether it be a scraped knee or as a partner to escort him for a walk out in the enormous gardened backyard, or just someone to read him his favorite bed time story, she was there. He had always looked up to her, both figuratively and literally speaking. It wasn't until he was well into his teens that he was finally able to look her squarely in the eyes, without the need of a chair or her loving embrace.

More often than not, he and his mother would dine alone, being that his father was always off tending to his many businesses. And it wasn't very often that they would venture out of their fortress-like walled in home out into the real world, for an occasional restaurant dinner. But no matter where they were, there were the bodyguards, multitudes of them. They were scattered throughout the inner grounds and inside the mansion. It seemed like they were everywhere. It had all been arranged by his father, for their personal protection. Because of their royalty-like wealth.

When at home he simply played around them and hardly even noticed them, really. When outside the walls of home he was always focused on the beauties and the coarsness of the outside world. A world far different from that which he was accustomed to and it scared him at first, but as he grew older the fear turned into intrigue and wonder and the people of the City of Angels began to interest him. His excitement grew with each outing, though they were few and far between. But still, soon he could not wait to be a part of it all. Yet he remained behind the walls of the fortress he called home.

***

The shutting of a car door broke his state of meditation. It was now 7:15 and there in the driveway of the Donaldson home set a dark blue sedan much like his own, next to the min van, already there. Daddy was home. By the time his eyes focused, Donaldson was inside the home with the door closing behind him.

He stretched a bit. Now their bright, happy little family was complete. It would be just a matter of time now before the night would be at it's blackest. Somewhere around the witching hour, when the neighborhood would be asleep. Then he would venture out and do his bidding. But for now, it was back to his meditation and the further recalling of his past.

***

Though it was a rarity that his father had the time to spend with him, and they saw so very little of each other, he always had been, and still was, quite fond of the man that he called father. It was just that his father was not the typical 9:00 to 5:00 kind of guy. His many business titles kept him a very busy man. Though his father was not as available to him as his mother was, When there was time to spend together, he was a very playful man, for being such a straight laced, top-notch business man.

At times, though very rare, his father would have consecutive days when he could spend time with him and his mother, from dawn 'til dusk. But again, those days were few and far between. Most of the time his father would be called away on business, only shortly after their time together had begun. There were many missed birthdays. Not only his, but his mother's and father's, as well. His first steps, his first words, missed all in the name of business.

At least he was always home for Christmas, Thanksgiving and New Years. Three days out of each year that he knew his father would be home. With a party on New Years Eve. They always let him stay up until midnight, when they would all three share a warm embrace of love, to ring in the New Year. A time that was shortly lived. Then he would once again begin waiting for Thanksgiving to come back around. That was how he had become so diligent in his waiting. Diligence brought about patience. Patience, brought about caution. Caution kept him elusive. And elusiveness kept him alive and from being caught.

In his adolescent and teenage years he had spent most of his time behind the prison walls of home. Whatever he wanted or needed was brought in to him. He had been home schooled by private tutors, taught proper manners and behavior by his many nannies. He was taught to be a gentleman, nothing less. His martial arts instructors not only taught him the fine arts of hand to hand combat, but instilled in him a sense of honor and discipline. To be strong, both mentally and physically. Well molding his mind and body.

Even most of his entertainment was funneled in from the outside. Friends of the family would drop by now and then with their children, for play dates and birthday parties. He was only allowed to watch so much television and even then, the programs were pre-selected by his mother. After his school work was done he would spend a good portion of his day reading. Only the classics, however. No Stephen King or Dean Koontz, and he was definitely not allowed to read any comic book tripe. Educated in classical piano, he spent many a nights entertaining his mother and some of the help, all the while imagining himself in the outside world. Not just existing, behind the towering walls of home, but living in the City of Angels. Living by his own rules, fulfilling his own dreams and desires.

***

2:00 a.m.

The Donaldson home was dark, just like all of the others on the block. The street, deserted. The entire neighborhood enshrouded under the cover of the blackened sky, the moon barely a slit to the eye. The only light being that from the street lamps, which did not intrude into the boundaries of the homes perimeters. It was time. His heart jumped a bit, elated. They would all be asleep now, snuggled cozy in there beds, the Sandman having already come and gone.

Leaving the sedan he crept down and across the street. His head was on a swivel, making sure that the night was empty, himself being the only exception. He didn't need to be seen by some insomniac, who later could become a witness.

Reaching the Donaldson's home unnoticed, he stepped over the quaint, thigh high white picket fence and scurried across the front lawn over to the side of the house, hiding behind some high hedges, there. Satisfied that he had not been seen he began to disrobe, dropping his clothes' to the ground. Once completely nude he reached into his pants pocket and removed a pair of surgical gloves. After pulling them on he retrieved a small metal wedge from the other pants pocket, using it to pry open a window that he stood directly under.

The wood of the sill and the window frame, both began to crack and splinter. Only seconds after which, the lock at the top of the frame gave way, the window opening up wide and easy. Soundlessly. He slithered his way inside, entering into the darkness of what he figured to be the family room. This room he chose for later use, when the ritual would begin. He removed some pictures from an otherwise empty wall, further preparing for the ritual that was soon to come.

Scouring through the pitch blackness of the home's lower layout, he finally found the kitchen where he quietly searched through the drawers until he found the knife drawer, from which he extracted a ten-inch bladed butcher knife. Dragging the blade across the counter top to check it's sharpness, the steel cut deeply into the laminate with very little force applied. It was good enough, he thought.

Skillfully navigating through the darkness he found the staircase where he made his way to the second floor. He had expected a squeaky stair or two, but dad Donaldson ran a tight ship. All of the little things that usually go wrong with a house over the years appeared to be fixed and or prevented.

Creeping down the hallway he came upon the first door, which set at his right. He turned the knob and pushed a bit. The door swung open wide, without any annoying squeak. Thanks, Dad. He moved further into the room. It was the boys' room. They lay nestled in their twin beds, nine feet apart, blissfully asleep. He had always wanted children. Boys. He had watched as these boys played in the front yard on several occasions, tossing around the football and wrestling. Their dad, spraying them with a hose. But alas, he had never found anyone special enough to share his life with. Therefore, he could only be a father in his mind.

Standing beside the eldest child's bed he stared down at the pre-teen, so innocent and peaceful. Lowering his hand he covered the boy's mouth and before the kid could even open his eyes, he fiercely plunged the knife down into his stomach, twisting the blade. The boy's screams went unheard throughout their duration, which wasn't long. Thus, his little brother remained asleep and the rest of the household remained undisturbed.

He walked over to the younger boy's bed, covering his mouth, as well. Then buried the knife deep into his abdomen, cutting his way up to the sternum. Gutting him like a downed deer. The boy's eyelids never even fluttered.

His pre-ritual was well underway. Leaving the boy's grisly remains behind, he walked further down the hallway, coming to the next room, also on his right. The door was not shut all the way so he just gave it a bit of a push and it opened wide. It was the parents' room and he wasted no time in moving to the bedside. The father's side. He looked down at the well maintained, healthy looking man of the house. Having watched him with his children and his wife he appeared to be a decent man and a good provider. Oh, how he envied him. Oh, how he hated him. He and his perfect little family.

He lowered his hand to cover Donaldson's mouth, just an instant before shoving the ten inch blade down into his heart. He didn't make a sound and his wife, still more than half asleep, rolled on to her side facing the opposite direction. The husbands never made a sound and the wives never woke up, he knew from past endeavors.

Extracting the blade from Donaldson's chest he moved around to the mother's side of the bed. She was a very beautiful woman and very affectionate toward her husband and their children. Attentive, so he had noticed from the weeks of watching them. She reminded him of his mother. He slid the knife blade flat, under her neck. She even kind of looked like his mother, and was oh so very beautiful, he thought.

In one quick, continuous motion he turned the sharp edge of the blade to her neck and planted his free hand on the side of her head, holding it in place. She opened her eyes just in time to see the intruder, but not soon enough to scream. He drug the blade deeply across her neck, from side to side. Nearly severing her head from her shoulders.

The flow of blood from the wound was enormous. It soaked the bedding as it gushed from the severed arteries, like water from a hose, covering his lower body in blood. Every muscle in his body tightened in ecstasy, the blood running down from his penis to his toes. Empowering him with the essence of her life and eternal soul. She was his now. She was in him. They were one. He wanted to remain by the bedside and prolong his rapture, savoring each passing second, but there was one more worshiper to be had before the ritual could begin. And she would occupy the next room.

He left the parents room behind and headed for the daughter's room. He was leaving partially bloodied footprints on the hallway carpet, but that didn't worry him, because you can't be identified by footprints. Unless of course, you became a suspect and the local CSI divison matched those prints to yours. But that would never happen. No one in his or her right mind, would ever suspect him as being Los Angeles' most productive serial killer, ever. And more than likely in the nation. To hell with that! He was the most productive and feared killer ever, just like the media kept telling everyone.

He reached the youngest child's room, the door was not even closed. The poor thing was probably afraid of the dark so her door was left open, so that her parents could hear her call out in the night. That was more than likely why their door was ajar, as well. Such a caring family, the Donaldsons.

He entered the room, slowly. Her blood would be the most powerful of them all. The younger the blood the more powerful the essence. He moved to her bedside and looked down at her, a sleeping angel. A joyous grin crossed his sealed lips. The two boys were young and their essences powerful. But she was another, entirely unto her own. Raising the bloodied knife above her, he then forcefully plunged it down into her torso. She awoke immediately, screaming in agony and horror. He plunged the blade deep into her body again, again and again. Her piercing screams turned into a gargle of blood, then stopped. He doubted that any of the neighbors had heard anything. Her screams, though piercing, had lasted no longer than a few seconds, by his estimations.

He stared down at the small child, whose open eyes peered back at him. He reached down in a moment of composure and closed them, though not a repentant bone existed in his body.

He left her room shortly after the butchery had ended and went back downstairs to the kitchen. He lay the knife on the counter top and ransacked the lower cupboards until he found what it was that he was looking for. A simple, household mop bucket. Removing the bucket from underneath the sink, he dropped it off in the family room on his way back upstairs. It was time now to assemble his worshipers.

With the ease of five men, he carried each member of the Donaldson clan down to the family room, where he sliced them open, gutting each one like a prize buck, hastily removing their organs and leaving them in a pile in the corner of the room just behind and to the side of him. Picking up Mr. Donaldson first, he held his hollowed carcass over the bucket, with each of the other family members to follow. Stealing their blood, their life essence. When he finished draining the Donaldson's toddler daughter, he placed the girl beside her oldest brother. Positioning her like all of the others, resting in a prayer like stance. On her knees with her forehead touching the floor and her arms stretched out in front of her. With the family all together again, it was now time for the ritual to begin.

He stood between his worshipers and the blank wall he had created earlier. Nude and bloody, the bucket of their blood held in his hands. His worshipers bowing to his all powerful entity.

"You, my sixth servants. You will witness my continued rising, and know that I am your Lord," he proclaimed.

Raising the bucket above his head, he tipped it and let the blood flow out over him, covering him from head to toe. He threw the bucket to the floor and rejoiced in the unholy union of his and the family's essences. Continuing the evolution of his soul, to a plain much higher above that of mere mortals. A plain equaled to that of the gods. A level no mortal man had ever reached before.

Wiping the blood away from his eyes, he faced the blank wall and with his blood drenched hand, he wrote with broad strokes, "STALKER."

Leaving his moniker on the wall for all to see and bloodied footprints for the police and the FBI to find, he moved back upstairs and found his way to the bathroom, where he showered the blood from his body. Allowing his body to air dry while walking back toward the staircase, he stopped along the way to straighten a family portrait on the wall between rooms. He then continued on downstairs, passing through the family room where he let his worshipers set, and climbed back out the window.

He dressed himself behind the cover of the hedges, then removed the surgical gloves and shoved them into his pocket. Then, under the cover of darkness, he crept back through the night like nothing more than a shadow. Back to his awaiting sedan and drove away, unnoticed.

CHAPTER TWO

7:30 a.m.

Revered psychologist, Dr. Nancy Webb sits at the center island in her kitchen, her nose buried in the morning newspaper. A nearly empty cup of coffee and a half eaten bagel set on the counter top in front of her, as the morning news sounded off from a near by radio. Laying the paper on the counter she focused on the voice of the reporter on the air.

"Police have reported that another family of five were found slain in their home this morning, in the Los Angeles suburbs. Discovered by a neighbor only half an hour ago. Police have released a statement to the press, which verifies that the murders are indeed the work of the fiendish serial killer, known only as the Stalker.

"The names of the deceased are being with-held by police, pending notification of the next of kin. Specifics of the crime scene are still sketchy at this time. A spokeswoman for the L.A.P.D. has informed us that the integrity of this scene, as well as all the others. Is being with-held, out of an on going fear, of copycat murders... In other news today... ."

Webb turned the radio off. She didn't need the media's outlook on the scenes of the Stalker murders, because for her the integrity of these scenes and other unreleased details had already been compromised. Shortly after the murders began, she had been enlisted by the police to help in the profiling of the killer.

Although the FBI already had their own profiler on the case, the killings were still a police matter. The FBI had not officially been called in. They were merely assisting the L.A.P.D. in it's efforts to capture the Stalker. But the L.A.P.D. had enlisted her to assist them. Thus she had full access to all of the written reports, all of the crime scene photos and every other piece of evidence that they had on the Stalker Murders. Which wasn't much.

Lieutenant Josh Morrow, the detective in charge of the case for the L.A.P.D., had enlisted her just after the third set of murders. Looking for anything that the feebs profiler might have missed. But as for now, her profile was no more help than the FBI's.

At this time, the federal profiler was clinging to a list of former prisoners and mental patients that at some time or another, held a similar interest in blood that the Stalker was exhibiting now.

Meanwhile, she was mostly focused on the prayer sites, where the victims would appear to be bowing to their savior. Facing a wall where ostentatiously written, in their own blood, was the single word, STALKER.

Drinking down the last bit of coffee, she stuffed the remaining bagel in her mouth and walked outside to her candy apple red BMW. Settling in behind the steering wheel she started it's whisper quiet engine and pulled out of the driveway. She cruised through the city streets in hopes of bypassing some of the heavier freeway traffic. It was a longer route, with traffic of it's own. But she always seemed to get there on time.

Changing the radio channel continuously, she tried to find a station that was not featuring the story of the latest Stalker murders, but her only true escape was just to turn the radio off. She rounded a corner and blew past a news stand where she was sure that the front page of each news paper, had some type of headline, featuring the Stalker. But she couldn't worry about that fiend now. She had a private practice with patients to worry about, and until closing hour they would be the only thing on her mind.

***

A medium height, dark haired man, attired in a dark Armani suit, picked up a copy of the Los Angeles Times, at that very same news stand. He handed the attendant a five dollar bill and walked away. He flipped the paper over, revealing the bottom half of the front page. Skimming through the article about the renowned psychologist, Nancy Webb, whom he had just now taken into consideration as a possible threat to his anonymity.

He thoroughly examined the picture of the good doctor that accompanied the article. He found her quite striking. Blonde, mid to late forties. She was quite the intelligent one. Her reputation preceded her. He remembered reading an article on her a few years back. She had worked with a man who had eighteen personalties and inside of two and a half years she had him completely cured. The papers called her a miracle worker, the best in her field. And now she sought out the Stalker. But did she really want to find him? He was going to find out. He dropped the paper into a trash can and pulled out his cell phone, dialing the number for L.A. Information. He wore a crooked smile, cold and evil. Dr. Webb had something coming to her and he was going to make sure that she got every little bit of it.

The operator answered. "Los Angeles Information, how may I assist you?"

"Hello, I need the business address for a Dr. Nancy Webb, please." He pulled out an electronic notepad.

When the operator came back on the line she not only rattled off a street address, but a building and suite number.

"Thank you, very much. You have no idea, how helpful you've been." He slid the cell phone back into his coat pocket, along with the note pad. After, he memorized the address.

There was a grin on his face, like the cat that had just ate the canary. "All right, Miss Webb." He spoke softly, only to himself. "If you want into my mind, you've got it. But you're definitely not going to like what you find."

He would toy with her for a while and then see just how much reality she could take. He was going to take her to the threshold of his exemplary veracity then let her go and together, they would see who had the mightier intellect and determine just how far it was that she was willing to fall.

CHAPTER THREE

Stepping off of the elevator on to the fifth floor of the medical professional building. The well dressed, dark haired man roamed the halls until he found a door with the letterhead: Dr. Nancy Webb, Psychologist.

He moved inside and made his way across the somewhat small waiting room, to a glass enclosed receptionist's desk. Behind an opening in the partition sat a beautiful young brunette.

"May I help you si… ." She cut off her sentence in mid word, her eyes showing her excitement. "Aren't you—"

"Bray Hamlin." he cut her off, softly.

She broke her stare. "I'm sorry, it's just that you're a celebrity, or the closest thing to a celebrity I've ever encountered up close."

"Well thank you. I think."

"You're so charitable, and the Los Angeles' Times man of the year and, most eligible bachelor. I'm so pleased to meet you." She was star struck. "My name is Brooke May."

I really don't give a rats ass, who you are, he thought. But he smiled, anyway. "Hello, Miss May."

"Brooke, please."

"Brooke," he indulged. "I'm hoping that you can help me."

"Sure, what is it that you need. I'll certainly try my best to help."

Well, I could use a blow job, right now. He smiled politely. "I hope that you can. I'm looking to make an appointment to be seen by doctor Webb."

May frowned somewhat. "I'm sorry, but doctor Webb's schedule is booked up through next year."

Fuck! "Next year." he marveled. Maybe he should be worried with her chasing his tail. She must be a lot better than he thought. "How is that so?"

"Most of her patients are booked several sessions in advance. The average booking is six to eight months and she has quite a few clients. Even if she did have some time open, I don't think that she could fit you in. There are just too many people ahead of you."

Shit! This was not good. In fact, it fucking sucked monster cock. He had plans for the good doctor. This was no good. No good, at all. He leaned in a bit on the small counter between them and asked suggestively.

"Well Brooke, would it be possible for me to leave my name and phone number? That way if anyone were to cancel on an appointment, you could call me and I could take their place."

She frowned again. "I'm not supposed to do that. Doctor Webb only takes patients by referral."

She looked him over. He was a bit shorter than she thought he would be, but just as handsome as his picture in the Times and all of the other magazines she had seen him in. But he did appear to be a bit bulky under the suit he wore and she knew for a fact that he was one of the wealthiest men in the world. She just couldn't help herself. He was just so unbearably nice and so charitable.

"I'm really, not supposed to do this. I could get into trouble, but I will take your number and call you if anyone cancels."

"Are you sure? I don't want to get you into any trouble, not on my account." He could give a fuck.

"Don't worry about it, I can work it out with her. she's really a push over, once you hit her with puppy dog eyes. She'll crumble, I promise and I won't get into any trouble," she assured him.

As he penned his phone number, May reiterated. "Remember, though. Even if she has extra time it may be filled by an existing client. But I'll give it my best shot at giving you a chance," she promised.

Hamlin handed the piece of scratch paper given to him by May, with his phone number on it, giving her a wink. "Thank you very much, for your help. Hopefully, we'll see each other again."

"Hopefully." she tried not to sound too sixth gradish.

Suddenly, from across the room to his right the door to Webb's office opened. He looked past his shoulder at the two women standing in the office doorway. One, he recognized immediately as being Webb. But the other one, he didn't know. She was older than Webb that was unquestionable. Maybe in her late sixties. He presumed.

Webb retreated back into her office and closed the door, while the older woman made her way to the receptionist's desk.

Hamlin stepped aside and gave her clear passage to the opening in the partition.

"Same time, next week."

"Don't you mean, same time for the next six weeks, Ms. Pierce?" May returned.

"Brooke, dear. You should know by now to call me Betty." the old woman reminded her pleasantly.

Hamlin took this time to sneak out and get away from this old coot. He didn't want to have to share an elevator with her. She smelled like heavily perfumed death. He couldn't stand heavy perfume.

***

The elevator doors opened up to the ground floor lobby. Hamlin stepped off and made a B-line for the nearest pay phone, using the phone book there. He flipped through it to the P section and it was there that he found it. B. Pierce. But as he had guessed there would be, there were more than one. Three, in fact. But two of them resided in parts of town that Betty could do better than. She was seeing a five hundred dollar an hour psychologist, and she still had six sessions to go. With that in mind, she must be the B Pierce from the Hollywood Hills neighborhood, and that was all that he needed to know.

Things were starting to look up. With Pierce's address he wouldn't need to chance fate that some weirdo would back out of an appointment. All that he had to do was take out the old lady and her remaining sessions would be his. Six weeks worth. Plenty of time to sufficiently sucker Nancy Webb in. Then give her a great big welcome into his world.

He tore the page from the phone book and shoved it into his pocket, then turned away from the phone, where he noticed Betty Pierce leaving the elevator and heading for the building's attached parking garage. He followed her into the eighteen tiered parking ramp and would loved to have been able to take her out, right then and there. A quick punch to the throat and it would be done. It was a rather slow and painful death, to suffocate within a matter of minutes. The pain, of course, coming from her crushed trachea.

Though there wasn't any blood involved, which usually deterred him from using such tactics. He preferred his deaths, bloody. Yet, he would have done this in the name of all that was sacred to him. Knives, blood and godliness. Oh, yes, he almost forgot. And pussy. But there were just too damn many security cameras around. So instead he would wait. Wait for the night to come. His, time. The Stalker's time. When he could move in and out like a shadow, under the cover of darkness.

He found his Mercedes amid the rows of parked cars and slid in behind the wheel, starting the engine, then slowly navigated his way out to the street.

***

5:00 p.m.

After another long days work, Nancy Webb locked her office door for the night then crossed the lobby and stood outside the glass partition, where Brooke May's desk set, enclosed.

"So, what's up for tonight?" Webb slung her jacket over her forearm. "Can I get my purse please, Brooke."

May handed over the purse. "Oh, just another TV dinner and Lethal Weapon, on video."

Webb shook her head as she spoke. "Not only is that movie old, but you've seen it about a million times. You do know that you're being obsessive compulsive, don't you?"

"I don't care. There's a lot of gun play and, I get to see Mel Gibson's butt, healthy or not. But my tape is showing heavy signs of wear. I think I need a DVD player, but not at my current salary. We'll talk later."

Webb laughed at her as she slung her purse strap over her shoulder. "Ah, a good man. Whatever happened to those knights in shining armor that we were supposed to grow up and marry?"

"We were supposed to grow up. So that's what I've been doing wrong." May teased. "So what are you doing, tonight?"

Webb grimaced a bit. "I'll be going over the files of the Stalker murders, again. Like almost every night, since the police dragged me into it."

"Oh," May sprung from her chair and grabbed a file from underneath the desk behind her. "The police came by a couple hours ago and dropped this off for you. They said that it was from the latest murders. As you can see, it's still all sealed up, so I couldn't look at it." She glanced around, pretending to look for any unauthorized ears. "So, can you tell me anything that the police might be holding back?"

"No," Webb said, bluntly. "But I can say that they're all the same. Every crime scene. He doesn't do anything differently. Everything is always exact. Totally obsessive compulsive. No offense."

"I mean, I go over and over each case file, night after night. Time and again, but there is never anything new and I'm sure that this one," she held up the newest file. "Will be exactly, like all the rest." She fussed, securing the purse strap squarely on her shoulder. "Well, good luck with Mel. I'm going home. I'll see you tomorrow." she began to back away.

"Oh, wait!" May blurted out.

"What is it? What's the matter?"

"No, it's not like that."

"Well don't do that. You scared me half to death." Webb approached the glass partition, a hand to her chest.

"Sorry, but I just remembered something I was supposed to tell you. Or ask you, actually."

"Okay, what is it?"

"Talk about knights in shining armor, I've got one for you. He came in today, looking to make an appointment."

"Who?"

"Guess."

"You're fired."

"Okay, okay. You don't have to be rude. Bray Hamlin." she was almost salivating.

"*The* Bray Hamlin? The multi-billionaire Bray Hamlin?" Webb appeared a bit enchanted.

"The very gorgeous, Bray Hamlin. The L.A. Times, Man of the Year, and most eligible bachelor, Bray Hamlin," May added.

"And he wanted to make an appointment, with me?"

May nodded.

"And what did you tell him?"

"I told him that you only take on new patients, by referral and that you were booked up, through next year."

"And?"

"And, I took his telephone number."

"What? Brooke, you know that's not the way we do business." She sounded a bit disappointed. But not too disappointed.

"I know, but I thought that we could keep his name and number on file, just in case someone were to cancel on you. Then he could fill in for them." May's puppy dog eyes were working overtime.

"Not the eyes." Webb glanced away, trying to defend against May's pouty face, but she was tired and didn't want to deal with it. "Okay. But only if someone cancels. I couldn't possibly fit in a new client right now."

"That's all that he asked for. Actually, you'll probably never get the chance to meet him. No one ever cancels on you. You're like a guru to these people," May told her, somewhat complaining.

"Okay. But remember, it's just this once. Just so you know, devil woman. And I mean it. Those puppy eyes won't save you, again. I mean, if Tom Cruise comes in here and wants the same deal as Bray Hamlin, what are you going to tell him?"

"Why don't you step behind my counter. There's no waiting at this window." She licked her lips, invitingly.

Webb laughed at her. "Slut."

May laid her head on her desk and laughed, hard. Webb couldn't take anymore, so she turned around and walked away.

"Good night. Don't forget to lock up, on your way out." she said over her shoulder, as she walked out the door.

Brooke May wiped away a tear drop from her eye and tacked Bray Hamlin's phone number to the bulletin board next to her desk. She was hoping that there would be a cancellation, and soon, so that she might get another shot at enticing this angel of a man.

CHAPTER FOUR

Bray Hamlin sat, patiently watching Betty Pierce's home from across the street. It was 1:00 a.m. and the entire neighborhood was dark, his kind of dark. Almost pitch black, barely a moon in the sky.

He had been in his car now for three hours, watching, waiting. He had had to duck and cover from the security patrols several times. Luckily though, his Mercedes fit in well with his Hollywood Hills surroundings. So there was no reason for them to stop and check it out.

He continued to wait patiently, trying to derive exactly how he wanted to take the old lady out, so not to seem like the work of the Stalker. He was long set in his ways of killing, but he needed to change his trademark, just for the night. That meant no knives and no blood. Two of his four favorite things.

It was slightly after 1:00 a.m. now. The rent-a-cop security patrol had just gone by ten minutes ago. It was time. Old lady Pierce had to die. He left his Mercedes behind and cautiously crossed the street, his dark clothing making him no more than a shadow. He needed to be cool about the old lady's demise. He knew that it would have to look like a robbery gone bad to keep the police where he wanted them, and to obtain Pierce's final six appointments, so that he may test Webb's intellect and fortitude.

He walked around the side of the house, and prepared to pry open one of the ground floor windows when he observed at the top of the pane of glass a set of two wires, almost unnoticeable. Pierce's house was equipped with an alarm system. Fuck! The old bitch! He was not prepared for an alarm tonight. Why wasn't he as prepared, as the Stalker usually was? He grit his teeth.

Okay, so plan A was out. Who was he trying to kid. He swung at the darkness, extremely pissed off. There was no plan B. Hell, there wasn't really even a plan A. The only thing that even came close to being a plan was this one thought. Break in, kill the old bitch and leave. Then the remainder of her sessions with Webb would be his. That was it, that's all there was. Fuck!

His initial thoughts on how exactly he would use Webb were merely to toy with her and string her along, then throw his godliness in her face, just to show her that she wasn't so fucking smart after all. Trying to match wits with him. But he had had a change of heart, while waiting for the neighborhood to sleep. He had remembered reading several articles about her brilliant mind, helping others. Especially, that poor fuck with the eighteen personalities. Maybe there was something to her intelligence, after all. Maybe she was worthy of his interest in her, as a woman. Not just a soon to be addition to his ascension. But a partner instead. Every king needed a queen.

He was not about to lose a chance to know this, or not. If she was as good as he believed her to be, she would understand him. He would finally have someone who would understand him. For now, at least, he needed Nancy Webb. He needed her to know him, to be one with him. And this fucking old bitch was not going to stand in his way. He didn't care if he had to trip the alarm, she was going to die. Even if he had to take half of the police force with her. She was going to die and her remaining sessions with Webb would be his.

Blinded and fueled by rage, he walked around to the backyard, where in a moment of clarity he found his way in. There was a second floor balcony and it's doors were wide open. Somehow, these doors were not secured by the same system because there they stood, wide open and inviting him in. The only thing in his way now was about thirteen feet in height discrepancy. But he was not going to be denied.

Looking around abruptly in the darkness. His actions, almost frantic. He discovered a wooden tool shed off to the side of the yard. He ran to it. With his patience nearing the breaking point, he pulled on his surgical gloves. It was a newer shed, so it wasn't going to be a problem. The older models were made of thick wood and would be a bitch to break into, especially since it had a new paddle lock on it. But the sheds of today were flimsy and made of half inch plywood. He could break that stuff with his dick. Not that he couldn't break the harder, thicker stuff. It's just that it would make a hell of a lot more noise, which would defeat the purpose of his silence all together.

He placed a fist to the door of the shed, right beside the lock and pushed.

Applying more and more pressure, the plywood began to crack. A moment later, the locks face plate separated from the door. He swung the door open and stepped inside. It was pitch black. The darkness forced him to feel around blindly, until he came across hedge trimmers, a shovel and a hoe. Before he finally came across what he was looking for. A ladder. He carried it out of the shed and set it up beneath the balcony, finding it to be far shorter than the lowest setting of the balcony.

The balcony appeared to be thirteen feet off the ground. Where as the ladder stood only six feet at the very top. With his own height and the ladder, it was still going to be a bit of a stretch. Besides extending his arms as far as they could reach, he may also have to risk it and jump for the edge of the balcony. If he were to make it, the old hag was as good as dead. He climbed to the top of the ladder, balancing himself there only for a moment, reaching up for the balcony's edge. But was still just short. So bending his knees, he jumped for it, catching the edge and pulling himself up and stepped over the railing.

He strolled into Pierce's home carefree. Walking down the upstairs hallway, opening each door as he came to it, until he finally struck gold. He found Pierce laying at the center of her bed, flat on her back. Dead to the world. He stood at her bedside and gazed down at her for a minute. She looked so peaceful, so calm. He shared in this peace. His mind and body consumed by this serenity. He had never felt quite so calm before. He had always exhibited it on a constant basis, but he had never really felt it until now. He drew in a deep, cleansing breath, exhaling away his rage. The longer he looked at her the more she resembled his grandmother, on his father's side. May she rest in peace. And speaking of resting in peace, he would be doing Pierce a favor. She was in her late sixties, and seeing a psychologist for fuck sake. She had one foot in the grave already.

He suddenly reached down, wrapping his hands around her throat and dragged her from the bed, viciously throwing her to the bedroom floor. She had awakened at Hamlin's first touch, but could not manage a scream because of his immensely strong hands being locked around her throat squeezing. She grabbed at her attacker's wrists and tried to pull his hands away, but he was far too strong. His grip like a vise.

She panicked, gasping for air. But each time she tried to inhale there was less and less oxygen to be had. Until finally Hamlin's grip cut off her breath entirely. She couldn't see the face of her attacker clearly in the dark. And her vision was blurring and dimming fast. Her eyes feeling like they were bulging and might pop right out of their sockets, from the immense pressure. Pierce knew that she was about to die, but for what reason and why? Or who might want her dead? She didn't know. Then suddenly, everything went black and her struggles stopped. Her hands slipped from Hamlin's wrists, as her arms fell spread eagle to the floor.

Hamlin kept his hands wrapped tightly around her throat, even though she was no longer moving and was obviously, dead. He kept the pressure on for several more intense minutes, before finally pulling himself away, releasing her. The Stalkers excitement was nearly unbearable. He wanted her blood. He wanted it on his skin. He wanted to cut her open and take just a little bit, even though there wasn't much essence left, in that old body of hers. It would be pointless and risky, possibly drawing unwanted attention to the Stalker and himself.

Instead, he began a slow deep breathing exercise that he had to use once before, after an evening of rough sex with one of those boring socialites, not too long ago. It took about twenty minutes, but soon his craving for her blood started to diminish, and shortly thereafter he was calm once again. As calm as he could be, anyway.

It was time to mess things up a bit, for the benefit of the police investigation soon to follow. He rummaged through her dresser drawers tossing their contents over his shoulders, leaving it strewn all over the floor. He dug into her jewelry box and took what looked most valuable. But to him, it all just looked like a bunch of crap. Probably not worth much at all. After filling his pockets with as much of the junk as he could he took a moment to look around.

Deciding that the room was trashed enough he stepped over Pierce's body and re-entered the hallway, following it to the staircase where he made his way down to the main floor. He opened the front door wide and moved outside to the front walk. The alarm system was going off like a high pitched, ringing bell. But he was in no hurry.

He wasn't worried about the neighbors, because they would just be waking up and their eyes would take a while to adjust to the light. And by his watch, the rent-a-cop patrol would be a few minutes from Pierce's house and they would be coming from the opposite direction, as to the way he would be traveling. So there were no witnesses to be had.

He crossed the lawn at a casual speed, then slowly jogged across the street and slid in behind the wheel of his Mercedes, while the lights of the neighborhood homes began to illuminate their interior. He could hear the sound of the sirens from the patrol cars, but he calmly drove away like it was just another day at the park, and by the time that they would arrive he would already be long gone.

Now all that he had to do was sit back and wait for Pierce's body to be found by the police. Thus, the wide open door and the ear piercing alarm. Then the news of her wrongful death would be broadcast, and the beautiful Brooke May would surely hear of the tragedy, then eventually he would be offered Pierce's remaining sessions, starting that next Tuesday. Then the lovely Dr. Webb would enter into his world and become more involved in the Stalker case than she ever could have imagine.

***

Bray Hamlin walked barefoot through the sands of Venice beach. It had been nearly forty-five minutes since his little chore. He loved to walk on the beach at night when there was no one around. It was so peaceful. But tonight he had an ulterior motive for being there. He was on the beach to rid himself of the jewelry he had taken from Pierce's house, and to watch the stars shine in the night sky.

He threw a handful of jewelry out into the ocean, about forty yards. The pieces were a bit heavy and would lodge themselves in the soft ocean floor, slowly digging themselves deeper, with the incoming and outgoing tides. He surely didn't need them. He gave better pieces than those to one night stands. He walked back away from the water and took a seat in the dry sand. There, he gazed up at the stars. He loved to sit outside somewhere wide open, like the beach and gaze into the sky, watching the beauty of the infinite universe. All the while knowing that his potency was quickly becoming just as immeasurable.

***

After a short while he walked back to his car and put on his socks and shoes. He was about to climb into his Mercedes when a sheriff's patrol car hit him with a spotlight, as it came to a stop horizontally, behind his car. The two deputies stepped out of the cruiser, approaching him. Both, carrying their night sticks.

He smiled at them. Just try it, his mind spoke to him. Just try those billy-clubs on me, he hoped. I'll shove them up your asses and turn you into a pair of bloody popsicles.

"Excuse me, sir. What are you doing out here so late at night? It is kinda late, don't you think?" the cop from the passenger side asked.

"I was taking a walk, I couldn't sleep. Is it a crime now to take a walk at night?"

How fucking dare they! Who did these fucking jackoffs think they were dealing with? He could easily have their badges for this. Or better yet their lives. He could take them both of them right here, right now. He started muddling through the hundreds of ways that he could take them and every one of them would only take a few seconds. The closest of the two would take a swift kick to the throat. Then the second one, the snide one. He would get a pair of thumbs to the eyes. Fucking bastards. Or, he could just... .

"Listen, sir. We're... ."

"You're Bray Hamlin, aren't you?" the second cop cut in.

"Yes, I am." He kept his cool, even though only one of the fucking pigs recognized him. His identity didn't really matter anymore, he just wanted their fucking blood and the blood of their families, for getting in his way.

"I'm sorry, Mr. Hamlin. We didn't mean to bother you, sir. We get a lot of addicts down here at night. We're just trying to keep the beach clean," the second cop apologized.

Hamlin smiled, just a bit. "That's all right. No harm, no foul." He leaned in toward them and read their name tags. "Deputies, Hoite and Jefferson. I'll be sure and tell the governor at lunch tomorrow that you two were on top of things, tonight. I'm sure that he'll be happy to know that." His threat was ever so subtle.

He opened his car door, much to the first cop's dismay. "Now, if you gentlemen will excuse me, I'd like to go home and get some sleep. The ocean air seems to have done it's job."

"Of course, sir. We'll just move our car and let you get on your way. Good night, sir."

The second cop licked his shoes again, while waving for his partner to get back into the car.

Hamlin slid into his Mercedes and started the engine, while the sheriff's cruiser backed out of his way. The Stalker pulled out of his spot and drove out of the parking lot, speeding off down the street.

"Who in the hell was that? Why did you let him go, so easily?" Hoite wondered.

Jefferson shook his head a bit, and said. "I know that you've only been in

California for a few weeks. So I'll tell you right now. Don't ever stop that man. I don't know if you have someone like him in Rhode Island or not. But do not fuck with that man. Don't get in his way, don't ever try to detain him for something as stupid as taking a walk on the beach at night. Always call him sir. As a matter of fact, instead of telling you everything that you shouldn't do, I'll just tell you what to do. Don't ever have anything to do with him, unless you're trying to help him."

"Why not? Who in the hell is, Bray Hamlin?"

"He is a god in this state. And a saint in this community. Not only is he one of the most wealthiest men in the world, but he donates millions to charity, every year. He has friends all over. The governor, the police commissioner and the chief of police of every city and county, in this state. The sheriff is a poker buddy of his, as are federal and circuit court justices. You name them, and he knows them. You see, he got into everyone's good graces when his father was still alive. And he's like family to them. All, of them. So just leave him be," Jefferson warned.

"I mean, if he pisses in your pocket and still has to go you'd better smile and offer him a dry one. If there is one person to watch out for in this town it's Bray Hamlin."

"Hell, we were only doing our jobs," Hoite protested.

Jefferson shook his head, and reminded his partner. "It doesn't matter. Bray Hamlin, is always in the right, so never cross him. Just remember that, and you'll do fine. Like I said, he's a god in this town."

***

The Stalker guided the Mercedes through the deserted streets of the City of Angels. His run in with the police had given him a rush. He had never killed a cop before, and his loins tingled at the thought of wearing their blood. If only they had known who he really was, they would have had to try and take him. He gripped the steering wheel tighter, doing all that he could, just to keep from turning around and going back. Just for their blood.

He rolled down the window for some fresh air and breathed in deeply, the cool night breeze rushing in through the open window. Deep, cleansing breaths, trying desperately to suppress this urge. Nearly turning around twice. He would have loved to have done it. His dick was hard, and nearly wet, just from the thought of it. But unfortunately the police were not exactly rocket scientists. He grinned, with a bit of a laugh. Dicks.

But he was wired, now. Wired, with nothing to do. He was going to have to go home and work out. The weights would help burn off some of the excess energy he had stored up inside of him. And if that didn't do it, he could practice his martial arts until he was sweaty and tired. But just for good measure, a good jackoff in the shower after a work out was always a nice sleep aide.

Speaking of getting off. All that he had to do now, was to sit back and wait for the very fuckable Brooke May to give him a call and offer him the now deceased Betty Pierce's appointments. Which probably wouldn't be for a few days, out of respect for the old whore. He would likely hear from them by Friday, so not to miss next Tuesday's session.

***

Brooke May turned off the radio in her glassed in cubical, after hearing the horrible news of Betty Pierce's death. She noticed Webb walking her 2:00 p.m. appointment back out into the lobby.

"You take care, Mr. Blank. I'll see you again, in two weeks."

The gentleman waved at Webb and walked out into the hallway. She was about to re-enter her office, when the sight of Brooke May waving her hands in the air, caught her attention.

Webb joined her at the receptionist desk. Smiling at her 3:00 p.m. "I'll be with you in just a minute Mrs. Roberts."

She leaned on the narrow counter between her and May, who looked a bit disturbed. "What's up?"

"Have you listened to the news at all today?" May asked, vaguely.

"No. And I didn't even look at my paper this morning. I'm so tired of hearing about the Stalker. He already fills my nights, every time I review his case files. I certainly don't want him filling my days, as well. Why, what's going on? Did he kill again?"

"I didn't hear it myself, until just now. Because I always change the channel when the news comes on. But Ms. Pierce. Betty. She was murdered last night."

Webb placed a hand to her mouth, aghast. "Really. My god, what happened?"

"They found her strangled to death, last night in her own bedroom. They figure that burglars woke her up, while they were trashing her room and killed her. The news said that there were three jewelry box's on the floor, but very little jewelry was found." May tried not to speak too loud, so that Webb's 3:00 appointment didn't over hear them. "But what was strange was, that they didn't even touch any of the other rooms. They passed up the TV, the DVD, and all sorts of valuables. It was like they wanted her to wake up, just so they could kill her." May's eyes showed her shock.

"The police said that they got in through her open balcony doors, using a ladder from her own tool shed. It was still standing under the balcony, but left through the front door. Her security alarm was going off and everything."

Webb shook her head, a disgusted and horrified look about her. "That's terrible. It's scary to know that we aren't even safe in our own homes anymore."

May raised her shoulders. "Speaking of which, take the Stalker for instance," she ominously pointed out.

"Don't remind me," Webb said, appearing drained, both emotionally, and physically. "Hey, why don't you take a look in Betty's file and find out who her next of kin is. We should send flowers."

"I'll take care of it."

"I have my 3:00 I need to get to. I'll check in with you later." Webb left the matter in May's capable hands, and escorted her 3:00 into her office. Even after hearing the bad news, Webb pressed on. Her work was vital, and had to continue.

***

The day after Betty Pierce's death, the morning news brought the word of the murder to light. Bray Hamlin slid a piece of peach into his mouth, the sweetness of the fruit enlivening his saliva glands. He sat out on the back patio of his mansion in Beverly Hills, staring out over the home's one thousand square foot backyard, listening to the less than graphic details of the murder on the radio.

All that the police knew at this time was that Pierce was killed around 1:00 or 1:30 in the early morning hours, and all that they suspected missing was some jewelry. How much it was worth, they didn't know. And they had no suspects in the killing, at this time.

Hamlin shrugged his shoulder's. "Well that wasn't very informative."

He chopped an apple in half and continued his fresh fruit breakfast. The news in this town sucked, he brooded. They even dumbed down his Stalker murders. They never mentioned anything about any of the good stuff, pussies.

He shrugged again. It didn't matter how much the police allowed the press to report. It wasn't notoriety that he sought. It was simply Pierce's time with Webb that he wanted. Actually, the more he thought about it, the more he realized that it was Webb herself that he wanted. Her understanding and eventually her mind, body and soul.

He was, after all. Still searching for the perfect mate. Who knows, he thought. He just may have found her.

CHAPTER FIVE

After a long day of probing the psyches of just a few of her many patients, Nancy Webb stood in the shower, her hands against the wall. Allowing the water to rain down on her neck, and roll off of her back. Easing her tensions, just a bit. But she still couldn't get the thought of Betty Pierce's murder out of her head. She couldn't even begin to understand what state of mind, drug altered, or otherwise, a person had to be in to take the life of another human being. A living, breathing entity. Just for a handful of lousy jewelry.

The Stalker was one thing. He was completely insane. Incompetent of mind. But the people responsible for Pierce's death, were nothing more than society's bottom feeders. They knew better, but they just didn't care.

She had spent eight years in college and graduate school, studying the human mind and the many illnesses that effected it. But still she could not understand the senselessness and horror. It just really pissed her off. Maybe she was losing her touch. It was strange. She felt strange. Someone she had been counseling weekly, for two years, was dead. Murdered. Someone that she knew, well. Yet, she had not shed a single tear for her.

Maybe she distanced herself too far from her patients. Too far, to where they had become no more than a name, face and case file. Meaning she knew of them, their thoughts, their fears and at times, their rage; but she didn't know them personally. She had never really taken sufficient time to do so. It was hard, with the volume of patients that she had, to find time to get to know each one a bit more personally.

She lifted her head to let the water softly pelt her face, while running her hands back over her hair. Wringing her wet locks almost entirely of water. She blamed herself for not having gotten to know Betty Pierce better. But wasn't that part of the job's requirements? Never get too personal with a client. But there was a difference between becoming personally attached to someone and knowing someone. It was a fine line, but there was a difference.

She turned the shower off and towel dried herself, then walked naked to the bedroom, being that it was only kitty-cornered to the bathroom. She slid on some panties, then covered herself with a short, silky nightgown, and finally a robe.

After a dinner for one, she retreated to her study where at her desk, she began thumbing through the case files of the Stalker murders. Including the latest one, there were six files, in all. She studied the grotesque pictures and examined every blood trail that the Stalker had left behind. Just foot prints, mostly. Accompanied by some drippings, from the bedrooms to the prayer sites. He never dragged anyone, he was tremendously strong. But by the size of his foot prints not exactly a giant. His size nine print suggested his height to be somewhere between five-eight and five-ten.

She reviewed each report, and the description of each scene again and again, but still couldn't come up with anything new that might help her to profile him any more which could lead the police and FBI to his capture. In comparison, she thought, he was like a modern day Jack the Ripper. There were never any witnesses to any of the murders, and he left no traceable evidence behind. The cover of darkness being used to enact his heinous visions of brutal death. Only the Stalker made Jack the Ripper look like a boy scout, going for his pen knife merit badge.

Hoping to find any shred of a clue that she may have missed before, she once again dove into the profile that she had provided for the police.

The Stalker was a white male, since all of his victims were white, and serial killer's tend to hunt within their own ethnic groups. He was twenty-eight to thirty-eight years of age. Highly above average intelligence. Very meticulous. Definitely obsessive-compulsive. A psychopath by nature, but possessed the ability to blend in with society. A chameleon of sorts. His victims are carefully selected, not chosen at random. He must watch them for a while, two to three weeks at least. Most likely timing them, getting to know their routines by heart. He was not a man who just kills when the mood strikes him.

With both the police and federal forensic's teams having tested hair and pubic hair samples found at most of the crime scenes not only prove that he has brown hair, but also establishes that he commits his murders in the nude. Though none of his victims have ever been found sexually assaulted. Further forensics testing also proved that the gutting wounds, from the lower abdomen up to the sternum and the emptying of the organs, are post mortem wounds. Though at times, the gutting procedure was the actual cause of death.

Which suggested to her that he desires each of his victim's blood. Because some time after death all of the body's blood collects in the stomach, and the only way to get to that blood was to gut his victims. But for what purpose he wanted the blood, was still somewhat of a mystery. Though she had theories on that subject.

There were usually quite a few blood trails left throughout each home. Mostly on the staircase and in the living room, or family room. Then there was the giant puddle of blood, left in front of the supposedly praying bodies.

Partially bloodied foot prints on the second floor of each home, appear to be left behind just after the killings begin. But leading out of the puddles of blood at each prayer site were fully formed prints. These prints, which led back up to the second floor bathroom, proved that the Stalker not only took his time in executing the killings, but also took the time to casually take a shower afterwards.

He was a very clever killing machine. A perfectionist. Clean and cautious. Pretentious, in the way that he left his calling card behind. But in leaving his self-appointed title with his worshipers, handwriting analyst's had determined that he was left handed.

In his mind he was becoming something. Something strong, that could not be stopped. So when he was found, the police and the FBI were going to have no choice, but to put him down to stop him. Because there was no way that he was going to willingly stop any other way.

Indeed, there wasn't going to be any way of helping the Stalker in recovering from his insanity she knew. He was simply too far gone and better off dead. Which was a shame, because she would love the opportunity to try and unlock the catacombs of his mind and study the essence of evil that dwelled within him. But he had too much of a taste for it now. The killing, and the blood. Mostly the blood. So yes, the best thing for him and the best thing for society was to end him, and put him in the ground. And any fool that might think different and try to reach him was destined to fail, miserably.

If the police were actually able to capture him alive no doubt they would call in the best in her field of medicine, maybe even her, to open up his mind and try to dissect what was inside. Actually, that would be exactly what they would want to do. Almost, immediately. But they would have to get someone else, because once he was caught, she wouldn't want anything more to do with the Stalker. In the name of psychological science or otherwise.

But there would always be someone, with a new technique that they would just have to try. But like all others before them, they would fail. Not only would they be unable to penetrate his outer defenses. But to enter and explore the deep, dark caldrons of his mind would be virtually impossible.

But if by some slim chance one were to succeed in tapping into his consciousness and actually reach him and somehow understand his logic would not only be a major coup, but it might connect the two together in a mind set, trapping whom ever might succeed in penetrating his cerebral defenses, in the dark void of his of his insanity that awaited them. A pure, black ball of evil, she was sure from which there would be no return.

But in her case, as a doctor and a member of society, she would feel much safer, knowing that he was in the ground. Rather than being locked away, behind the walls of a maximum security mental institution.

Webb flipped through the file of the very first family, to fall victim to the evil, of the Stalker. Family name: Jacobson.

The way it all began and possibly, the way it might all end. She searched through the file, hoping to find something there that was not in any other case file. Something that the Stalker had done differently, or left behind that was not in conjunction with all of the others who followed. But her quest to find a difference was to no avail. He was like a machine in his methods, with never a single discrepancy at any of the crime scenes. He was unique. A stone cold killing machine, sneaking around in the dark, issuing his own brand of silent death. It seemed to suit him. It seemed to suit him too well. He may be former military. Special forces, maybe. Lieutenant Morrow, the officer in charge of the Stalker case, was already investigating that theory further. She could only hope that he would come across a suspect and end the Stalker's reign of terror, before many more lives were lost.

But as for why he only kills families of five? She suspected that he may come from a similar background. Only it was not a happy time, for him. Most likely the middle child, of three. He did not receive the attention from his parents that he so desired. He may even have been abused by his parents. Which fueled his hatred for families of this size.

This said abuse could also have been the work of a foster family of the same size. And in that case, the abuse may not have been limited to the adults. The other children may also have had a hand in the making of this monster. This evil.

As for the positioning of the bodies in the prayer-like stances, in which they were found. His childhood may have been guided by the firm hand of religion. He likely saw himself as some type of devil, or something else that was just as evil that should be worshiped, due to possible and constant reprimand by one or both parents. Making him believe that he was, in fact, evil.

She reviewed the files over and over, again and again, one by one. Knowing that there had to be something there she was missing. Something that would expand her profile. Something that would help narrow the list of suspects, for the authorities. If indeed, they had any suspects at this time. She wasn't exactly sure. It had been a few days since her last contact with Morrow.

Something was there, she was sure of it. She just wasn't seeing it. It was quite possible that it was right there in front of her eyes. There in plain sight. She scoured every inch of the gruesome pictures, but nothing seemed to jump out at her. No differences. It was like they were all the same pictures. All just copies of the first murders.

Sleeplessness started to overcome her. She glanced at the clock on the corner of her desk. It was 12:08 a.m. She had been up since six that morning, and putting in these long hours at night was not helping her to get up in the morning. She reassembled the files and stacked them neatly at the center of her desk. That was enough for tonight. Beleaguered by her inability to shed new light on the case she went to bed and left the Stalker for another day.

***

Bray Hamlin slid out of the ground floor window of the two story, white suburban home. Naked as the day he was born he had already showered the families blood from his body and left his bloody moniker behind. Normally he would not have taken two families so close together, but his chance to do so arose and he took it. It had only been three days since his last sacrifices, and their essences were still adjoining with his own life force. Now, there was even more power to unite with his own.

He feared nothing, but had always toyed with the notion that too much power at one time might prove to be dangerous. But instead he felt fantastic. Infinite. He could feel the power swelling inside of him, more so than usual. It was almost orgasmic. Yet another successful step in his ascension into godliness. He dressed beside the house in the shadows. There was a slight chill in the air tonight, and he didn't like the way it made his balls feel. He checked his watch. It was 2:41 a.m. Time to go home and have a nightcap, and warm his nuts, before turning in for the evening.

He wanted to get up early and get his workout out of the way, because he was expecting a call from the office of Dr. Webb and he didn't want to have to stop his workout to answer the phone. He hated that. He could just let the machine answer it for him. Only, he didn't have one. He hated answering machines, even more than something disturbing his workout. He grinned wide, devilishly as he pulled his coat on. The mere thought of the good doctor at her best, with him. Understanding him. It warmed the area where his heart should be. But even he wasn't quite sure if he had one or not.

He was going to take his time with Webb. He would allow her into his world, only so much at a time. Just enough to grab her, startle her, arouse her. He wasn't above a little mind fuck, either. Then, when she was ready, he would open all doors for her. He would show her what the Stalker held in his mind. Unhinged. Then she would understand. Or at least, she'd better. He was hoping she would, anyway. But if she didn't or couldn't, he would have to wear her blood as a conciliation prize.

He scurried across the street, the night covering his departure. Climbing into his awaiting Mercedes, he drove a block before turning on his lights. He was going to bypass the beach tonight, down a few shots of whiskey, and go straight to bed.

His ascension was on the rise. It was sky rocketing. His power was mounting and soon the sand would be his, the stars would be his, and the air. The world would soon revolve around his axis. But the most important thing of all, Webb would be his. He shrugged, and lowered his brow. What was the world, if you had no one to share it with?

***

The next day came and went, with no call from Webb's office. He heard nothing from Brooke May. She said that she was going to put in a good word for him. Lying bitch! He should find her home and fuck her with a ten-inch blade of steel. In a rage, Hamlin sought out the basement of his five thousand, three hundred square foot home. Where he moved to a portioned off area, filled with gym equipment. He had already worked out for the day, but after being fucked by May he suddenly had a bit more energy to dispel. He laid back on the bench press and took hold of the weighted barbell above him.

Lifting the bar off of it's roost, he began pressing it.

Just thinking about what he might do to May and Webb made his work out nothing more than a blur. Before he knew it his heart was pounding. He was sweating like he had just spent the night with six virgins on prom night. When he replaced the barbell on the bench, he had pressed three hundred pounds, thirty three times.

CHAPTER SIX

A brigade of black and white police units, swarmed the property of the Carey home. Red and blue lights, flashing. A barrier of yellow crime scene tape, sealing off the area.

The unmarked cruiser driven by lieutenant in charge, Josh Morrow, arrived and took its place amongst the units already on scene. Morrow worked his way through the crowd of swarming media. Not even bothering to utter a "No comment," to their multitude of questions. Bowing beneath the yellow tape he joined the nearest plain clothed officer he could find.

"Is it our man?" he asked the cop.

Staring down at his notepad, the cop spoke outright. "It's our boy all right. The place is a bloody mess. He left his calling card on the wall. Victims on their knees, their guts all dumped into a corner. You know, the usual," the detective told him oh so casually.

Morrow shot him a cold stare. "You look, before you talk about a crime scene." His voice shocked the cop into looking up from his notepad. "What if I had been a reporter? That would make one hell of a head line, you just gave me," he scolded.

"I'm sorry, sir. I wasn't thinking," he apologized.

"That's exactly right. You weren't thinking. And if I ever hear you speaking so caviler about a dead family like that again, you'll be handing out parking tickets along Melrose."

He pointed to the house. "There is a father, a mother and three children in there. Mutilated, because some fucking psycho can't get his rocks off, any other way. Even if you have no respect for the dead, you could at least try to fake it, for God's sake," Morrow growled.

"You know a case like this could make or break a career. Even if you're only assisting. Well Blaine, you just pissed your way off of it, you're no longer on this case. You're not ready for the Stalker. Go go back to the station and have sargeant Monroe find you something else to do. Now get the fuck away from my crime scene."

He left the officer licking his wounds and made his way inside the house. Immediately upon stepping through the doorway the stench of the prayer site hit him like a ton of human feces, tucked away inside a bloated, rancid dead skunk. A fouler smell he could not remember.

He turned back out the door, inhaling deeply the non-toxic air. Trying desperately not to show the media, set up outside of the yellow barrier, the other side of the investigation, he pulled a white handkerchief out of the breast pocket of his suit coat. He held it over his nose and mouth and ventured back inside, where he passed a uniformed cop leaving the house, his hand covering his face, just as Morrow was. The lieutenant heard him speak from beneath his hand.

"A little further back, sir. On the left." then he left the house rather quickly, thereafter.

The closer Morrow got to the prayer site the more pungent the stench became. He thought just entering the house was difficult. He could feel his stomach turning over, as saliva began filling his mouth. He swallowed repeatedly, trying to avoid the dry heaves. Fortunately, he hadn't had the time to eat breakfast this morning, because of his abundant workload. Hell, he rarely even had the time to go home at night to change his clothes. The Stalker was the biggest case of his career. Unfortunately, seven families, thirty-five people, most of them children, are dead. And he hadn't a single clue as to the identity of the raving, fucking lunatic responsible yet. He could just feel his career slipping further and further away, as the body count continued to rise.

He held the handkerchief tighter to his face. He was breathing through his mouth, but it wasn't doing any good. Not only could he still smell the pungent odor, but it was so powerful now he could taste it. The spilled blood and spoiled organs. Morrow looked across the room and spotted the two federal boys that were assisting the police in tracking the Stalker. He shook his head. He was dead tired and barely lucid, but he couldn't afford to rest. If the feebs were to catch up with the Stalker before he did his career would go down in flames. He had three weeks on them and nothing to show for it. It wouldn't be the first time he had to take early retirement. But he didn't want, nor did he need that scenario, clouding his mind. Not now.

He joined the medical examiner, Harold Minor, who stood amongst the corpses. Morrow kept his distance as best he could, but still his eyes began to burn and water, because of the over- powering stench of the blood plastered, organ strewn prayer site. Minor looked up at him. The M.E. had a mask covering his nose and mouth. And a pair of what appeared to be swimming goggles, protecting his eyes.

"Goggles, huh," Morrow admired. "I should have thought of that."

"How are you, Josh? You look like hell, have you been sleeping?" Minor wondered.

"Not much. Please tell me that you've got something new on this sick bastard."

Minor shook his head. "Sorry, but it doesn't look like there's anything new. I'll have to wait until I get them back to the morgue to be sure. But the prayer site, is all your's. All I can tell you right now, is that they've been dead for about three or four days. Probably killed just before the weekend to give us this stale mess to work with. You know how he works."

Minor shrugged. "And there are no telling signs that any of them have been sexually assaulted. Just like all the others."

Morrow motioned toward the federal officers across the room. "Have you already told them, what you just told me?"

"Oh, yes. They got here about five minutes before you did."

"Dicks," Morrow mumbled.

"Oh, they're not too bad. Besides, I like some of the equipment they brought with them from their facilities. Some high tech stuff. Too bad it's not doing us any good."

"High tech. It used to be your brain was the only high tech thing you needed. Now they come around with their profilers and nice suits, and high tech gadgets that don't get you any closer to your suspect, than before," the lieutenant grumbled.

Minor looked around, cautious. "There is a little something that I saved for you," he confessed.

"You saved for me. What?" Morrows muffled voice asked, through the handkerchief.

"It's a small detail, really. But it is something. We've always known that the bastard was strong, right. Now, there have always been blood trails.

Drippings, when the bodies are moved, but never any smears to say that at any time he has had to drag any of the bodies to the prayer sites."

"Yeah, so?"

"Well, that's what we have here. But Mr. Carey here, by the looks of him and by his driver's license, weighs in at three hundred and twenty pounds. But like I said, there aren't any smears of blood to say that the Stalker had to drag him down here. And his organs were removed, post mortem. He carried him, Josh. Just like all of the rest of his victims. Down a flight of stairs and placed him here in the living room. Which makes him massively strong. Especially since it's dead weight that he's lifting. It's all relaxed, dead weight, which makes it even harder to carry," Minor observed.

"So we're looking for an extremely strong psychopath. We sort of already knew that, Harold. But thanks, for sharing." Morrow rubbed the back of his neck, with his free hand.

"Yes, that's true. But the piece of the profile distinguished by the foot prints he's left behind, suggest that he's between five-eight and five-ten, correct? That means more than likely he has quite a body builder's build. Big and bulky. Either that, or he has a partner."

"Don't say that. Don't even think that. Besides, the feeb boys have already profiled him as a loner. So has doctor Webb. All of the evidence, points to one man. Well, the evidence of the profiles, anyway. Thanks for the initial heads up, though."

Morrow mulled it over. "So he's got quite a build on him, huh. That's just great. So we're looking for a psycho with a big, bulky build. Do you know how many men in Los Angeles fit that description. The build part, anyway. A lot, and there must be hundreds of gyms in L.A. Hell, he might even work out at home. It's very slim, at best. Don't get me wrong, doc. I will modify the build, on the description. But it is, more or less, a shot in the dark."

Morrow looked across the room to find his partner, and secondary officer on the Stalker case. Jonathan Price, standing near an open window. Price too, as everyone else inside the house, was holding a handkerchief to his nose and mouth. Trying in vain to block the decaying stench of death.

Morrow rubbed his eyes with his free hand. He was extremely tired, damn hungry, and short on time, with the feebs hanging around. But the Stalker was being a prick. He was hiding himself too well. And was being too damn clean and careful. He hadn't slept in over seventy-two hours. And even when he did, it was only ten to thirty minutes, here and there.

He had examined every angle of this case, over and over again. But to no avail. It always seemed like the Stalker was two steps ahead of him, and he just couldn't catch up.

"You look like, hell. Why don't you go home and get some rest. I'm sure that Price can handle things for a while," Minor suggested.

Morrow shook his head. Looking over at the two federal agents, talking amongst themselves. "I don't have the time. This fucking case, and those God damn feebs, are driving me to drink. And I haven't had one of those in three weeks. Besides, I know that if I go home somebody will catch this fuck. And I want that somebody to be me. Otherwise, my career will be worth less than a pile of dog shit."

"I don't know, you look terrible. I can prescribe something for you. It would do you good to sleep, at least a couple of hours."

"No thanks. I don't care much, for sedatives." He wasn't about to go through that hell, again.

He shook off the old memories, before they could invade his thoughts. Because now, he had a killer to find. A vicious, sadistic psychopath, who liked to cut up families and wear their blood, as some type of retarded ritual. And he didn't need old demons clouding his head at this time. He needed to be sharp in his thoughts. Something that he couldn't be with his troubled past returning to haunt him.

"I'll be fine." he told Minor. "I'd better go check in with Price, before I get accused of sleep walking. Just give us a call if you find anything out of the ordinary. Stalker ordinary, that is. Otherwise, I'll have someone stop by your office later on and pick up your report."

Minor simply nodded in recognition.

Morrow left the medical examiner with the mutilated bodies of the supposed worshipers. Joining detective Price near the open window, which was no help in alleviating the stench of the bodies, and their displaced organs.

Price held an open notebook with his free hand. Looking over his notes about the scene. The family and the questioning of the poor little bastard who found them. His handkerchief still pressed close to his face.

"What have you got for me, Price? Anything new?"

"Not a damn thing so far, lieutenant. Just a water diluted smear from his taint meat, that he left on his way out. A bloody, gloved hand print on the knife handle. The bucket was completely drenched in blood. No surprise, there. And as always, a ground floor window that has been wedged open. No witnesses." The detective filled him in. "We've dust—"

"Wait a minute. Taint meat?" Morrow wondered. Though he knew he shouldn't ask. Price was always coming up with stupid shit. Usually to lighten the mood.

"Yeah. The space right between the legs. It taint dick, and it taint ass. Taint meat."

"I knew I should've let it go. Go ahead, keep going." Morrow shook his head.

"Like I was saying. We've dusted the windowsill, inside and out. The family will be printed at the morgue, to see if we have any matches. We'll have the bodies checked out for finger prints, just in case he took his gloves off to touch anyone. Which we know he never does. You know, the usual on all of that. We've been checking the grounds outside the window, ever since we got here. But it looks like another, clean scene. Just like all the others," Price told him.

"Who found the bodies?"

Price grimaced a bit. "A friend of the oldest child found the bodies. He came over for a ride to school after being away with his family for the weekend. No one answered the door, when he knocked. So he started to walk around to the back yard. Apparently quite often they didn't answer the front door in the morning. So he'd go to the back door, where the kitchen is."

Using his free hand, Price wiped his forehead with the sleeve of his suit coat. Even standing next to the open window, it was still as hot as hell in there. The Stalker had purposely shut off the air conditioning some time before leaving the scene. He was just that kind of prick. He loved to let the prayer sites stew for a few days, before the police got there. A joke he had pulled, before. Just to make it even more difficult for them to sweep the scene. He was truly a royal pain in Morrow's ass.

"So when he passed by the window that was left open a crack, that's when he caught a whiff of the stench. So he took a look inside, and that's when he found them."

"So, did you tell those dicks? Or did you let them find out, for themselves?" Morrow motioned toward the federal agents.

"Yeah, I didn't want the kid to have to go through being questioned a second time. Not yet. So yeah, we've already collaborated on that. If you can call them asking me a bunch of questions, a collaboration."

"What about the kid. What could you get out of him.?"

Price shrugged. "All that I've got, I already told you. And I barely got that. He was pretty much in shock. They had to sedate him, after he puked all over himself, the side lawn, and all the way back home. He's resting at home now. I was going to wait and see what I can get out of him later."

"Give him a day, or two. This fucker is working my last nerve."

"You and me both. Hey, you look terrible. Why don't you go home and get some sleep. I can handle things around here. Go on, go home. I can take care of things for a few hours. We've got nothing here. So it's not like we're going to find him, as soon as you close your eyes."

Morrow rubbed the back of his neck. He was so tired, he almost took Price up on his offer, but he couldn't just leave the investigation. This case was far too important for him to just leave. He had to be there when this bastard was taken down. He'd just grab a nap on the couch in his office later.

"Believe me, I'd love to. But right now... ." He let his sentence trail off, as the two FBI agents approached them.

Special agent Scott Ross, and agent Charles Bicket, joined Morrow and Price, near the open window.

"Lieutenant," Ross nodded, receivingly.

"Ross," Morrow returned his greeting. Though not quite as pleasant.

"You look like shit," Ross observed.

"Thank you, for noticing." He glanced at his partner. "And people say that the FBI is cold and discourteous."

Price smiled along with him, underneath his handkerchief.

"Hey, why don't you take it easy. We're all on the same side here." Bicket joined in.

"Oh, we're on the same side. So that's why you keep questioning my people for your information, instead of finding thing's out for yourselves." Morrow laid into them. "My people have better thing's to do than to be your personal data banks."

"I didn't know that it bothered you so much. We'll just start asking the witnesses the same question twice and leave your people alone. Fair enough? I mean, we are working together on this, aren't we?" Ross said.

"What difference does it make, if you ask the same questions twice. Hell, we ask the same questions more than once, ourselves. And what do you mean, witnesses? There aren't any witnesses. Ever." Price jumped in.

"It's true that we're working together. And the L.A.P.D. has extended the bureau our every courtesy. You know what we know. But do we know all that you know?" Morrow accused.

"What in the hell is that supposed to mean?" Ross shot back.

"What I believe the lieutenant is trying to say," Price came to Morrow's aide. "Is that you're the ones with all of the high tech gadgets, and infinite resources. What do you know that you're not telling us? Just so that you can take the Stalker down, and show us up. The FBI always gets their man." Price recited their creed.

"He read my mind." Morrow agreed. "I owe you a dollar." He fooled with his partner.

"We're not hiding shit. Are you?" Bicket took exception to their allegations.

"We know what you know. That is, if you only know what we know." Morrow entangled his reasoning.

"All right, let's knock this shit off," Ross intervened. "We all have the same God damned information that the other has. Can we cut this bullshit out, now?" he adjusted his collar.

"You think that we're cutting into your investigation, and we feel that you're impeding, ours," Ross added.

"We're impeding your investigation!" Morrow growled.

"Yes, you are."

"How so?"

"The way that you insist that our forensics team work out of your labs. So that we have to shuffle in our own people and our own equipment. It's a pain in the ass. We do reside in the same city, you know. Your people constantly get in our way. We should be able to examine all of the evidence in our own facilities, using our own people. And whatever we might find, we'd be sure and let you know," Ross argued.

Morrow's eyes widened, and he lowered the handkerchief from his face. The stench of the stewed organs were ineffective, at that time. He was pissed.

"Look, you C.I.A. flunkies. This was our case for nearly a month, before the governor, in his infinite wisdom, decided to call you in to help in our investigation. That's right, help. Not to take it over. So the way I see it. We don't need you here, nor do we want you here. This is our case! And if you want to help, you'll do it in our facilities, with our personnel. We are not incompetent, you know."

"Well, to be fair. There was that O.J. thing." Bicket was more than happy to remind them.

"Mmm. I seem to recall a place called, Waco. Ring any bells?" Price chucked back in his face.

Morrow looked at the feeb, like he wanted to take out his gun and shoot him in the head. Even after, Prices' retaliation. But instead, he grit his teeth and spoke as calmly as possible. "This is the L.A.P.D.'s case. If you want to work it. You'll do so through us. And right now, you know what we know. So why don't you take your nice suits and your crew cuts and get the fuck out of my face."

"You know, you guys really ought to get some sleep. Because you're being way too fucking paranoid," Bicket observed.

Ross pulled at Bicket's coat sleeve. "Come on, we've got all that we're going to get, from this crime scene. If they find anything more, I'm sure they'll let us know. Let's go to the lab." The special agent pulled his partner away from the near confrontation. And the feebs left the scene.

"Dicks," Price said, a little heated. "What exactly was that all about, anyway?"

Morrow agreed with his secondary on the name calling, with a nod of his head and a bit of a hiss of contempt. "I have no, idea. Do you think it could be stress, related?" the lieutenant continued his banter.

"No…can I have that dollar, now?"

Morrow gave him a double take. But before he could continue their little mood breaker, he suddenly realized that his nose and mouth were no longer covered. He raised the handkerchief to cover his face again, looking at Price. His eyes peeking out over the top of his makeshift mask. And when he spoke again, his voice was muffled, just like before.

"Why in the hell, did you let me do that?"

Price shrugged. "You were on a roll."

He just let it go. "Well anyway, I've got to get back to the station. I've got to brief the chief, the commissioner and the governor about our progress. And the news of these new murders. We'll be lucky, if we're assisting the FBI after all of this. Anyway, when you get the results of the finger printing and the rest of the search, go to the coroner's office and pick up his report. Then pick up the pictures of the scene from the lab and bring it all to my office. I'll be there. Hopefully, someone will find something that the son-of-a-bitch left behind, that we don't already know about. I gotta get out of here. I've got twenty minutes to get back to the station."

Morrow started to leave, but turned back for one final instruction. "Oh, and send a copy of the whole mess, to Dr. Webb's office."

"Gottcha. What do you want me to tell the press?"

Morrow glanced at the Stalker's signature on the wall, thinking. "Tell them that it's definitely our boy. You can give them a rough time of death. How they were found by the kid. But for God's sake, don't tell them his name and don't give them anymore than that."

"I'll take care of it. Hey, let me know if we still have jobs after your meeting. I may want to sleep in tomorrow," Price yelled after him.

Just after leaving the Carey home, Morrow lowered his handkerchief and tugged at his collar. It was hot outside, but it was even hotter inside. The stench of the decaying organs could still be smelled, up to halfway across the front yard. So the press was getting none of it and that was fine with him. If they were to get a whiff of what was left inside the Carey home, they may begin to speculate on what mutilate meant, exactly. And that would give the rest of the psychos in L.A. something to work with, in attempted copycat murders.

As soon as he ducked under the yellow tape he was swarmed by the press. There were so many people, asking so many questions all at the same time. They all just seemed to mesh together, into one distorted howl.

"I have no comment. Detective Price will be with you shortly." He plowed his way through the crowd to his car, with a little help from a few uniformed officers.

The sea of reporters slowly parted, as he coasted through them to open ground. He drove away, pissed. Mostly, because of the Stalker. The rat fuck couldn't have picked someone else's town to carve up for blood. No, it had to be his. The blood sucking media worked his every nerve. And the FBI had a hand in his misery, as well. Plus, he was just so fucking tired.

CHAPTER SEVEN

It was Tuesday, 10:00 a.m.

The week following the blood bath of his seventh set of worshipers. Hamlin had spent the whole weekend pissed off because Brooke May had not called him on Friday, as he had expected she would. To offer him the remaining sessions, of the late Betty Pierce. But that call didn't come until just a few minutes ago. On the very day that he had expected to be seeing Webb for the first time. It turned out that they were contemplating on not filling the available time in Webb's schedule at all. But then they remembered him, considered him and gave him the call.

Not only did he accept Pierce's remaining sessions, but he offered up his deepest condolences on the old whore's passing.

Soon, he would have Dr. Webb right where he wanted her. Then, class would begin. She thought that she knew the mind and motive of the Stalker. But she knew nothing. He would teach her, though. And if she was smart enough she would learn and understand his plight. No longer labeling him the psycho she believed him to be.

She was a very intelligent woman and he believed that she would understand that the sacrifices he made were merely stepping stones on his way to his ascension into godliness. He expected her to understand. Because once he made himself known to her, he would give her but one chance to join him. And she damn well better not disappoint him.

There was always the possibility however, that she would turn him over to the authorities. In that event, her blood would be an acceptable substitute for her understanding.

With his first session with Webb coming up next Tuesday, the Stalker only had time now to begin his research on his next set of worshipers. Because he had already taken the Carey's. The family that was originally set for worship, this week. So he was ahead of schedule. Staying ahead of the game was not necessarily a bad thing. Now he had a little more time, for other things. For example, he could hit the night clubs, score himself some pussy and have a good time. Or cruise up the coast for a little R&R. Life couldn't always be about business.

***

Nancy Webb entered into the police station squad room, and made her way to lieutenant Morrow's office. She entered, unnoticed. Morrow was talking to his secondary officer on the Stalker murders, detective Jonathan Price. Both men she knew from before, during their one and only meeting in her office, a little more than a month ago. Though she did have contact with Morrow over the phone, trying to decipher the lunacy that scrambled the Stalker's mind. All that they had ever talked about was the Stalker, and she knew he was no doubt the topic of the two detectives conversation this time as well. Actually, he seemed to be all that anyone ever talked about.

She moved further into the office. "So, we meet again." She caught their collective attention.

"Doctor Webb. Please, come in." Morrow stood.

Price was already standing and nodded his head somewhat, greeting her.

Webb returned Price's acknowledgment, then stepped up to Morrow's desk and set down her briefcase on the corner. She opened it and extracted a stack of files, setting them at the center of his desk.

"Here are your files. All seven of them. I'm sorry, but I can't add anything more to my existing profile that might be of more help to you. The last four sets of murders are the exact same, as the first three. He never does anything differently. He is extremely meticulous. Picture perfect. A classic case of obsessive compulsion."

She sat down in front of the desk, opposite Morrow.

Price crossed his arms. "Too bad that there isn't a data base for foot prints. We'd have him in a heartbeat, with all of those size nines he's been leaving around.

Morrow sat down again, his lips pursed. Then indulged himself in Webb's presence. "Detective Price and I were wondering about a point or two, concerning the case. Maybe you can help us out, while you're here."

"Of course, anything to stop this man. Or should I say, monster. That is what he is, isn't he? Well anyway, what is it that you want to know?" she expressed her disdain.

"Well, the last two families that the Stalker has killed were taken closer together than usual. Do you think that he's stepping things up? Is his time frame that induces the killings almost up?"

"To tell you the truth. I'm not certain of anything when it comes to him. He doesn't really seem to have any set time between the killings. I know that we've talked about this before. But I don't believe that there is any type of cycle that he is going by. Lunar or otherwise," she offered.

"Okay. So you believe that he's wearing the blood of his victims so that he can become God-like, right?" Morrow tried to piece it all together. Sleep deprived and all.

"Yes. He's trying to become omnipotent. I think that in his mind he believes, that in some way if he wears enough blood he can take the inner power of his victims, and become this God-like being." She refreshed his memory.

"But it could be that his fetish for blood is increasing," Price speculated. "Maybe he is on some cycle. A cycle of his own concoction. Something that we wouldn't think of. And I know that we've talked about this before, but maybe he isn't trying to become God at all. Maybe he's just trying to appease some kind of cult figure, and his fear of this figure is his motivation to kill. Now it wants more… souls, at a faster pace. So he's stepping things up."

"No detective, he isn't afraid of anyone, or anything. He is the Stalker. That's why he leaves his signature behind. To make sure that we know exactly who he is. He wants us to believe in him, to fear him. There is no other cult figure. It's him and only him. He is the only cult figure that he is trying to appease. Like you said, we've already had this discussion. I'm afraid that you're just grasping at straws now," she told him.

"But you were right in suggesting that the only reason that he would be stepping up the frequency of the murders is because he believes that he is getting closer to achieving his goal. And that is omnipotence. Godliness, I do believe," she agreed. "And it scares me to death to think of him in this way, but like I said, he doesn't hold fear for anyone. Not even God himself, I'd say."

"Okay, so he's fearless." Morrow sit up straight, opening his eyes wide for a moment, trying to remain alert. "So what happens when he reaches his goal? Does he continue on, slaughtering family after family. Taking things up a notch. Or maybe he just disappears, into thin air."

Webb stared at him. A look of fear, and uncertainty in her eyes. "To tell you the truth. I don't think that he will disappear, at all. He has too much of a taste for it."

"Well, if he doesn't just disappear, may God help us, if he makes it as far as he wants to go," Price added.

It was quiet for a moment. The only noise, coming from the busy squad room through the open door to Morrow's office, before Webb broke the silence.

"There is one thing that might help us, if he reaches his goal. He will likely believe himself to be unstoppable and will likely become brazen and careless. Possibly leaving clues behind. He may even become so bold to where he may try killing during the day. Becoming sloppy."

"Yeah, but how many more families will have to die, before he makes a mistake?" Morrow wondered.

A moment of intense silence came over the room. It appeared that no one wanted to chance, answering that question. But the silence only lasted thirty seconds, or so. Then Morrow spoke.

"Jon, why don't you go home and get some sleep. Spend some time with your wife. And I don't mean just talk and sleep. Get in some of the good stuff, while you're at it. You never know when the chance might come again." Morrow looked at Webb. "Pardon me."

She shook it off. "Don't worry about it. I'd be thinking the same thing, if I were in either of your shoes."

"There you go. Doctor's orders," Morrow added.

"I'm fine. Why don't you go home and get some rest, yourself," Price suggested. "You've been awake a hell of a lot longer than I have. I can handle thing's while you're gone. It's not like you're going to miss anything. We can't find the fucker."

"You just want to sit at my desk. I've got your number." Morrow yawned.

Price snapped his fingers. "Damn, you got me. I was planning a coup with the third shift. We were going to take this joint over, and I was going to lead them and sit at your desk." Price went along with Morrow's jest. It was nothing more than a tension breaker. "Go home."

Morrow shook his head, wearily. "No, I think I'll just catch a nap on the sofa." he pointed at the vinyl couch, against the wall. Far off to the side of his desk. "You go home to your wife… or I will."

"All right. All right, I'm going. But you make sure and wash up a little, before I get back tomorrow. You're getting just a bit funky."

"Get out of my office."

Price backed away. "All right, I'm going. I'll see you bright and early. Good night, doctor." He left the office and disappeared somewhere into the squad room.

Webb gazed at the lieutenant glumly. "You do look dead tired."

"You have no idea." he rubbed his eyes.

"You really should get some rest. It's not good for you to stay awake so long."

"I have too. I really have, no choice. I can't allow the body count to go much higher. I'm walking on thin ice already. The chief and the commissioner are both breathing down my neck. And the governor is threatening to hand the case over to the FBI if I don't do something, soon."

"They can't possibly blame you for what's going on. And besides, the FBI doesn't have anything more than you do. So what could they possibly gain by taking you off this case?" Webb protested.

His eyes were half-closed. "Have you ever heard of the term 'scapegoat'? Hopefully, they'll only blame me and leave Price out of it. He's a hell of a good cop. He doesn't need a black mark on his permanent record because of this damn case."

"Don't worry, I'm sure that you'll catch him and put him away before long. I know that so far he's been perfect. But he has to slip up sometime. He won't be able to help it. He's insane." She tried to be optimistic. But deep inside she feared that Morrow's career would be over, before the Stalker case would be closed.

Morrow looked down at the files on his desk, and shuffled them into a neat stack.

"You know, doctor. It's all getting to a point to where I don't care anymore, why he does it. I just want to put the fucker in the ground. That's all that matters to me, anymore. I don't care to know any more about him. What he thinks, why he's doing it. It just doesn't matter anymore. I just want him in the ground." He rubbed the back of his neck. He was so tired.

"I suppose you think that I'm a little off my rocker myself, for thinking that."

"No," she confessed. "To tell you the truth, I wish the same thing, every day. Just to end his madness. Just for it to be over. I'm right with you on that.

And I haven't been awake for the better part of a week."

Morrow smiled, a bit groggy. "Well thank you for all of your help, doctor." He widened his eyes again, trying to perk himself up. "I know that this case has taken up a lot of your time, and I would just like to thank you, on behalf of the department. We appreciate your time, and effort. I know I do."

"I wish I could say that it's been a pleasure. But under the circumstances, that wouldn't be a fair assessment. Although it has been quite nice, meeting you. If only it were under better circumstances." She threw out a line to him, but he was far too weary to catch her drift.

True, he was a bit older than she was. But there was something about him that stirred her insides, and made her feminine wiles wild again. Maybe it was the authority he projected. Or his sincerity and sensitivity toward the victims of the Stalker. Or maybe it was his fatherly like relationship with detective Price. Or maybe it was just because he was so damn handsome. Likely, it was all of the above. He was simply the type of man that she wanted.

"I'm positive that sooner or later the profile you've given us will help us to catch this crazy son-of-a-bitch." He was completely oblivious to her tenuous flirtation.

She smiled, somewhat shyly. Embarrassed. Even though he did not catch the line she was casting out to him. Her eyes drifted away from Morrow to some pictures on the wall, behind him. Pictures that exhibited Morrow competing in martial arts competitions. In one of them he was standing alone, wearing what appeared to be a championship belt.

"You're a martial artist." She pointed to the pictures.

"Yes, I am."

"It looks like you were a champion," she noted.

"Yes, I was. Heavy weight champion of the world. Retired."

"You look rather young in those pictures. How old were you when you retired? If you don't mind my asking."

"No, not at all. I was thirty-five."

"Why did you retire so young? Didn't you care for the sport anymore?"

He kept his mouth shut, and seemed to be trying to avoid the question.

She became suspicious of his silence. She had, and still has, many clients that were reluctant to speak about certain things. But she had found that the healing process worked much faster, when the patient put all of his cards on the table. And Morrow was holding something back.

"Lieutenant, I have a question. If someone has been awake for more than seventy-two hours, why would they turn down a chance to get some sleep?"

He raised his shoulders. "I just want to be here in case we get a fresh lead on the slippery bastard. And, I'm needed."

She stared at him, a knowing look on her face. "I've been here for twenty minutes, and I haven't seen you do anything, but try and stay awake. Why?"

"Why, what. I'm needed."

"For what?"

He was slow to speak. "...Stuff."

She shook her head. "No, there's something troubling you. Something about those pictures. Am I right? What happened, while you were fighting?"

"I can't afford, five hundred dollars an hour." He tried to escape.

"I'll give you this one, free of charge."

"Okay, I might not quite be as needed as I may have led you to believe," he confessed.

"What happened, while you were still fighting?" she pressed.

He released a very weary breath. "It's not just, what happened while I was still fighting. I've been having these recurring nightmares."

"About the Stalker?"

"Sometimes." He wasn't offering up the whole story.

"Lieutenant. I can't help you, if you won't let me."

He stared into her beautiful blue eyes and felt partially, relieved. She had such a soft, caring look about her. He tilted his head off to the side, like a dog or a cat might do, out of curiosity. He was still unsure whether he wanted to offer up anything or not. But in the end he told her anyway.

"It was my last title fight." he spoke suddenly. "To make a long story short, I had to kick my opponent one last time, to put him out and take the victory. So I threw a kick to his head. He hit the canvas hard, and died on the spot."

"Oh." She winced. "I didn't know. I'm sorry."

"So am I." he turned in his chair to look at the pictures on the wall. "But it was a long time ago and a complete accident. But still, I killed him. His life he couldn't win back. But the title, I could have," he said, critical of himself. "It was fifteen years ago, ancient history." He tried to tuck away his obvious guilt. "Then the rest of my sleeplessness belongs to the Stalker."

She felt for him, but she had run across this type of self-inflicted punishment before. Many times.

"Look, Josh. This is all, very simple. You're allowing the weight of the Stalker case, and your own fear of failure to come down hard on your shoulders. And this pressure is triggering an identical feeling of helplessness, like you felt when your opponent died in the manner that he did. But his death was not your fault then. And the Stalker murders are not your fault now."

She leaned forward, laying her forearms on his desk. "Are you going to allow the Stalker to make you out to be the bad guy, for what happened fifteen years ago? Because you're not." She reached out and touched his hand, softly.

He paused for a minute, looking at their hands together. Her skin was so very soft. But before he could come up with something to say, she slowly pulled her hand away.

"I hope that what we've touched upon today will be of some help to you with your dreams," she said, sincere. She suddenly appeared to be a bit uncomfortable, because of her unbusiness-like touch. "It's getting late, I really should get going."

"Of course. Don't let me take up all of your free time. I think we've taken enough as it is. And like I said, it's ancient history. And as for the Stalker, we'll catch up with him, eventually." He shook her hand. "And thank you for the advice, it was well taken."

She smiled. "I hope that it helps you with your dreams. Goodbye."

"Goodbye."

They released hands, and Morrow sat back down, as Webb disappeared into the squad room.

Once outside and in her car, she guided her BMW out of the parking lot to the street, leaving the station house behind and headed for home, as the night sky set in. Wary that the Stalker might very well be out tonight.

CHAPTER EIGHT

Nancy Webb stared across her desk at her new patient. The well known and widely famed multi-billionaire, Bray Hamlin. Brooke May was right, Webb thought. He was quite handsome. The pictures of him in the newspapers and magazines did not do him justice. He was far more attractive than any picture that she had seen. He was also quite generous in the many donations that he continually, awarded. No cause was too small, or so hapless.

He was a bit shorter than she had expected, at only about five-eight. But she could tell by his tailor made suit, which fit him perfectly, that he was carrying a bit more weight than a man his size normally would. It was not fat, though. It appeared to be thickly dense muscle mass. Which made him appear deceivingly smaller than he actually was.

The thought of her not having been with a man in eight months suddenly popped into her head. "Oh my God." She couldn't believe that she had just thought that, while interviewing a new client. It was simply unethical. But Hamlin stirred something inside of her, as Morrow had, the previous week. Something deep down inside of her. It was no big deal to be attracted to two different men, in two weeks. But she wasn't the type to ache over every body builder, model type that came along.

But after an eight month dry spell, her needs were beginning to surface. She didn't even know Hamlin or Morrow. That's what made the whole thing so sordid. But it had been such a long time. It was her own fault, though. She allowed her work to dictate her life, and that wasn't good for her mental status either.

Why couldn't she just knock off work a little early one Friday, and have just a bit of a long weekend. Just for her, to get away from it all. She could take a ride up the coast, and spend the weekend at a nice little bed and breakfast. No interruptions. No cell phone, no pager. Just a beautiful view of the ocean. Total relaxation. No worries, no commitments. But especially, no Stalker. No radio or televison would assure her of that.

That would be perfect if she just had someone special to go along with her. A well maintained gentleman, with no financial or personal baggage. Especially someone without any troubled faculties. The latter of these requirements counted out about ninety-eight percent of the men that she knew. Maybe more.

Case in point. Sitting in front of her was not only an attractive man, but a brutally handsome man. Well mannered, very generous and kind hearted. With no seeming ulterior motive, behind his generosity. He just wanted to help.

One of the wealthiest men in the world. His financial future was more than just bright. It was blinding. But there were two problems. He was a patient of hers. So almost positively, he had some dysfunction of the mind. Or some past baggage of some sort, from his childhood. As to what extent, was unclear. And secondly, he was a patient of hers.

Though on the surface, and knowing only what she had read about him in the news papers and magazines, he appeared to be everything she wanted in a man. But still, his true self remained a mystery. So maybe now was a good time to start to get to know her patients, more personally. It couldn't hurt. Could it?

Well, either way she couldn't just start off with very personal questions. She couldn't just reach out and physically touch him. But she could and would have to settle for, metaphorically speaking, reaching out and touching his mind, to come to know his inner self. What was Bray Hamlin's motivation? What made him tick?

He was only a temporary patient, with only five sessions. So maybe he would be the perfect candidate to begin her direction to get to know her patients more personally. And then when their time as doctor, patient was over, who knows what could happen. She caught herself in a fairy tale-like daydream. An improper daydream. She shook it off. Luckily, Hamlin had not noticed her staring off into space. She opposed herself. He wasn't paying her to fantasize about her non-existent sex life on his time. But thus far, his initial session had been nothing more than silence. They had been sitting across from one another for nearly ten minutes now. But Hamlin hadn't said a word since the two had exchanged greetings. And her own daydreaming, caused by the silence. Had led her away from starting the session herself.

So it seemed that he was no more prepared than she was. Instead, he was just sitting there casually, looking around the office. At times, appearing to have the words right there in his mouth, but never broke his silence.

She cleared her throat a few times, hoping that it would spark conversation. But he just looked at her briefly, each time. Then continued to familiarize himself with his surroundings.

He knew that she wanted him to talk, so he held back. She needed to believe that she was in control. And his silence was taking that away from her. He would return her control back to her, shortly. But over time, he would take it away, all together. For good. During her directive however, he would show her his true self. Not so much the Stalker, at first. But the identity he had been born with. His true feelings. Preceding that of the beginning if his ascension.

She stirred in her leather chair. She was a very patient woman, and never liked to rush her patients along. She would let them open up, on their own accord. But Hamlin's silence was fast becoming nothing more than a waste of her time. It was clear to her that she was going to have to speak first, to get the ball rolling. And so she did.

"Mr. Hamlin… ."

"Bray." He quickly cut her off.

"I'm sorry. Bray, isn't there anything that you would like to talk about today? I am here to listen. And I get paid five hundred dollars an hour to do so."

He cracked a bit of a smile, but Webb could tell that it was forged.

"I'm sorry, I've just been trying to decide what to talk about, first. There's so much I'd like to get off my chest. I just don't know where to start." He smiled again, uncomfortably. He already had her. Such gullibility.

"That's okay. Just pick anything at all to start with, and we can move on from there," she encouraged. "I've had a lot of patients that were the same way, but once we got started, it just began to flow."

"Okay." He paused, still uncertain. "My parents died in a plane crash when I was twenty-five." He offered up a true, event.

"And you're how old, now? I know I've read it somewhere, but I can't seem to remember."

"Thirty-eight."

"That is, a terrible tragedy. And not having any siblings, must have made it even harder to take. Being alone, and all."

He cracked what appeared to be a nervous smile. "You even know that I don't have any brothers or sisters. I guess my whole life is in those papers and magazines."

"How does that make you feel? Knowing that there are millions of people out there who know quite a bit about you, but you don't even know their names. Or that they even exist."

He shrugged. "It can be overwhelming, but I try not to think about it. At least I'm not stalked constantly by the media, like celebrities. I very rarely come across a photographer. Even then, I just keep walking and eventually they leave me alone after while."

"What about having to deal with the death of your parents alone. Or did you have someone to lean on? An uncle or a cousin, maybe?"

"Well, as for the loneliness, I think that I adjusted quicker than I thought I would. Then again, I was kind of prepared for that."

"How do you mean?"

"Well as a child, besides my parents, that is, I had no one to play with most of the time. So I would play by myself. I read to myself." He paused for a minute. Pondering his next response.

"Lets just say that I have adjusted to being alone. I'm just having a hard time adjusting to the loneliness." There was a saddened and glassy look in his eyes, with a slight break in his voice.

"Loneliness. I thought that you were Mr. Goodtime," she spoke up spiritedly, trying to uplift him. Maybe it was lonely at the top. "But you have all of these friends. The governor, several judges, high ranking police officials," she rattled off just a few.

"Well, yes. But they're all more along the lines of being acquaintances. I mean, we're not exactly best of friends, or anything like that."

Friends. Yeah, right. He wouldn't be friends with any of those people, even if his life depended on it. But pretending to be, to keep powers like theirs on his side, was another thing all together. You never know when you might need a favor from a supreme court justice. Or staying two steps ahead of the police, as the Stalker always was, from tips about the investigation from the rambling of the police commissioner. But favors like theirs would only be necessary until his ascension was complete.

He had just gotten to know them and their predecessors through his parents, once he got older. But he certainly didn't care for any of them. As a matter of fact, they could all die in a fiery plane crash for all he cared. He would just go on and make nice with all of their replacements and start all over again. Friends. Yeah, right.

"Don't you have a girlfriend?" Webb probed.

"No. I don't even have a dog," he confessed.

"Why would you relate a dog to a woman?"

"I wasn't. It's just like the saying goes. Man's best friend, is his dog. So I would guess that it would be easier to get the dog, than it would be to get the girlfriend."

She swayed her head, just a bit. Accepting his comparison. "So I take it that you haven't had any long term relationships."

"Actually, that would depend on what you would consider long term."

"A few years or more."

"No, never. Not any longer than two or three months."

"Why not? After all of these years alone, can't you handle someone being a constant in your life? I know through a few of my patients that being alone for an extremely long period of time, then to suddenly have some one there on a constant basis does somehow throw you out of wack. Disturbs your cycle, so to speak.

"But you must try, or forever remain alone. It can be frightening I know, but we have to adjust; there's just no other option. Life can be scary, so why not have someone there to lean on if you need to. It makes life so much more pleasant," she reasoned.

Frightening. Scary. She didn't know the meaning of those words. In her wildest imagination, she couldn't even come close. But eventually, she would come to know their full definitions. Because he was going show her. He was going to take her to the heights of terror, where she would either come away with a broken mind or a complete understanding of his plight.

It would be then and only then that she could come away with him and be his. A queen, to rule beside his godliness. Yes, she was right. He was tired of being alone. And even in retrospect of all of the headlines that had been spurned about him by the police, through her profile. Calling him a "madman." He knew that once she understood him, her first impressions of him would fade away and she would come to know his genius.

Even though her profile had caused him much mental anguish, by way of newspaper headlines and constant badgering by the radio and television news shows, he forgave her. He had to, he had no choice anymore. He needed her now. His original plan was just to mind fuck her for a little while, then scare the hell out of her and wear her blood. But it seemed to him that she might be the only person in the world who could actually give him a run for his money, in the intelligence department. And he had a lot of "money," to run with. Her beauty and body, were a plus as well.

"Oh no, you misunderstood me. It's not that I can't handle having someone in my life, I would love that. Having someone to hold while we sleep. Someone just to talk to. To lay around with, looking like murder victims, while we watch T.V. Or just to know that somewhere in the house, there's a warm body, waiting for my touch. Someone to love."

My fucking God. She was actually getting to him. No one had ever asked him questions like these. Not in serious conversation, anyway. Sure, he had unbridled sexual fantasies. Two, three women at a time. And he made them happen, whenever he wanted. But that's not to say that he didn't want someone special to live out the end of time with. He had never had anything quite like that before. An intelligent, beautiful woman. Someone who could not only understand him, but make him feel safe and warm. The way his mother could.

"But relationships, just don't work out well for me."

"How do you mean?"

He sat back, firm in his chair. "It's just that women know how wealthy I am, and after about a month or so of dating they suddenly want to get married. They make it seem like such a grand idea. Like, 'Let's fly to Vegas and get married. It would be so romantic, like we're eloping.' Or, right after sex. 'I have a crazy idea. Let's go get our blood tests, then our marriage license and get married, right here in the house. With only our closest friends as guests.'

"Bull shit. Pardon my French. They don't want me, they just want my money. So the concept of a real relationship just doesn't work out for me. That's the bottom line." He appeared, somewhat heartbroken. Even he couldn't tell for sure.

He stood suddenly and began pacing about the office. Staying always within Webb's view. "But it's not just about the money. Although that is the main issue. Trust me, doctor. If I could find a woman that actually loved me, I'd give it all away." He snapped his fingers. "Just like that."

He gazed at her from across the room. Not a stare, but a casual look instead. She was quite striking. Her blonde hair, hanging like a frame around her face. Her deep sea shimmering blue eyes. Her skin, a soft vanilla. And her body a perfectly proportioned, sculptured piece of art. And lastly her lips, just under pouty, yet full and inviting.

Besides his parents, she was truly the only person that he had ever met that he didn't have the urge to kill. She was exactly what he needed. A graceful beauty, with such a soft voice. So soothing. Like his mother's. Yes, she was going to be his. He would possess every fiber of her being, lovingly. And he would rule the world, with her by his side.

***

"Have you ever tried a disguise? You know. Going out, incognito," she suggested in a lame attempt.

"I've actually tried that. It didn't work. Every time I donate money, the damn paper puts my picture on the front page. Then the Times, names me Los Angeles' most eligible bachelor. That really helps. I just can't escape it. Disguise or no disguise, what do I do, stop handing out donations? Go to some third world country, and drop off the face of the earth?" He appeared helpless. And for the first time in his adult life, he actually felt that he was. He wasn't screwing with her, but she sure as hell was doing a number on him. And she didn't even seem to be trying.

"Maybe I should try leaving the state. Do you think that they've heard of me in Michigan?" he stared at her, a sorrowful, glassy look in his eyes.

"I'm truly sorry, Bray. I don't know what you can do about it. I wish that I did. But I really don't have any suggestions... . Say, have you ever tried dating women that are already, wealthy?"

He shook his head. "That doesn't work, either. So called high society women are uppity, boring snobs. Boring as hell with their 'I'm better than you are' dinner parties, luncheons, and all of that crap. They're no better than anybody else. Even if they're already wealthy, it's always nice to mix money with money."

"Don't you think that your being a bit over critical when it comes to the whole dating process? I mean, not every woman in Los Angeles is looking for wealth."

"How long have you lived in L.A.?" Hamlin wondered.

"All of my life."

"Then how can you be so naive. Everyone is looking for wealth out here. This is Los Angeles. Hollywood, and all that. Everyone is a screen writer, or a singer, or an actor. Or already wealthy. This is La La land. The city of dreams. They're crawling out of the wood work. If they're not already wealthy, then they certainly want to be. That's it. That, and/or famous. That's all that's out there." He sounded upset.

Webb disagreed. "No, that's not true. Not everyone wants to be wealthy. Some people see it as a curse. Somewhat like you. And would much prefer to be middle class."

"Well, they sure as hell don't live around here. If you want to find someone who would prefer to be middle class you go to Iowa or Indiana. But this is Los Angeles. The home of money and fame."

He paused, collecting himself. "That's just the way it is, out here. That's the way it's always been, and that's the way it will always be. I can't change that. You, can't change that. The best that you can do, is hook up with someone and hope they can at least make you happy. In one way or another, you may never truly get what you want. But one thing is for certain: You can always get what you pay for." He was overly discouraged.

"It all just depends on how much you're willing to spend… . Oh, and by the way, I don't consider myself cursed. I wouldn't want to be middle class. Middle class sucks. I like the perks of having wealth. It just so happens that true love doesn't happen to be one of them. Otherwise, my life is just peachy."

"I'm sorry, Mr. Hamlin. But I have to disagree."

"Bray," he cut her off again, forging a slight smile.

She returned his pleasantry. "I'm sorry. I always start off formally with my patients. I've found that it makes them feel more significant," she apologized.

"Where was I. Oh, yes. All of your worth may work well for you. But you really can't speak for everyone. Now, what you said about true love not being one of your perks, I'd have to agree. If you're going to look at it in that way, then that is how it will always be. You really need to trust, more. You can't just give up. Everyone deserves to be happy."

"Oh, I'm not giving up. All I'm saying is, you really have to be careful about who you trust. You know. Just make sure of any motive they might have, before you totally commit."

"Motive?"

"Well, most people. Maybe not all," he conceded, "are untrustworthy. At least that has been my experience. I mean, you just mention money and everyone's eyes seem to glaze over."

He sat down again. "You of all people, must know what I'm talking about. You make five hundred dollars an hour. That's twenty thousand a week. One million dollars a year, for God's sake, assuming you take a two week vacation. How do you know that your boyfriend doesn't just want you for your money? I say boyfriend, because I noticed that you're not wearing a wedding ring."

He fished for information.

She sat quietly, watching him. Trying to decide if she should share that information with him, or not. She was trying to be closer to her patients. What was the harm, really? "I don't have a boyfriend."

He made a mental note of that. "Why not?"

Now that seemed a bit personal. But if she was going to know her patients better, they would have to know her as well. At least, a little bit.

"It's because I'm very busy. I don't really have the time to meet new people. But that's enough about me. We're here to talk about you."

She sit back in her chair, regaining control. "Why don't we leave your relationship woes, for another time. I'd like to talk more about your family. I know that you don't have any siblings, and your parents have past on. What about the rest of your family? Aunts, uncles, cousins. Do you keep in contact? Are you close?"

He shrugged. "I was my parents' only child. So when they died, the entire family fortune came to me. My father told me once that it would all be mine, someday. I just never knew that it would be so soon." He paused, remembering. "The money all came to me also in part, because my father didn't like the way that the rest of the family spent money. It was like there was no tomorrow. He would give it to them and they would have it spent in days. They didn't even work for it. I was the only one that properly handled what I received, responsibly. And I worked for my money. I worked very hard. Everyone else just wanted the money for doing nothing. And that's what my father did. He gave it to them. They were family. He didn't want to just turn his back on them. Then came the plane crash.

"They were all at the reading of the will, just waiting to see how much they were getting. You should have seen the looks on their faces when it all came to me. It was priceless.

"I have three aunts, two uncles, and several cousins. They don't come to me for money. They came to me, once. But they got nothing. I gave them jobs instead. The money that they get from these jobs is quite a bit less than what they were used to. But they make a nice living. Like I did." He paused just a moment to reflect. "I get a Christmas card, now and then."

She wrote in her notebook. "That's too bad. Everyone needs family. Now, what you said, about not having any friends. There's no one from when you were a child that you keep in contact with?"

"Like I said, I only have acquaintances. I was home schooled. I didn't get out very much. The friends that I did have in my youth were play dates. They were brought in to me, when it was time to play. They were the children of my parents' friends. My father's co-workers. There were different kids, for different days. But as we grew older they slowly stopped coming over, and we grew apart."

"So you have no idea as to where they might be? Or maybe you've seen a few of them around." She finished her sentiments, from before he cut in. Even though Hamlin was shaking his head at the time.

"Well, actually. I do see some of them from time to time, when I visit my businesses. I check the books. Sometimes I'll sit in on a staff meeting. They work for me. Well, they work for their fathers, who work for me. Their always pleased to see me." He used his fingers as quotations.

"No, the best thing that I can do is to pick someone up in one of my clubs. But that's just to serve my needs. It only lasts a few nights, at best. I play poker, with some judges. Or take lunch with the police commissioner, just to have someone to dine with. But there is no one special that I feel close to. I thought that we already established that."

"Yes, we did. Sorry, I was just looking for a clearer definition." she glanced at her watch and scowled. "Wouldn't you know it. We just get a dialogue going, and we run out of time. We're going to have to pick this up next week."

"No. Actually, I have something else that I'd like to talk to you about next week. Since I don't have that many sessions, I'd like to do some hit and runs, first. Then if we have time, we can talk some more about this. If that's okay with you."

"Of course." They stood, and shook hands. "I'll be waiting until then."

So will I. He owed her for making him feel… too human. She had dragged him down from his ascending godliness. Too far down.

"So will I," he promised.

CHAPTER NINE

2:00 a.m. Tuesday night.

L.A.P.D. firing range. Josh Morrow slid on a pair of protective glasses and a muffler headset. Then loaded a clip into his .9mm. He had tried to sleep on his office sofa, but he had far too much on his mind to be able to fade off. Not only was the Stalker a permanent fixture in his thoughts. But now, there were his dreams. Nightmares of the past, returning to haunt him. The death of his final opponent fifteen years ago hung over his head like a giant, darkened storm cloud.

Webb had given him a crash course therapy session the previous week. And made him realize that he was not responsible for the Stalker murders. He was simply, at the time, falling short of capturing the psycho. But she couldn't quite make the guilt for the killing of Dewayne Harper, his last opponent, dissipate. It was just a fight. A controlled fight. No one was supposed to die. But Harper, did. He was married, with children. And was just trying to provide for them.

Harper's death, and so much more, was clouding his mind. He just couldn't sleep. So he said, fuck it. And came to the firing range. He pointed his .9mm at the target silhouette of a man, which hung fifty feet away. As flashes of his final title fight, came alive in his mind's eye. His opponent's bloody face, appeared as clear as day.

He had sixteen shots in his weapon. A full clip, and one in the breech. More than enough fire power to clear away the interference from his mind, so that he might finally get some sleep. And if by some chance that wasn't enough, he had two more clips available.

He squeezed the trigger and the slug pierced the target through the right shoulder. He was off. He was trying for the heart. He sighted the target, again. When he suddenly recalled his opponent's final flurry of kicks and punches that had backed him onto the ropes. He pulled the trigger, and the slug tore through the target at the base of the throat. Again, he was off. He was going for a head shot. He sighted the target a third time, as a flash of his opponent's bloodied face, stole his vision for a millisecond. He squeezed the trigger twice. Both slugs penetrated the silhouette through the upper right pectoral. Again, he had been trying for the heart.

He closed his eyes and shook his head slightly. Trying to clear away the cobwebs. The instant of him landing the final blow to his combatant's head flashed before his eyes, as he took aim on the target once more. He fired five clean shots. The slugs created a nice grouping through the center of the chest. Finally, his hand-eye coordination was coming together. The slugs had grouped almost exactly where he had wanted them to. And it was a very loose grouping. His mind suddenly displayed the moment that his opponent hit the canvas, for the last time.

The mob was on their collective feet. And the roar of the crowd was so loud he couldn't even hear his own prayers for Harper to pull through. Blood was seeping from Harper's nose and mouth, as the ring side doctor turned him over, trying to bring him around. He tried smelling salts, but Harper did not respond. And when the doctor tried to check his pupils, he found that his eyes were rolled up inside of his head. He wasn't breathing, and there were absolutely no vital signs. No motor functions except for some sickening, involuntary twitching.

All that the fight doctor could do was wait until the EMT's got down to the ring, but he held no hopes in reviving Harper. He was literally dead before he hit the canvas.

Morrow shook his head a bit again, trying to clear away the cobwebs. It was not his fault. Everyone had told him that, repeatedly. But before he even reached the locker room, he knew that he was finished. His career was over. And the very next week he announced his retirement to the media. It was quite unexpected by everyone, but him.

After dealing with his drug and alcohol dependency, he wondered what he would do for the rest of his life. But he didn't wonder for long. He held a degree in law from U.C.L.A. And his new path in life was clear to him. Now, fifteen years later, he was a lieutenant with the L.A.P.D. And was facing his toughest case to date: the Stalker murders.

A burning sensation ignited in the pit of his stomach. Just the mere mentiong of the psycho's self-appointed title sickened him physically. And pissed him off, to no end. He fired two quick and clean, head shots. A third shot fired only a second later, struck the target directly in the center of the forehead.

Thirty-five people, seven families, men, women and children, were dead. Slaughtered by the Stalker. For what reason? Well, Dr. Webb had a pretty good theory on that, and he felt inclined to follow her lead.

Right then and there, he vowed that the body count wouldn't get much higher. He couldn't promise himself that there wouldn't be anymore deaths. Because they still had no leads and no suspects. But he was bound and determined to find the fucker, and simply put him in the ground. Then the City of Angels' nightmare would be over. And so, likely, would his. He fired his final two shots. They pierced the silhouette, directly through the heart. Perfect.

***

2:30 a.m.

Bray Hamlin positioned the Baxter's eldest son on his knees, next to his mother, and stretched his arms out in front of him. Then adjusted his forehead to touch the floor. The family, his worshipers, were finally together again. He removed a few pictures from the wall that they faced. Flinging them across the room, in a frisbee like fashion.

He stood before his worshipers nude, and ready for his blood bath, as shadows of light filtered in through the window shades, from the street lights outside.

There his worshipers knelt, to praise him. In all of his unholy glory. Their lord and master. He was already partially covered in blood as it was. He had cut the eldest child's throat, which caused a gushing of blood from his severed carotid artery.

His mind was in a blissful, yet frenzied utopia, while he shook with an intense anticipation of their essences blending with his own. An evil twinkling in his wide and animated eyes. His continuing ascension, was in full swing. And he hadn't even doused himself with the bucket of their blood yet. He dipped his hand into the bucket, nearly three quarters to his elbow. The tenuous yet dense, dark redness that covered his forearm, enraptured him, quickening his heart. Facing the wall behind him, with broad strokes, he left his signature in his worshiper's blood.

Smiling like the devil himself might beam. He picked up the bucket, lifted it above his head and tipped it. Dousing himself in his worshiper's essence. He emitted what sounded like a low howl of shear delight. As the blood engulfed his form, and streamed down his body into a puddle on the floor, where he stood. His power was already immense, but was still, ever growing.

CHAPTER TEN

Bray Hamlin entered the lobby of Nancy Webb's practice, and made his way directly to the open partition of the glassed in receptionist's desk. There sit the beautiful Brooke May. She sat at her computer, with her back to him.

He hadn't really noticed May's hair the first two times they had met. It was long, black and silky. Shiny, and appeared soft to the touch. Which he would never really know for sure. Unless May became a later insurance policy, to keep Webb from turning him over to the police once he revealed to her his true identity. It was a thought. A damn good one, too. He played drums on the small counter, between them.

She turned suddenly, noticing him there. "Hello, Bray." She welcomed him with a bright smile.

She was a bit too cheerful, for his taste. But Jesus Christ, she had a body on her. Yes, she would be the perfect insurance policy. "Hello, Brooke. Is she ready for me?"

"Almost. They should be coming out anytime now. The hour is just about up."

"Thank you." He began to pace.

He glanced at his watch. The hour had just expired. It was time for his appointment. Unless his watch was wrong. Fuck that! It was Swiss quartz. It was never wrong. Whoever this prick was, he or she, was cutting into his time. And that, he would not tolerate.

"So, how are things working out, with doctor Webb?" May's voice, turned him in her direction.

"Just fine, thank you." When he could actually fucking get in to see her. Whoever was taking up his time was walking on dangerous ground.

"Yeah, she's really very good. She's great. The best, really. You've only just started, seeing her. But she'll get to the root of your problem, before your last four sessions are over. I'm sure of it," May said, in a perky, happy way.

She made him sick. He hated constantly happy people. Because most of the time, there was nothing to be happy about. But there they were, day in and day out. It was his wish to take these people and slowly cut their hearts out with a spoon. That would make him, happy.

Where in the fuck was Webb? He was becoming angered. He wasn't paying her five hundred dollars an hour, so he could talk to her fucking receptionist. Even though May was beautiful to look at and factored into his future plans, and what Webb made in a year was mere pocket change to him, none of that mattered. He just wanted his equal time. And he was about to go and take it.

May pondered her decision on whether or not to ask Hamlin out. She had chickened out when he had come in for his first session. It was against the rules, and she could get into serious trouble if Webb found out. But she had to take her shot. She just couldn't resist. She wasn't after his money. Even though not having to work for the rest of her life sounded quite appealing. But her attraction to him was more than just a bit physical. Plus, he really seemed to have a heart of gold. With his many donations to charitable causes. He was well bred, intelligent, handsome. She just had to ask. She couldn't chicken out again. And miss out on an opportunity to be swept off her feet, by a true, knight in shining armor.

"Bray."

He turned to look at her. She was sitting forward, leaning on her desk. Showing off her low cut blouse. He looked down at her. Nice tits. He smiled. Great, pouty lips. He could see her as a pretty mean dick sucker.

She leered up at him, with bedroom eyes. "You know. I'll probably get into trouble for this. That is, if you were to accept."

"Sounds dangerous. You may want to put more thought into it, whatever it is. But if it's very important. Go for it." He opened up to her.

She sit up straight to further accentuate her breasts. "I was just wondering, if maybe you'd like to get together, sometime. Like maybe tonight, after I get off work. We could go out for a drink, or maybe dinner," she tempted him.

He scowled, ever so slightly. She was hot. And he would love to fuck her. Cumming so deep inside of her that she could brush her teeth with his spew.

She was going to come in handy, but not just yet.

He gazed down at a ring that she wore on her right ring finger. It was so very beautiful. A diamond angel, surrounded in an eighteen carat gold setting. She must have paid a pretty penny for that. But on a receptionist's salary? No. She must be fucking the boss. His thoughts paused, while he dreamed up that scenario.

"Bray." She broke his concentration. "What do you think?"

He shook off the picture of May and Webb, together. "I'm sorry. I'm very flattered, but I don't think that it would be such a good idea. You being my doctor's assistant and all," he politely declined.

Although he would still, very much like to fuck her. And make her squeal his name, in ecstacy and pain.

"I understand, completely. It was really wrong of me to ask, because of your situation with doctor Webb. Besides why would someone like you want to go out with a receptionist."

"Don't sell yourself short. If I weren't seeing doctor Webb, I just may have taken you up on that. Who knows, really. I've only got five more sessions." He looked at her, pleasantly.

As he focused on her pouty lips, there was a stirring in his pants. He was starting to get warm. He loved women, and he would have his pick of the litter, once his ascension was complete and his godliness was assured. That pick, of course, would be Nancy Webb. But that didn't mean that he couldn't have some fun while he waited. Maybe he would go out with May. Once, and only once. Then she would become a pawn in his dealings with Webb, to keep the good doctor quiet, until his ascension was complete. Then there would be no need to keep her quiet, any longer. He would be far to powerful for any mortal man to handle, at that time. He would own her. He would own everyone and their precious little world.

May was absorbing Hamlin's suggestive speech, when the door to Webb's office opened, and she escorted out the patient that had taken up five minutes of Hamlin's time.

Hamlin tried to cool down, while he watched her talk to the man for a minute longer, then sent him on his way. His cool down was interrupted by the tight skirt that Webb wore. She was just as stunning as May. Only May had slightly better tits. But her body was shaped with curves in all the right places. That was one thing that he had to hand to the big guy. He sure crafted some great pussy.

Webb motioned for him to come her way, as she re-entered her office. He passed the other man on his way to following her inside. He could have ripped his heart out for taking up so much of his time. But instead, he just followed the beautiful doctor inside her office. When he stepped inside, she was already seated at her desk.

"I'm terribly sorry that I took up a little of your time. But it's hard to stop Mr. Anderson, once he gets going," she apologized. "Please Bray, have a seat. We can get started, right away."

He closed the door. "I would prefer to stand, right now, if you don't mind?"

"Of course. However you feel the most comfortable."

She watched him, as he slowly began to pace back and forth. He was clearly trying to think of what to start with. Just as he had done, during his previous session. But she was not about to sit through that silence again. This time, she would begin.

"Bray, I know that it can be hard to make up your mind on what to talk about, but I remember from last week that you said, you didn't want to talk about your social life, anymore. But you did have something else that you would like to discuss. Does that ring any bells?" she started him off.

"Yes. Yes, I do. I just had my mind on business."

"Speaking of business. What do you import and export? And you own quite a few other businesses as well. Can you tell me what they are?" she tried testing his faculties and competency.

He put his hands on the upper back of the chair, finally stopping his pacing. He raised his shoulders, with a look of boredom on his face.

"We import, foreign cars. Export American cars. We deal in diamonds and furs, and much more. As for the other businesses, I own four night clubs, six five-star hotels, and all of their chains across the country. Two of the largest real estate chains across the country. Should I go on?"

"No, that's fine." She just wanted to test his faculties, not hear a laundry list of his financial conquests. "Why don't we just go ahead and talk about what you mentioned before ending your session last week."

"Okay." He began pacing, again.

"We can start now. Or after you've broken a sweat," she said, lightheartedly.

He stopped pacing directly in front of her, behind the chair. And shot an icy cold stare, deep into her eyes.

She blinked erratically, as though she were trying to deflect his stare. Then sat up straight in her chair. "I'm sorry, Bray. I was only joking, to try and lighten the mood. You seem so tense, I thought it might help you to relax.

I meant nothing by it," she apologized. A very slight hint of fear in her voice.

"That's all right. I'm sorry about that. I'm just a bit moody today is all. There's nothing to it." He stopped her from asking, why. "I always get this way, around the anniversary of my parents' death. Please, don't read anything into it. It starts the day before and ends the day after. This is the day before. Let's just not talk about it, please. I have something else on my mind to talk about today."

He paused again, as if trying to find the words. "When I was younger, from birth until I was seventeen, everything was brought to me on a silver platter. The best of everything. Brought right into my home. I was rarely allowed outside the grounds. And when my mother and I did venture out, there were at least twelve bodyguards with us. I don't ever remember a time when we were without them.

"My parents were very protective. They wanted to shelter me from the violence and profanities of the real world." He walked around the chair, and sit down.

"In my first seventeen years, I was allowed outside the walls that imprisoned our home exactly thirty-seven times. Always with my mother and our bodyguards. And very seldom with my father.

"I was never allowed to read anything but the classics. *Moby Dick*, *Tom Sawyer*, *Hamlet*. But never a magazine, never a comic book. There wasn't even a T.V. Guide around to skim through. And the only television that I was allowed to watch was some educational tripe that my mother had preselected for me. Even then I was only allowed to watch for about an hour. You know how you let your mind wonder while the commercials are on, until whatever you were watching continues? It was just the opposite for me. I wouldn't watch the crap that I was supposed to. I wanted to see the commercials. Brief glimpses of the outside world that I got to see so very little of. I was amazed by a simple, soda commercial. Or a monster truck rally.

"Don't get me wrong. I loved my parents, more than anything in the world. But they were far too cautious and protective in their raising of me," he confessed.

"Why do you think that was? Why were they so afraid of letting you experience life? So afraid that they made a little boy a prisoner in his own home. What could have scared them so badly?" she wondered.

He shook his head. "A fear of kidnapping. Corruption of a small child." He shrugged. "Who knows." He cracked a bit of a smile. "But I'll tell you what. You've never seen a little boy with as many imaginary friends as I had.

It wasn't until I was thirteen that I finally got rid of all of them." He released a whispered laugh, appearing somewhat embarrassed.

"Some were funny, some were friendly. And then there were some, that were just angry and mean. Very, very mean and nasty." He stopped for a minute, a somber look on his face. Remembering. "They may have only been pretend, but they were the only true friends that I ever had."

Focusing on the name plate at the front of her desk, he continued to reflect. "How in the hell was I supposed to ready myself for the real world, if I didn't know how to survive in it? How was I to know, what society deemed right or wrong. Luckily though, I started getting out a lot more after I turned seventeen. Fortunately I was a quick study. I mean, I turned out all right, didn't I?" he overly dramatized.

She leaned back in her chair a bit. "Of course you did. I don't know how, but you did it. I have never seen anyone as well rounded as you," she praised.

"I don't know, myself." A slight smile, broke through his tight lipped, expressionless face. "I guess I just got lucky."

He had her. She was hanging on his every word. She was mentally his. And he wasn't even lying. Everything that he had told her, in these first two sessions, was completely true. He still had a bit of a mind fuck in mind for her. He wasn't sure. Maybe he would, maybe he wouldn't. Because so far, the truth was doing the job.

He was slowly pulling her into his world, and soon she would know his plight and would join him in his ascension, into a power. To rule Heaven and Earth. The devil might even have something to worry about. Because like in business, he always did like to expand.

"Okay, there may have been a little luck involved. But I think you're just being modest. To tell you the truth, I don't think that I could have come out of a situation like that. And adapted to society as quickly as you did. Please, continue."

She wrote in a notebook that rested in the center of her desk. Waiting for him to move on. Just a bit spellbound. These notes she could rewrite into a paper for the New England Journal of Medicine, a paper that could change the way that social anxiety disorders were treated. But she needed more from Hamlin. Much more. And of course his permission to use him as a test subject. She believed that he would do this, because of his generous nature. He was always looking to help someone, in one way or another.

Hamlin relaxed a bit more in the firm leather chair. He watched Webb as she jotted down her thoughts about his life, to date. She appeared very interested. That was another reason why he wanted her. Her sincere interest in him. Yes, she would make a fine queen.

"My father was always wealthy. He was born into it, as I was. And he wasted too much of his life, looking after his businesses. Not really taking the time to live.

"My grandfather founded and built Hamlin's import, export. From the ground up. Before my father was even born. But he past away, before I was born, slaving over the many companies he had founded. Not wanting to see them, swept away... . God damn him. He taught my father to be the same way. And I'll be damned, if he didn't take up right where my grandfather left off."

"My mother and I rarely saw him, because of business. Then suddenly, they were both gone. I barely even knew the man. I was born of his seed. Yet, over the twenty-five years before his death, he was mostly a stranger to me. But I loved him, just as much as I loved my mother. Who was always there for me. Be it night or day. Twenty-four hours.

"I may hold the family fortunes now, but unlike my father, and my grandfather before him, I will not let them govern my life. Each business has a president, who runs things. I drop by every now and then, to spot check, how things are going. I feel that my more laid back approach is easier on the heart.

"As for my mother, she came from a well rounded, middle class family. Lots of love, all around. When she was fifteen she was discovered by some photographer, and boom. She became a super model. It was her dream come true. But when she was twenty-three, and my father, thirty-one. They met, fell in love, and got married. A year and a half later, I was born. So my mother quit her dream job to raise me," he said, guilty.

"She was a one hundred percent devoted mother. The most loving woman to ever grace God's green earth. She never, not once, showed any ill will toward me. She loved me deeply. And cared for me, like Mother Theresa would the masses."

"But your father, wasn't always there."

"No. Like I said, he wasn't always around. But when he was, we had some premium quality time together. He was a very busy man, though. I think that he believed that he, himself, was supposed to keep the family businesses afloat. That was a tough job. There was always some type of business, going on. It was never ending, and I accepted that."

She wrote in her notebook again. "Did your parents ever tell you why they only had one child?"

He bowed his head a bit, on that one. Then again, connected with her eyes. "I asked my mother why I didn't have any brothers and sisters, once. She told me that they had everything that they ever wanted in a child in me. So they didn't need, anymore." His features were chiseled and nostalgic, yet somewhat saddened.

Again, she wrote in her notebook. "A while ago, when you said that everything was brought to you, like what, for instance? I know about the schooling tutors. But what else?"

He raised his shoulders. "Instructors. Play dates. Everything."

"Instructors. What type of instructors?"

"Piano. Violin. Martial arts. Things of that nature."

"Martial arts, huh. I know a retired world heavy weight, kick-boxing champion," she boasted.

"Really, who might that be?" He already knew. You get to know someone, when he's been tracking you for a month, or so.

"He's a lieutenant, with the L.A.P.D."

"Ex-boyfriend? Future boyfriend?"

"Sorrowfully, no. On the latter of the two."

"Sorrowfully, no." What the fuck was that? Morrow was nothing. "World champion, huh." It was more like a heavy weight pussy. He beats one guy to death in the ring and can't even continue his career. He was disgusted just by the mere mentioning of his existence. He had more respect for the guy that cleans your windshield on Hollywood and Vine, than he did Morrow. Pussy.

"Have you ever had to use what you've been taught?"

Now they were getting to the good stuff. "Yes, I have," he reminisced. "When I was seventeen, my mother set me up with a friend's daughter. She had been over for play dates, in the past. But it had been years since I last saw her. It was the first time that I had ever been allowed out by myself. And the first time that I was ever near a full grown young woman. Needless to say, I was more than just a bit nervous. Very, nervous." He paused, clearing his throat.

"Please, go on," she urged.

"Well, I picked her up in one of my father's limousines. When she came down the stairs, and I saw her all dressed up like she was. Man, was she radiant. Then I got even more, nervous. I didn't exactly know how to act around her. I think I did okay. I mean, she never looked at me like I was retarded, anyway."

"Where were you going?"

"We were going to a friend of hers coming out party. High society, and all that crap." he stood, and began pacing about the room again.

Webb continued to write in her notebook, while keeping a trained eye on him.

CHAPTER ELEVEN

He appeared a bit hesitant to continue. As though he were ashamed of what he was about to tell her. He was quiet for a minute. Maybe, two. But then, he finally spoke.

"As soon as we arrived at the party, you could tell right away, just by how loud the music was, teenagers running rampant all over, that the party was unsupervised. It turned out that it was her coming out party, before her coming out party. A party just for her and her friends. Before the party with all of her parent's friends, family and their children. Well, I didn't know what to do. I had never in my life come across such a circumstance like that one before.

"I thought that we should leave, but my date talked me into staying. She promised that we wouldn't stay for too long, so we stayed. We were there for about an hour, when I finally started to relax, and have some fun. There were a lot of pretty girls there. Pretty and filled out. I had never seen so many beautiful girls, obviously. Then I noticed that the one girl that I was supposed to be paying attention to, my date, had disappeared. I looked every where, for her. I finally found her in the back yard, behind the cabana. She was surrounded by these eight guys. My age, maybe a little older. These were big guys."

He tried to show her, with his hands. Comparing them to his own, medium height, thickly muscled frame.

"They had been drinking a little, and were feeling bullet proof. They were trying to get her dress off, pulling at it and ripping it in spots. She was screaming bloody murder, but with the music being as loud as it was, no one could hear her. Except me and them. So I stepped in."

"Did you hurt these boys?"

His eyes glistened, excitedly. "Oh, yes. Severely. They all ended up in the hospital. Let me see if I can remember it correctly." He paused, suspensefully.

"Okay. There were eight of them. I ended up breaking a total of six arms, three noses, one jaw. Fractured one cheekbone, broke eighteen ribs, and bruised or fractured ten more. A lot of the breaks were compound fractures. They all ended up with concussions. And there was blood everywhere." He was speechless, for more than just a minute. Appearing quite animated. Stimulated.

His face suddenly grew somber. "I never told my mother all that had happened. My father boasted to all of his friends and workers. He was very proud. My mother was proud, just not in the same way as my father. She knew nothing about the details of that night, until we went to court. That's when the whole ugly story, was told. In fine detail." He paused long enough for her to get in on the conversation.

"You went to court. Sure, you harmed the boys. But you were just defending your date. She was going to be raped."

"That didn't matter to the parents of the eight guys. They filed a joint civil action lawsuit against me." He noticed the anticipation in her eyes. "They charged that I attacked their sons with a deadly weapon." He tapped his chest. "Me."

She shook her head a bit. "It's okay if their sons gang rape this girl and shatter her life. But it's not okay if they get hurt while trying to do so." She wore a look of disgust. "I'm sorry, Bray. I didn't mean to cut you off. Please, continue."

She was fiesty. He knew that she would understand him. She didn't mind hearing the explanation of the occurrences of that night. She didn't mind hearing about the breaking of bones, or the amount of blood that was spilled. And she wanted more. He bent his neck from side to side, a cracking noise accompanying each movement.

"There's not really all that much left to tell. Pictures of each boy were taken into evidence. So were their medical reports. There was testimony. At which time, they all managed to tell the same story. Almost exactly. You see, they said that they were merely engaging in some odd form of dance. In which the girl would stand at the center of the circle. Moving from guy to guy. Dancing, nothing more. But the police had taken pictures of her torn dress."

"My date testified on my behalf. As well did I. Only we didn't sound quite so rehearsed. But anyway. The jury didn't buy their story. I think what really got them, was the dance. A dance that had never been heard of before. And, like I said, they just sounded too well rehearsed."

"They were later all found guilty of attempted rape and did some time. Not much. But some, anyway. I mean, my father's attorneys tore their story apart." His features saddened.

"What's the matter, Bray?"

He stared across the desk at her. Despondent. "It was during those few days of testimony that my mother had heard just how dangerous her little boy had become. She was still there for me when I needed her. But our relationship was never the same. I think that she had become afraid of me. Yeah, I know that she was. I could see it in her eyes."

He collected himself. His eyes were beginning to tear up, but they never did flow. "The only woman that I had ever loved, feared me until the day that she died. No mattered how much I tried, I could see, there in her eyes, that her fear never faded."

He stared off into space, out the window behind Webb. "I don't think that her fear was caused just by what I did to those guys. I think that it was topped off, by my not sustaining any injuries. I mean, there was this fighting machine that put eight guys in the hospital, without suffering so much as a scratch. I was untouched. And I think that that was what scared her the most. I was a deadly weapon. And she was not only the one that had suggested that I take up the martial arts. But she urged me to. I wasn't interested, otherwise. I think she believed that she was responsible, for what I had become."

His expression lightened. "Well, in any case. I was deemed a hero, by my date's parents. And because of my chivalry, I received many more dates with the daughters of my parent's friends. And out of all of those dates I was rewarded with quite a bit of sex. I enjoyed that, very much."

His features suddenly went blank, again. But the glimmer of excitement, remained in his eyes. She tried to connect with him. Waving her hand in front of his face.

"Bray. Are you in there?"

But for that moment, he was off in his own world. A world where fighting and fucking were the only thing's that mattered. A world where rivers of blood flowed into a sea of crimson. A world where the Stalker ruled. And his worshipers, thus far. Awaited his arrival.

A sudden blink of his eyes, returned him to Webb's office. He shifted his stare to look her squarely in the eyes. And in an eerie calmness, he admitted his sentiments on his conduct.

"But what I liked even better than the sex was hurting them. Those boys. Hearing the sound of their bones breaking, the screams of their anguish. And the blood. Yes, I enjoyed it very much. All of it. It was, at the time, like I was someone else. My chivalry, turning into a bloodlust that not even I could control. Nor did I seem to want to. I didn't want to stop." He stared out the window behind her.

He was almost salivating. Appearing to revel in this memory. Savoring it. Replaying the events of that night over and over again, in his mind. A distant, vacant look in his once charming, caring and warm stare.

Her spine tingled, as she faced off with this intense new version of Hamlin. This blood lusting doppleganger, of L.A.'s most popular, kindest, angelic man. And it scared the piss out of her. She could suddenly feel a black evil emanating from him. An evil like no other she had ever experienced before. And she had worked with some of the most desolate, insane and evil minds ever to be institutionalized. Most, without any chance of ever being released back into society. Minds that made the fictional Hannibal Lecter seem to be nothing more than a villain in a child's fairy tale. But at that moment, none of them could hold a candle to what she was experiencing from Hamlin.

"It didn't stop there, though," he confessed.

"What do you mean, that it didn't stop there? What, didn't stop there?"

He started pacing again, crossing his arms. Then stopped on a dime. Looking into her awe struck, deep blue eyes. Causing her to nearly wet herself.

"For the next five years I beat up on my sparing partners. I mean, I beat the hell out of them. One, sometimes two a day. Even then, I wasn't satisfied. Then when I was twenty-two, and had finished my home schooling, my version of graduating college. I moved into my own home. That's when my obsession really began to soar," he divulged.

"That's when what obsession began to soar?" she asked, intrigued.

She was hanging on his every word, and he wasn't even lying to her. Sucking her in was going to be easier than he thought. His past life was interesting enough. So he would just keep her there, hanging until the right time came along. He just had to be careful of what he confessed to, for now. He needed his anonymity just a bit longer. Then, when he was too powerful for his true identity to pose as a threat to him. He would then reveal his true self to her and only her. He didn't need a fan club. He just needed Webb.

"Haven't you been listening to me? After I moved into my own place. I started paying guys five thousand dollars to fight me, no holds barred. Until one of us was unconscious, or just couldn't continue," he told her.

She was shocked. She couldn't believe her ears. His admittance to such brutish behavior quite frankly stunned her. Never had any of her patients, in the past or present, had ever done that before.

He witnessed her shock and asked, before going on. "Do you want me to continue?"

"Yes. Yes, of course." She ran a hand back through her hair. To her surprise, she was becoming somewhat stimulated. And wanted more. "So you paid men to beat up on you. Go on."

"No. Not just anyone. I found these guys coming out of gyms and dojo's. These were muscled men, black belts, street fighters. I never once led a lamb to the slaughter. There were over two hundred and fifty, in all."

"Two hundred and fifty," she echoed, aghast. "How long did you do this? It's not still going on, is it?"

"No, it's not still going on." He recalled, but for a minute. "I only participated in it, for about fifteen years."

"Only fifteen years. Only," she echoed herself. Still somewhat staggered. Afraid.

He nodded. "Yes. Only, fifteen years. But then, after a seven month grace period. You might say that I found another outlet."

"Were you ever beaten, by any of these men?"

Her interest seemed to pique at that moment, with the knowledge of his no holds barred, fighting matches. So it seemed that way, to him. But if it was, she was repressing her feelings very well.

"No. No matter how big they were, or how high a black belt. Not one of them, ever came close to beating me. Most of the time, I never even got touched. Pretty soon, it got to be too easy and I got bored with it. That's when I took my little grace period. Then I found this new outlet."

"So what is this other outlet, you have? And what exactly, is the outlet for? What are you releasing?"

He sit down, again. "Anger. Pent up energy. I just like to fight," he offered.

She wrote in her notebook. "I see. But tell me, Bray. What kind of an outlet can help you release these types of impulses, when you just like to fight? There are a lot of thing's to do to release pent up energy. But as for a penchant for fighting, wouldn't fighting be the only outlet for that? Am I right?"

He wore a somber look as he stared at her. Deep and cold, like he had done before. It sent chills down her spine. She really wanted to know more, that was her job. And yes, a little part of her might even be a bit stimulated, by all of the talk of his dominance over his opponents. The bad boy image, and all that. But Hamlin was not for her. She needed someone who had his dominant side under control. And didn't scare the hell out of her. She didn't know why she had even considered, him. Maybe it was because she hadn't had sex in eight months. He was handsome as hell and she was physically attracted to him. Like millions of other women were. But once again, he was a patient. Untouchable. And now, far too scary.

There was a part of her that just wanted him to leave, and never come back. He was really frightening her. Just sitting there, calm, after having confessed to more or less, loving the thrill of a good fight, and the spilling of blood. The breaking of bones. So calm. His once sensitive demeanor appeared to disappear from her radar. And he now emitted a soullessness. An emptiness of being. It was like he was dead inside. Like squaring off against the devil.

Even when he had spoken of love, in his first session. There was a wickedness, about him. Even though his pain was quite heartfelt, and he was an angel when it came to things such as contributing to the community. His donations were notoriously large in sum. He had a large heart, and billions and billions of dollars that he didn't mind sharing. Still, every man held a secret. Be it good or bad.

In his own words, he liked the sound of breaking bones. The sight of blood. And the fact that he had paid men to fight him, no holds barred. It was all just too much. It was chilling. And yes, it frightened the hell out of her. He was far too calm for such confessions. With that stare. That vacant, evil stare.

He was staring over her shoulder out the window, behind her. Like he had done before.

"Bray, did you hear me?" she spoke softly.

He blinked and broke his concentrated stare. "Yes. But that will have to wait until next week."

She looked at her watch. "But your time isn't up yet."

She wasn't really sure at that moment, if she really cared if he left, or not. She wasn't even sure if she wanted him to come back next week. As a psychologist she was intrigued by him. But as your average Jane, she was becoming terrified. He was definitely not the type of person to run into in a dark alley. Yet, she would have no fear against taking that same alley with him by her side. As if in two separate wolf packs. She would rather run with him, than against him.

"I know, but I have business to take care of. You might say that I'm running a background check, on a new client."

"Are you expanding one of your businesses?" she pried.

"I'm expanding, yes. But it's nothing that you'd want to know about, right now. I have to go."

She barely got out, "Goodbye," before he closed the door, behind himself.

She relaxed after he left. Her petty fears subsiding, along with her tensions. But now that he was gone she felt the need to delve deeper into his psyche. But of course, she had allowed those moments to slip away. As for probing his mind deeper, it seemed that he was only willing to give up bits and pieces of his past and inner demons. Like he had the events of his life arranged in some strange order, as to when he wanted to discuss them. Which was nothing new, really. Many of her patients carried on in some type of order. But in Bray Hamlin's case, the order in which he was progressing, seemed to be pressing on to more and more dangerous ground.

Again, though. Many patients had an order in which they progressed. But most of her clients couldn't stick to one subject long enough, to focus on it's origin. Much less arrange them in some order. An order that he not only controlled, but dished out in small doses. Making a diagnosis almost, if not totally, impossible.

Yes, Bray Hamlin was a mystery. At first, he appeared to be one of those lonely and loveless people that were so alone, that they were willing to try almost anything to find love. But now, with his second session under his belt, she didn't exactly know what to think. She just hoped that the nature of his continuing visits did not worsen, as his sessions progressed. Like she was expecting them to.

She suddenly noticed that her tensions had not subsided, after all. She was sitting back in her chair. A very comfortable chair, but her body was rigid, not relaxed, at all. He had been gone for five minutes now and her heart was still pounding. He really got to her. She held her hands up in front of her. They were noticeably trembling.

His demeanor had been terribly unsettling. He was a tremendously gracious and caring man. Yet, he had managed to terrify her. Over the period of one week's time, he had gone from someone that she had had the urge to share herself with to a monster of a man that she didn't even want to share a room with. Was she just being foolish? Or was her fear justified? She really wasn't sure what to feel. During his first session his loneliness and helplessness had appealed to her sympathies and she genuinely felt for him.

But now, after session two of his brutal recounts of past aggressions, his vacant, empty stare, and his emotionless conscience, brought terror to her heart and mind.

He had assured her that these past aggressions, this violent side of him no longer existed. But his calm demeanor was heavily counteracted by the emptiness behind his eyes. It was like nothing that she had ever witnessed before. It was like he was two different people. And she knew about split personalities. But the difference between the two Hamlins was not caused by that specific psychosis. In one case, he was a kind and gentle man. In the other, he appeared to be a beast without a soul. But at the same time, he remained himself. Not Bray Hamlin, and John Doe. Just Bray Hamlin.

The sudden terror that had gripped her mind, would not release her. She tried her best to relax, but she couldn't help but to wonder what Bray Hamlin might have in store for her come the following week. Would he revert back to the helplessness he had exhibited in his first session? Or would he show an even more violent side? It was all up to him, and the demons trapped within the gray matter of his seemingly demoralized mind.

***

After leaving Webb's office, Bray Hamlin made his way to the receptionist's desk. He leaned on the small counter between him and Brooke May and she looked up at him, with a smile.

"Brooke. I've been thinking about what you asked, earlier. And I've decided that I'm not going to let my seeing doctor Webb stop what could be a good thing. So if you're still willing, I'm able." He smiled, charmingly.

Her face lit up. "Yes, absolutely. What time? I get off at 5:00."

He frowned. "I won't be able to make it tonight. I have some business to take care of. How about Friday? I have one meeting, and then I can pick you up at your place. Is that good for you?"

She wrote her address on a piece of paper, and handed it to him. "Yes."

"Okay, then. I'll see you Friday. Oh, and why don't we keep this our little secret. I don't want you getting into any trouble on my account."He smiled. "Bye, now."

"No problem. My lips are sealed." She waved as he walked through the lobby and left the suite.

May trembled with excitement. Her heart, pounding. She was actually getting a shot, at Bray Hamlin. The kindest, most gentlest and caring man in the country. He was the most charming man she had ever known. True, she didn't really, know him. But all of his charitable donations and a few magazine interviews that she had read about him. Made her feel as though she already knew him. He had been voted Man of the Year by a national survey. Several times over. And of course, the L.A. Times most eligible bachelor. He was truly a kind spirited, angel of a man. And she was going to be fortunate enough to spend an evening with him. Maybe, even longer she hoped.

***

Bray Hamlin unlocked the door to his Mercedes, which he had parked, in the structure adjacent to the medical center. He was about to slide in behind the wheel, when one of the buildings maintenance men approached him.

"You know, you shouldn't park in a handicap space, unless you're handicapped." He pointed to a clearly visible sign, on the concrete wall in front of Hamlin's car.

Hamlin glanced at the sign. "I'm psychotic."

"Yeah, you go ahead and poke fun. But next time, I'll be calling the police. You know, just because you've got a lot of money, doesn't mean that you're above the law. It just ain't right."

You fucking piss ant, Hamlin thought. He could squash him like a fucking bug. But he had balls, he'd give him that.

He drew in a shallow breath. "Point taken," he conceded. "Let me ask you one question though, before we part ways."

"What's that?"

Hamlin's eyes glistened, stone cold. His voice, bland. Almost robotic. "Do you happen to have a large family? Wife, three kids."

The guy shook his head. "No. I'm not even married."

Hamlin pursed his lips, disappointed. "Huh. That's too bad."

CHAPTER TWELVE

Wednesday. 2:30 p.m.

Bray Hamlin stood before a league of people, at a podium on the stage at the Los Angeles Civic Center. The audience was applauding the recent announcement of Hamlin's donation of five million dollars to the National AIDS Foundation.

He beamed a bright smile for the cameras. Truly basking in the praise of his soon-to-be worshipers. Just as soon as his ascension was complete. After a moment the applause died down and he was finally able to speak.

"Some people ask me, why give so much? The answer to that query is quite simple. Because, it is needed. This disease is not just going to go away. It needs to be defeated, medically. And the only way to do that is to study it. Understand it, and come up with a cure to eradicate it. Erasing it, from the face of the Earth." The applause bellowed out again, cutting him off.

His mind was allowed to wander now that he was once again, forced into silence. He looked out over the auditorium. There had to be thousands in attendance. That was a shit load of blood. He wondered how many there, could lead him back to their five member families. More than enough, he knew, to fuel his ascension to its peak. He trembled slightly, unnoticeably. He wanted their blood. All of it. But now, was not the time. He fought back his lust, and remained secure. Barely.

He continued looking out over the crowd. If his lust for blood could not be quenched this night, his lust for female companionship would be. He noticed a few high class seductresses, staring at him like a deep pocketed trophy husband. But he was looking for less than that. A one, or maybe two nighter. That would leave them breathless and throe stricken. A night or two that they would never forget for the rest of their lives.

The ecstasy and pain, of being fucked by Bray Hamlin. A night that they would never speak of again. Unless they happen to drop the fact that he was not only a magnificent, rough lover, but that they had been joined by another woman. Unless they were into that sort of thing. He could give a rat fuck, himself. He loved a good threesome and he didn't care who knew it. Yet somehow his escapades were never publicized.

He continued to comb the room, looking for those lucky ladies that would be accompanying him home tonight. And there in the front row, he singled out a strikingly beautiful brunette. She wore a very short skirt and a low cut blouse, showing off her magnificent body. He could feel himself getting harder, the longer he looked at her. She would be one of his guests tonight. That he was certain of. And what a time she was going to have. A night never to forget. Yes, he was going to put her in front of a mirror, just so that he could see the look on her face when he jammed his cock in her ass.

But she was not going to be alone. She would have some company. There was a sea of beautiful ladies out there to choose from. All of them just waiting to give up some pussy to a nice guy. And you don't get much nicer than giving away five million dollars to a worthy cause. Yeah, he was going to be balls deep in some socialite pussy before dinner time.

Once again, the applause died down and Hamlin spoke. Trying hard not to laugh. They all looked so God damned inspired and attentive. He really did love making public appearances. The audiences were always held right in the palm of his hand. Just waiting for him to squeeze the blood right out of them.

"But can this cure be achieved, without the proper funding? No, it can not be done. That's why, I give so much. As a gesture of good will and faith. That some day soon the AIDS nightmare will be over. Thank you."

He concluded to a roar of applause from the zealous crowd as he left the podium, taking his seat on stage.

Fuck this. This fucking disease never would have started if some African monkey fucker would have kept his dick in his pants. Or loin cloth. Which ever.

"You could run for governor, and go unopposed. They love, you," his publicist whispered, leaning in from the next seat over.

Hamlin smiled. You stupid, fuck. The hell with governor. He was going to rule all states. All nations. The world. Just as soon as his ascension was achieved.

While the foundation's president took to the podium to start her babbling. Hamlin once again, looked out over the audience. He was definitely, going to score some pussy tonight. But again, not just any pussy. But wealthy, refined and highly educated pussy. Hell, for a five million dollar donation. He was very sure to get at least two ladies, who would be willing to accompany him home tonight. It was just a matter of which two. He grinned. He always did love having an extra set of tits around.

***

On the ride home from the civic center. Bray Hamlin relaxed in the back seat of his limousine. He could feel the power swelling inside of him. His ascension was near. Closer than he had anticipated it would be by this time. Yet, he hadn't worn the blood of his worshipers in a little over a week. There was still a ways to go. And a lot more blood needed to be shed, before he could truly attain his godly potency. But that blood would not be shed tonight.

He wondered about Nancy Webb, however. Was she as intelligent as she appeared? Intelligent enough to understand his quest for immortality? Intelligent enough to join him in his ascension? Above all others. To rule the world, and beyond, as he was hoping she would. Or would she rebel against his rule and die with the masses?

He allowed his muscles to totally relax, and released a deep, cleansing breath. Those questions would be answered just as soon as his Tuesday appointment with the good doctor, came around the following week.

Right now, though. He sat at the center of the limousine's back seat. Flanked on both sides by beautiful socialites, whom he was allowing into his world. For this, a night or two of unbridled pleasure. In ways they never thought possible. On his left sat the beautiful, short skirted brunette, Nikki. And on his right, another enchanting brunette, Celine. Both of which upheld high social standings within the community. Were quite wealthy. And were now willing to attempt, what they may had feared to experiment with in college. Just for him.

Expanding their sexual horizons. Giving each other a guiding hand, and a tantalizing, slippery tongue. To lead one another to the heights of ecstasy. That they could only have fantasized about, until now. And he would guide them. Just as he had done in the past. Whenever his slick tongue and good looks got him into the love triangles he so desired. For nothing more than his own perverse amusement. And tonight, would be no different.

His intentions toward Webb, however, were honorable. With her by his side he wouldn't need any other. There would be no one else but her. To stand by his side, in all his majesty.

CHAPTER THIRTEEN

Griffith Park. Thursday. 12:07 p.m.

Nancy Webb sit at the entrance to the park in her BMW, awaiting the arrival of a friend. A friend who was a fellow psychologist. The two had attended school together. They met at the park bi-weekly for lunch and singular counseling. Even psychologists need someone to talk to now and then. And they had promised each other that they would always be there for one other. In the case of need.

She hadn't waited long before his Jaguar took the space next to her. She promptly joined him out in the sweltering afternoon air. Nathan Corbit. Psychologist to the stars. Not only her oldest friend from graduate school, but one of just a few of her classmates that she still kept in touch with. They hugged, and walked side by side. Each carrying a sandwich and a cold drink.

"So, how's Beth?"

"She's just fine, thank you."

"What about your practice? Doing well?" she asked.

"Business is booming. There are a lot of disturbed celebrities out there. Singers, models, actors. A lot of producers. Some directors. You know what it is with actors. They're always pretending that they're someone else. So out of all of these personalities that they project, their own sometimes gets lost in the shuffle.

"Directors tend to get this God complex. You can imagine why. And the producers come in totally stressed out. Almost on the verge of breakdown. Because they have to deal with the actors and the directors, all of the time.

That's why they're all on Prozac," Corbit joked, but noticed that his former study buddy didn't even crack a smile. "What's wrong, Nancy? We're here for each other, remember? So come on, spill it."

She wrapped the arm of her drink toting hand around his arm. Satisfying her need for security. "It's just this patient I have. He has a long history of violence. By his own, admission… ."

"Let's be careful, now. We don't want to over step our boundaries," Corbit cut in, reminding her of the limits of their oath.

"I know, don't worry. It's not going to go much further than this."

They stopped and faced one another.

"It's just that this patient told me that he doesn't indulge in these acts of aggression, anymore. But I'm not so sure that I believe him… I think that he could be a danger to others."

"Why shouldn't you, believe him? How dangerous, do you think he might be? Has he made any threats?"

"Well," she was indecisive. "No, he hasn't threatened, anyone. But when he told me about these acts. He seemed to be enraptured, just by the mere mentioning of them. And he was so very cold and distant. Almost entranced, just by the thought of these past blood lettings."

"Whoa, that's enough. I don't want to hear, anymore. We can't do this, Nancy. Not without a signed release form. We can consult. But not until you get that form signed. You know that."

He grimaced. Sorry that he couldn't help her. "Look, I don't want to seem like I don't care. But I can't help you in that respect. All I can do is give you some advice.

"If you really think that this guy is dangerous, then by all means. Notify the proper authorities. You have to do what you think is best. But you better be damn sure that he's the threat to society that you think he is, before you go telling anyone, anything. You don't want to lose your license over a misunderstanding. You have to be absolutely sure about this guy. Are you? Absolutely sure?" Corbit warned.

"Well, no. But if only you could talk to him, and see for yourself… . What I'm trying to say is, that he is far too peaceful. Even when he talked about those violent acts. He was as still as a coma patient. Emotionless. Except for his eyes. You can see the vacantness, and rage in them. A merciless, fiery stare. Like he is this powder keg, just waiting for the right moment to explode. And I'm afraid that it's going to be all over me." She just couldn't put his eerieness into words, and was quickly becoming unhinged. "I haven't even been able to sleep all that well since his last session, two days ago. I just keep seeing that soullessness, behind his eyes everytime I close mine. And I've had to look at the Stalker's handy work, continuously. But not even that, has kept me awake at night."

Corbit bent his knees, to look her square in the eyes. "Don't put your trust in a stare. Don't lay your career on the line for a look in some guy's eyes. A lot of people have cold, even evil, eyes. But that doesn't make them dangerous.

"Look, feel this guy out for a while. Give him a few tests. Then come to an honest, medical opinion on his mental status. Then, if you still feel that he's a danger to others, by all means call the police and get him some treatment."

"I was thinking about testing him, but he's only going to be my patient for three more sessions. Trust me, I know how that sounds. Very impotent. But he scares the hell out of me. He didn't, at first. But now, I can't get him out of my mind. He haunts me, constantly. So why shouldn't I just humor him for another three weeks, then dump him off on someone else. I just don't know what else to do. For some damn reason he just gives me the creeps." She shivered a bit.

"Nancy, what do you think professor Mamet would say, if he heard you speak like that?" He spoke of their college professor.

"Fuck doctor Mamet. We're not in school anymore. And he's not the one trying to care for this patient." She stopped, to regain her composure.

"Look. In public, he is a very generous and revered man. But being in a room alone with him, makes you want to wet your pants. You look into his eyes, and you can see that he's dead inside."

Corbit knew that he shouldn't. But his friend needed him. No one would be the wiser. "What was his situation like, growing up?"

She looked surprised. She always knew that Corbit was a great friend. But she never thought that he would break their code of ethics just for her.

"Are you sure that you want to do this?" she wanted him to be positive.

"Yes. No one needs to know. So just tell me what was his situation like, growing up?"

"Quite controlled. But in an attentive way. Loving and guiding," she let slip.

"And what about his parents, now?"

"They're deceased."

"Older brothers, or sisters?"

"No."

Corbit nodded a bit. Believing he had the answer. "Well then, maybe that's what he wants from you. He wants your guidance. You say that he's well revered?"

"Yes, but that doesn't explain his demeanor."

"Well, like you suggested. Maybe he is dead inside, of sorts. He has the attention he craves. But he lacks the leadership his parents provided for him. Maybe he just needs a friend. And as for his demeanor, maybe he feels that if he's too animated and shows his true feelings, you may think of him as disturbed. Maybe he's just being cautious."

"That does sound familiar. In his first session he said that he has no friends, just acquaintances. But why come to me?" she was stumped.

"He might have done this before. It's just that the other therapists didn't fit the bill. Maybe he thinks of you as his intellectual equal. And that maybe he can make some kind of a connection after his sessions are out of date." He raised and lowered his eyebrows, abruptly.

"Don't be retarded." She shied away. "I no longer consider myself on the market."

"Whoa. My best friend gets herself some, and I don't even get a heads up?"

"I haven't gotten myself anything. It's still a work in progress. He doesn't even know." She refrained from mentioning, who he, was.

He pointed at her. "You know we're open to each other about stuff like this. Remember? We can tell each other anything. And the other will not judge. Who is it? Anybody I'd know?"

"Let's get back to my patient." She changed the subject.

"We're not even supposed to be consulting on your patient. Who is this mystery man?"

She gently scoffed at the ground with her leather pumps. "It's Josh Morrow. The lieutenant in charge of the Stalker case."

"You know, I never thought that a psychiatrist could meet anyone at work. But I've got to hand it to you, you've managed to do it."

"Anyway. There's one other thing about this patient of mine. He seems to want to control our sessions. I know that it's up to the patient to decide what to talk about. But he seems to have a clear agenda. Once he's done talking about something, that's it. He's done. I get a very clear picture of what it is that he's trying to get across. But I really can't come up with a diagnosis. Because he never wants to talk about things any further than when he decides he's done."

"Sounds like a classic control disorder. One that seems to go both ways. He wants you to control, or give him a solution to whatever it is he wants solved. It's just like any other doctor, patient relationship, really. It's nothing to worry yourself over. It's basically a double standard. He simply wants to have control over what he wants you to control." He shook his head. "It's a bitch, isn't it."

She agreed with a half-hearted smile, "It sure is."

"Like I said, maybe he's testing you to see if you've got what it takes to equal him. To see if you're as good as everyone says you are. That could be a probability, couldn't it?" he asked, knowingly.

"I guess so." She smiled a bit wider and seemed to relax. "Yeah, I guess I just got kind of spooked. It's just his eyes; they seemed to pierce my soul."

Corbit agreed. "It happens to everyone, at one time or another. It may take years, and one thousand patients, before that person comes along. Or it could be that very first one. But sooner or later, it happens to everyone." He tried to comfort her.

He changed the subject to get her mind off of this mysterious patient. But unfortunately, the best that he could do off the top of his head wasn't much better.

"So how is the Stalker case coming along? How are the police doing with your profile, do they have any suspects yet?" he pried.

"None that I know of. Actually, I'm not even sure that my profile is helping. I mean, the death toll is up to eight families now. But when I was brought in to consult, there were only three." She turned away, a look of defeat on her face.

"Hey, don't talk like that. If the authorities are following your profile they'll get him eventually. You're one of the very best," he praised.

"I wish I could believe that. Hell, I've cured people in less time than it's taking to find him." She was frustrated, and tense.

"Things like this take time. They'll get him. You can't expect to find him in a day, or even a month. A lot of the time you have to wait until they slip up. And I'm sure that when he does, or the police just get a break and nab him, he'll fit your profile, exactly."

She shook her head. "I don't know. He's just so methodical, and extremely cautious. He never leaves any trace of himself, behind. Just a few strands of hair, that's about it. Nothing distinguishing. But for two exceptions, that I can't reveal."

She spoke of the bloody footprints, and the writing of his name on the wall, in his victim's own blood.

"He's cold and calculated. The police and the FBI all believe that he is just a total, psychopath. But I knew better. He is a total sociopath. But when it comes time for him to kill, he loses all touch with reality, and that's when he becomes what they already believe he is. But he is clearly in a controlled state of mind, or all of the crime scenes wouldn't be so picture perfect. He would mess up, somehow. But he doesn't. Psychopath, sociopath. I really can't tell anymore. I don't know what he is. All I can say for sure is that he has one hell of a blood lust, and he's not going to stop until he gets exactly what he wants. And I believe that is omnipotence. I know that I shouldn't be telling you all of this, but that's it. He wants to be a god."

"He wants to be a god?"

"Yes. Don't let on to anyone that you know. Not even Beth. I can get into serious trouble. Well, you already know that."

"Oh, yeah. You're preaching to the choir," Corbit assured her.

She smiled. "Thank you for all of your help, Nathan. It's just that this patient really put one over on me. I actually had never felt so scared before. It was just his calmness and his chillingly cold demeanor. It freaked me out."

"No problem, that's what friends are for. I hope everything works out."

She glanced at her watch. "Oh, no. I have a 1:00 appointment that I really need to get to, in twenty-five minutes. I'm terribly sorry. I hate to run off on you like this."

"It's okay. But remember, next time it's all about me," he kidded.

"You've got it."

They picked up their pace, walking back toward their cars.

He checked his, watch. "Ooo, I have to get going myself. I have an appointment with a celebrity control freak. I know what you're thinking. Which one? But some things must remain a mystery."

She smiled and opened the car door, kissing his cheek. "Thanks a lot. I owe you, big."

"It's no problem. Anytime," he said, graciously.

She put one leg in the car, then stopped. "I'll see you and Beth for dinner sometime. Love you, bye." she slid in behind the wheel of her BMW and drove off in haste. Waving as she went.

Corbit waved after his friend, with a smile on his face. But deep inside he was worried for her. She was overloading herself, and that was not a good thing. Especially when she was helping to track one of the most feared serial killers in U.S. history.

***

Friday. 8:22 p.m.

Bray Hamlin handed the valet driver a ten dollar bill. Then climbed in behind the wheel of his Mercedes, with the beautiful Brooke May joining him in the passenger seat. They had just finished a delightful meal, at one of L.A.'s finest restaurants. And now, at Hamlin's suggestion, they were going back to his place for a nightcap.

May was beaming. Dressed in her finest low cut, hip hugging dress, she looked very, appealing. But then again, she always did. Her smile was wide and constant. Like the corners of her mouth had been taped back. She was truly having the time of her life.

"So, are you having a good time, so far?" Hamlin asked.

"Oh, yes. The restaurant was fabulous. So was the food. You wanting to know all about, me, letting me talk while you actually listened. I've never been out with a guy who actually wanted to know all about me. And didn't stare at my breasts the entire time that I was talking." Her laugh was a bit out of breath. "So, when are we going to talk about you?"

"Oh, maybe later. You know a lot about me already, from the newspapers and magazines. I'd like to know more about you."

"Really? It seems like I've been talking about myself, for hours."

"You have, but I like it when someone wants to talk about more than just my wealth and popularity. So please, go on."

She wouldn't be talking about herself for much longer. Just until he could shove his cock down her throat, would be sufficient.

"I dropped out of school, after just one year in college. Luckily, I found Doctor Webb. Nancy. Or actually, she found me."

"What do you mean, she found you?"

"Well, I had been putting in applications all over the city. I didn't really have any qualifications. I'd done a little in retail sales. But nothing else. But she saw something in me. She helped me to learn more about computers than I already did. Huh. She trained me herself. She was a life saver. I was getting low on rent money so she gave me a little advance in salary so I could keep my apartment. She really helped me. I've been with her now for six years, and for being just a receptionist, she pays me very well. But I always kid her about needing a raise."

She stopped talking, as she looked at the houses in Hamlin's Beverly Hills neighborhood, her mouth hanging open a bit. Her eyes got big and wide when Hamlin turned up into his driveway, and she could see his home. She was excited beyond her wildest dreams. She had never been this close to a house of its magnitude before. And soon she would be inside, possibly staying for the night.

Hamlin parked at the edge of the lawn in front of the doors. They left the car behind and the Stalker led May to the doors and inside. He switched on the foyer light, and May was dumbstruck.

"It's... overwhelming."

"This way." Hamlin led her to the left of the foyer. Into the living room. He turned on the lights, and May's jaw dropped.

"This is the most beautiful place I've ever seen."

"It's nice. But it's not as beautiful as you," he complimented her.

She grinned, turning around. "Thank Y... ."

Just as she faced him. Hamlin hit her hard, with a right cross to the jaw. She fell to the floor like a bag of rocks. He bent down and moved her hair out of the way of her face.

He suddenly became enraged. "Shit! I should have at least fucked her first," he said aloud, to himself. But he just couldn't take any more of her fucking mouth. Besides, he had what he needed now to keep Webb on a short leash, once he identified himself as the Stalker. She wouldn't dare go to the police with her good friend, Brooke May, in his grasp.

CHAPTER FOURTEEN

Bray Hamlin entered the lobby of Nancy Webb's office, and walked over to the glassed-in receptionist's desk. There was an older woman at May's desk. She looked like she may have been in her fifties. She suddenly looked up from the stack of paperwork on her desk. Looking directly into the soulless, hazel eyes of Bray Hamlin.

She nearly jumped out of her seat. "You scared me. I didn't hear you come in. Can I help you?"

"Yes. I have an appointment, with Doctor Webb… ."

Before he could finish his sentence, the older receptionist said, "You're Bray Hamlin." She was dumbstruck.

"Yes, I am. Is the doctor ready for me?" Of course she wasn't ready for him. No one was ever ready for him. But she caught his drift.

She stared at him, awe struck. But blinked and broke her stare. "Oh. Umm. She should be coming out any second."

"Thank you. I'll just wander aimlessly over here while I wait."

She smiled. "Okay."

She picked up the phone and turned her back on him, as she dialed. After a pick up on the other end, she began talking to whoever it was. He couldn't hear what the conversation was about, because of her whispering and the glass that surrounded her. After a moment though, he heard his name mentioned. He stepped with purpose, back up to the opening in the partition.

"You know," he turned her in his direction. "You're not supposed to talk about the doctor's clients with persons out of the medical field. Even then, you need a signed release form," he told her, sternly.

"I've got to go, Anne. I'll talk to you later." She hung up the phone. "What do you mean?"

"Don't play dumb, it doesn't suit you. I may not have heard the entire conversation. But I know my name when I hear it. Doctor Webb could fire you for that."

The old woman looked like a fish out of water. He could tell that she was racking her brain, looking for something to say. He laughed inside. She looked like she was ready to shit her pants. Or adult diaper, which ever the case may be.

"I'm terribly, sorry. I just wanted to tell someone that I knew that I had met you," she apologized.

He appeared to mull over her apology. "That's okay. But you should never do that. Not from here, or your home. People like to keep their identities a secret, when it comes to seeing psychologists."

All that she could do, was repeat herself, "I'm sorry. It won't happen again."

He smiled. "Don't worry, about it. I won't tell."

She returned his gesture, as he once again began to pacing. Waiting for Webb to finish with this other patient. He glanced at his watch. That same fucking old man from last week was starting to cut into his time again. And he wasn't liking it.

This was pissing him off. Every fucking time he got there, ready for his appointment, he had to wait while some mush brain, knot headed, dumb fuck finished their session. What was the fucking problem?

The door to Webb's office opened and she escorted out her previous patient. He passed the old bastard on his way toward Webb's office. Glancing at him. He sure was an ugly motherfucker. God damn, was he ugly. He didn't need a psychologist, he needed a fucking plastic surgeon.

"Hello, Bray. Come on in and we can get started, right away," she greeted him. Following him into the office, closing the door behind them.

They each took a seat on opposite sides of the desk. Webb welcomed him, with an uneasy smile. There it was again, the heart pounding fear. Two hours before he had even arrived, once she remembered that he was scheduled for today. She started to feel physically ill, right down to her soul. She knew that he was coming, but she didn't know what to expect out of him. She remembered all of what her college friend had told her, but she couldn't make her fear go away. It loomed over her, like an ominous storm cloud.

"Where's Brooke today? At home, sick?" he asked, knowingly.

"No, she never showed up yesterday. I called her apartment several times, but she never answered. I had to call a temp service to get someone over here to handle the phone, and do some computer filing. I even went by her apartment after work, but she didn't answer the door. If I can't get a hold of her by the end of the day, I'm going to call the police. Since they can't do anything for forty-eight hours anyway. But I am very worried. She's never done anything like this before. I hope that there's nothing seriously, wrong," she said, troubled.

"I'm sure that she's fine. She appears to me to be someone who can handle herself." He tried to ease her. For now.

She was concerned. Very, concerned. "I hope so. I don't know what I'd do without her. She's like a little sister to me."

He was calm and collected. "Don't worry. Like I said, I'm sure she's just fine."

She sat back in her chair. More worried than scared, now. "Well, we should get to your session. I haven't cancelled anyone else's appointments today. And I don't intend to start with yours. So how are you today? How's your self-aggression therapy, going?" she appeared distracted.

"Are you sure that you don't want to cancel? It's okay you know, to stop work early to check on a friend." He was understanding.

"No, that's okay. The work day is close to being over with, anyway. I'll check on her later. Like you said, I'm sure she's fine."

"Okay, if you insist." He was quiet for a minute. Looking over the contents of her desk top, noting every item. There were the usual stapler, glass paperweight, a coffee cup full of pens, a letter opener, and a rolled up newspaper, off to the side. But he could only make out three partial words of the headline, and one of them was "Stalker."

He beamed, inside. He loved to read about his escapades. His triumphant steps toward becoming tyrant of the world. Then this beautiful creature before him would be his. To rule by his side.

He noticed that his silence was frustrating Webb a bit. She sighed a few times and checked her watch three times, during his three minute pause. She may be impatient now, he thought. But soon she was going to be appalled and shocked. Maybe beyond her senses, or maybe beyond her innermost fantasies.

Webb was about to speak up and get things rolling. But when she looked at Hamlin, her fear that had subsided out of worry for Brooke May had returned suddenly. Although he was just sitting there, nonchalantly looking over the room, he emanated a volatile and rancorous presence. He just felt wicked to her, though he had shown concern for Brooke and his normally chiseled features were softer than in his previous session. She couldn't help but to stare at his eyes. His eyes that screamed out, "Beware."

But before she made any snap decisions. Like Corbit had told her, test, then diagnose. She already knew that much. But Hamlin had scared her so much, she needed her good friend to remind her of the simple ways of getting to the roots of such problems. She couldn't believe that it took the suggestion of one of her peers, to kick start her mind into remembering the basics. Testing. Good 'ol testing.

"Bray... ."

"You want to know what I do now, to relieve my aggressions, right?" he cut her off.

"Yes. Or we can talk about whatever you want."

Or we can talk about, whatever you want. Yeah, right. She was hot to know what he did now instead of fighting, to relieve his aggressions. He would let her know, in due time. And now was not that time. He'll fuck with her a little, first.

"I had this frog, once." He began what was going to be about a fifteen minute story. About nothing really.

Oh, God. A frog. He went from losing his parents, and loneliness, to an uncontrollable fighting frenzy, to a frog. No way. She was going to have to sway him in a different direction. Maybe the testing. Yes. This would be the perfect time to mention the testing. Or so she thought.

"I don't mean to cut you off, Bray," which she did, "But I have something I'd like to run by you."

"Okay. But I really would like to get this thing about Herman off my chest." He was hysterical inside. Trying not to allow his laughter to break out.

"Sure, we can get back to Herman later. First, though. I was wondering if you would take a few tests for me? Does that sound okay with you?" she tried to sound as enthusiastic, as possible.

He raised an eyebrow. "You want to test me? What's the matter doctor, do you think that I'm crazy because I like to fight? That is what the testing is for, isn't it? Are you trying to get me off the streets, is that it?" he accused, nonviolently. But he did enjoy watching her squirm.

"No. No, not at all." She recovered. Looking like a deer caught in on coming headlights.

"Then why test me?"

"There are many reasons for someone to be tested. Tests are not only to discern whether someone is or isn't inept, or dangerous." She tried to regain control. "Testing is also a medium for finding disorders that might otherwise go undetected. And at your own admittance, you have had your share of peculiar behavior, over the past fifteen years." She thought that she had made her point quite clear. But... .

"So you're saying that I have some type of disorder? What kind of a disorder, doctor? The dangerous kind? Or just the inept kind?" he had appeared to become agitated.

But he quickly sat back into his chair and slipped back into silence and composure instead. He began looking the room over, again. Appearing relaxed and without a care. Any expected outbursts on his behalf just didn't happen. No ranting or raving. Just calm.

But she couldn't forget his self-proclaimed, disturbing accounts of his penchant for breaking bones, and striking blood. She felt like she was trapped in the eye of a hurricane, waiting in its stillness for the second half of the storm to raise its ire, and continue its destruction.

But Bray Hamlin sat quietly. Appearing to mull over his next response. Never once becoming threatening. Just calm. Like she had told Corbit. Emotionless. Like he was dead inside. A soulless, barren black void, who had filled her with lasting terror in less than one hour's time. She believed that there was a fire storm brewing inside of him, just waiting to be unleashed. But on who?

She was going to try to change the subject away from the testing. But he beat her to it.

"You know, doctor. You're a very beautiful woman." He smiled, warmly.

She was dumb struck. He had caught her completely off guard. And she froze. Both physically and mentally. Causing her heart to pound out of control.

"Did you hear me, doctor?"

She thawed, a bit. Just enough to answer him. "Yes. Yes, I did. That was very nice of you to say. But Bray, we really need to talk about the things that more involve you."

He smiled, again. "I am."

Her stomach dropped in unrelenting fear. But somehow she managed to keep from trembling, noticeably. "What do you mean by that, Bray?"

He raised his shoulders.

That's when the words of her colleague and friend, Nathan Corbit, sounded off in her head. Maybe he was looking for someone to issue guidance. Or to take over his dilemmas, and solve them for him. All of them being a byproduct of his childhood. But if that was what he was trying to gain from his sessions with her, she just had to set him straight, right now. That that could not be.

"Bray, I think I know what you're looking for and I'm sorry, but I can't take the guidance role that you seem to be shopping for. The guidance you lost when your mother died. You need to take the responsibilities for all the facets of your life into your own hands. And just care for yourself as best you can. No one can lead your life for you but you. I mean, I'm flattered… ."

His laughter cut her off. "I don't want your guidance, Nancy. I want you."

"Me. What do you mean, me?"

"You. I want you." He smiled, enchanted.

"To guide you." She still couldn't see.

He shook his head. "For being such a brilliant psychologist, you're not very quick. Do you know that you have the most beautiful, deep blue eyes and I love the way your hair frames your face. Your lips. Those full lips. Painted so beautifully, in my favorite color. Red." He admired.

His admiration sickened her. Psychically and physically sickened her, leaving her speechless. Noting her loss for words, he took advantage.

"You're so very beautiful. And I know that you could have any man you might want. But I was hoping that you might give me a chance." He seemed so sincere. Even his eyes now appeared earnest.

"Won't you give me that one chance and go out with me? We'll have dinner and then hit one of my clubs. I promise, you'll have a good time." He tried to charm her.

"Thank you, Bray." She lowered her head somewhat. "But I couldn't possibly. I'm your doctor."

"But only for two more weeks." He smoothly led her further.

She froze. He was calling her out. And he was right. In two more weeks she would no longer be affiliated with him professionally. Which left her open to his social advancements.

"I really don't think that would be a good idea."

"Why not?"

"Because I've done it once before. A patient once quit seeing me, professionally. So that we might get together socially," she lied.

"How did it go?"

"Terribly. I knew too much about him. I knew too much about what plagued his mind. And I practically had to take him by the hand and counsel him, just to get him through each day. It just became too much of a burden. And when the relationship became sexual, he had some definite issues," she deceived him. "But enough about that. We're here to talk about you."

"Not us?"

"No. Just you."

He shrugged. Apparently taking her words, to heart. "Okay," he conceded. "Now, what were we talking about?"

"You and me."

She exhaled, frustrated and fearful. When suddenly, she thought about something else to talk about.

"How about we talk about that five million dollar donation you made last week, to the AIDS foundation. It was very sizable, and quite generous. I know that you have made donations to that foundation before. Have you ever known someone with AIDS before? Or was it just from the heart, like all the others?" she tried desperately to change the subject.

CHAPTER FIFTEEN

"Naw." He sat back in his chair. "I just did it, to get women."

She chuckled, but noted that he made absolutely no attempt to smile back. He just stared at her with those eyes. The warmness was now gone, and the cold, callous, dark void was back.

"You're not kidding, are you," she realized.

"No, I'm not. I do that from time to time. Whenever I feel like a good threesome with a few refined socialites. They always seem to fall for it, too. I mean, I have hundreds of billions of dollars; what's five million to get a good socialite sandwich going on. And it's all tax deductible. It's win, win." He appeared so smug and self serving. Cracking a devilish grin.

"A threesome. You gave away five million dollars for a threesome?" she was disgusted and appalled.

"No doctor, you misunderstand. It wasn't just the idea, of a threesome. I could have hired a couple of whores for the night if that were the case. No, Nancy. The idea was to show off my wealth and good standing in the community. Then snag a couple of high society thoroughbreds. Intelligent ladies. Or a facsimile, thereof.

"Women who had never entertained such a notion, not even for a second. In college, where it is wide spread, experimental. Women who are at first repulsed by even the mere mentioning of such a thing. And then I not only charm the skirts off of them, but I charm them into eating a little pussy for the night, while I fuck them. Hard. That's what it's all about. Control," he told her. Savagely and straight forward. "Hell, I'm getting hard just thinking about it."

She shuddered at this announcement. Looking confused. "I don't get it. After all that you said to me two weeks ago, about not being able to find true love because of your wealth, yet you flaunt it so flagrantly. How do you expect to find love that way?"

"I don't, doctor," he said, blandly. "I gave up on trying to find true love a long time ago. I got smart, you see. The ones that I want I can't have. So, like after the fund raiser, I take what I can get." He shifted his weight around in the chair. Finding a comfort zone.

"But you know, Nancy. I'd give all of that shit up if the right person were to come along. It's true. But if shallow, meaningless sex is what they want, then that's what I'll give them. And yes, if I have to use my wealth to get the physical love I so desire, then so be it." He seemed to be grievous.

She felt for him, in a way. But the chills running up and down her spine pulled her in a different direction.

"Bray, you make me very uncomfortable. When you say things like you said, just a few minutes ago, I can understand your pain. But could you keep your depictions just a bit less graphic?" She asked, soft and polite. Not wanting to irritate his darker side.

"Oh," he whispered. Then his voice raised to a more noticeable octave. "Fuck, I didn't know that you didn't like my fucking language. You should have fucking said something, before we fucking began. I mean, I'm not a fucking mind reader, or any fucking thing like that. So it's a good fucking thing that you fucking told me. Because I can be a real vulgar motherfucker, sometimes." He sat back in his chair, and smiled. "I'm just fucking with you."

"I meant in reference to me," she corrected him, just a little too late.

"Oh, sorry. Well then I guess that's enough about you. What do you think of me, doctor? You keep writing things about me in that file of yours. And I for one would like to know what it is. What do you think of me, doctor? Do you understand me? Or do I disgust you? Do I scare you? Or am I arousing you?"

She shifted her stare away from him, so not to look him in the eyes. Even though at one time she had considered his company. The thought of such a thing now disgusted her. She looked at him.

"It would be impossible for you to arouse me into something like you've just talked about. I find it repulsive. But I'm not here to judge you. I'm here to diagnose any psychological problems you may have. No matter how small or large. I'm just here to assess you. And maybe come up with a solution that might alleviate your symptoms of rage, controlled or otherwise. Plus, your fear of commitment," she told him.

"Okay then," he said, calm. "Wait a minute. What fear of commitment? What is your full diagnosis?"

"Well, let's talk fear of commitment first. You say that you can't find anyone worthy enough of your trust. Because you believe that all they want is your money. You use your wealth as an excuse for this. An excuse to stay away from the company of others, except for more than a day or two. But it's not your money you're worried about. Not if you're willing to give away five million dollars just to get some kinky little sex thing going for a day or two. Those few days, here and there. That's all you really want. And when you told me otherwise, you were simply blowing smoke.

"You have absolutely no desire for a long term relationship. You have never had one. And I believe you have no intentions of getting into one ever, no matter what you might say. Not the way you continue to throw your money around." She held nothing back. Giving it to him, exactly how he wanted it. Or so she thought.

"Blowing smoke." He smiled, chillingly calm. "Look doctor, I know that how I go about my relationships isn't exactly the way to find a love for the ages. I know that. But it's a hell of a lot better than spending every stinking night alone.

"Yes, sometimes I have to go about using my money to get what I need. But I'm certainly not just going to give it away. And since I've come to find that there really isn't a true love out there for me, I take what I can get, when I can get it. And I've simply come to accept that. What about you, doctor? Can you actually say that you believe, with no doubt, that there is a true love out there for you? And you can remain vigilant in waiting for it? Or would you just like to get stuck, every now and then." His mood swung, vulgar. With a wicked grin.

Before she could respond, he asked once again. "What is your full diagnosis? I think that I've made it quite clear that I have no fear of commitment."

She was upset. "Bray, I asked you once not to speak to me like that. One more time and this session is over. And you will not be welcome back for your final two. Your payment will be refunded."

"All I said, was that I have no fear of commitment," he said, innocently.

"Before that. You know, what I'm talking about."

He bowed his head, for a moment. "Okay, I'm sorry. So what's the rest of your diagnosis?"

She seemed a bit skittish. "Are you sure that you would like to hear it now? We're only three sessions into your five. My diagnosis is not yet complete. I wouldn't want you to get the wrong idea. Why don't we build on last week's session and you tell me what your new outlet for your excess energy and anger is." She tried gingerly to change the subject.

Hamlin thought about her request, for about ten seconds. "No, I'd like to know the rest of your diagnosis now. I do have that right, don't I?" he said, his mannerisms care free.

She paused for a long minute. Very scared of what he might do once he read the report. She would prepare herself for the worst. If that was possible. She opened the file, turning it around and slid it across the desk into Hamlin's full view.

He gazed up at her from under his brow, sending chills down her spine. The hair on the back of her neck stood on end.

Hamlin lowered his eyes. Now holding the file just inches off of Webb's desk, he began reading. Wondering what the woman that would rule by his side really thought of him. Minus his foul thoughts and language.

He read about her fears for the safety of others that might cross paths with him in the future. Though she thought he was still at this time able to manage his rage. But it was these mental instabilities and violent tendencies that made up most of his file. There were even writings in the margins of this report. Little messages that detailed her fear of him, at different moments of his therapy. All of which had occurred during his second session. Mental instabilities, violent tendencies, and desperate fear.

He didn't need to read anymore. He closed the file and slid it back across the desk. There was a burning in the pit of his stomach. How could Webb sit on an ivory pedestal beside him, in rule of the world, if she thought of him in that way? She couldn't. But she could be taught. And he was a very good teacher. If he could teach a sixth degree black belt in Kenpo, a man much larger than he in stature, not only to beg, but to beg for his very life and soul for an hour, before he snapped his neck, he could teach Webb how to be his. How to sit quietly by his side. Clearing her mind of those gross exaggerations of his well being.

"Close." He smiled. Chilling her to the bone. "Close." Once again he glanced at the folded newspaper on Webb's desk, and motioned toward it. "The Stalker strikes again, huh?"

She followed his motion to the paper and unfolded it across her desk. "No. Actually, this headline is in reference to the police search for him. He hasn't killed, as of late." She was thankful that he changed the subject.

He stared at the paper, then look up at her. "What do you think of him?"

"Who, the Stalker? I really can't say. My profile is confidential."

"No, I don't want to know all about that crap. I was just wondering. What you thought might have driven him to all of this. No wait, let me guess." He nearly leapt from his seat, so excited. It was time.

"Let's see. He comes from a family of five. Possibly the middle child, who didn't get the attention he so desired. Oh, and maybe his parents were abusive." He acted as though he were mulling it over. "And that is why he only kills families of five," he concluded, with a tight-lipped grin.

Webb stared at him, dazed. Completely stunned. "How did you know… ."

He smiled. "Because that's the diagnosis any psychologist worth their weight in snack cakes would have come to. Did I mention that while I was being home schooled, I was taught psychology… . Anyway. I'm here to tell you you're wrong. What's your favorite, anyway? Cup cakes? Or Twinkies?" he stood in front, yet off to the side of her desk in full view.

"Let me run something by you, and you tell me what you think." He began pacing. Stroking his chin, as though he had a beard. "When he was a young boy, he developed many imaginary friends, because he was kept locked up inside his castle of a home. Never allowed outside the walls that surrounded this castle. Well, not much, anyway. Now, about those imaginary friends. Most were nice and played well with him. But there was one that was not so nice. And upon ridding himself of these imaginary friends, somewhere during his fifteenth year, not all of them left. No, one remained. Its essence joining with his own. Together they became stronger. Then and there, they decided to remain as one. Strong and complete."

He continued a slow pace from right to left, in front of her. "Then, at seventeen years old he went to a party and got into a fight. It was during this fight that the first blood was spilled. This life essence energized them. Him." He caught himself. "And made him stronger."

He grinned, evil. "That was when he knew that the blood was his salvation. It would heighten his potency to a level above mortal men. And the more blood that they, he, wore, the stronger he became." He stopped pacing. Standing behind the chair directly in front of her desk.

Nancy Webb stared at him. Her mouth almost hung open. She was petrified with fear. Her heart was nearly in her throat. She now knew who this man was that stood before her. It was a one word name. The most feared name, yet in contrast, the most revered name in Los Angeles history. Though trembling almost uncontrollably, she was not yet sold, on Hamlin's near confession. She needed more proof.

"That's... a very unusual... view on the subject. But I know the truth, as far as the Stalker is concerned," she baited him.

"Really." He started to pace, again. "His worshipers are killed in their sleep, mostly. Then carried. Carried, mind you. Not dragged." He defended the thought of a lack of strength on his behalf.

"He carries them, one by one, down to the living room or the family room, which ever it may be. Gutting them from abdomen to sternum."

Webb's fear intensified into sheer terror. Her eyes widened like saucers. It was him. She could barely keep from wetting herself, and had to coach herself just to keep breathing. There they were, one on one. No more than four feet apart. She couldn't speak. She could actually feel her voice, leave her. Her breath growing shallow and quick. All that she could do was stare at him, as he stared back at her. She was petrified and couldn't look away. She could only stare into the dark void of evil that loomed behind his eyes. And pray that he would at least make her death quick.

"Hollowing out their carcasses," he continued his tale of horror and gore, "leaving the organs in a corner of the room. They are left kneeling side by side, in worship. Facing a wall, where in their own blood, mind you, is my name: Stalker." He ran a hand across the air, in front of him. Mimicking a star-lit headline.

"I've always loved reading my name in bold print." He smiled at her, starry-eyed. His forged delight only a cover for the evil held within.

She squeezed her legs tightly together, holding back the urine that her bladder threatened to release uncontrollably.

"Why?" she suddenly spoke. But that was all that would come out.

"Why, what?"

Her breaths were rapid. "I believe I know why you wear their blood. And I know about the worshiping. But why families of five?"

"Are you sure that you know about the blood and the worshiping? Tell me your theory. If you're right, I'll tell you why families of five," he offered.

She swallowed, hard. Her breaths, still quick and shallow. "My profile, is that you wear the... b... blood, to get stronger. Which you even confessed to, earlier today. And they are worshiping you. As... some type of god."

He pursed his lips, seriously debating her profile. Then perked up like a game show host. In a matter of a heart beat. "Very, good," he toned it down. "Just one thing. I'm not some type of god to them. I am their new Lord and Savior. As for why families of five." He scratched his chin, looking somewhat amused. "I'll give you three guesses."

"You're sick, Bray. Terribly sick. Turn yourself in. We can get you help. I'll help you. Together, we can return your mind back to its normal state. You can go on to live a very productive life. Please, let me help you," she pleaded for his abstinence.

"No, no, no!" he was becoming agitated. "That was not a possible answer, in your three guesses. Try, again."

She was trembling uncontrollably, her heart pounding so hard she thought it may burst in her chest. Her voice was quite shaken, when she spoke. "You've already nullified my profile on that subject. I really, don't know."

"Wrong. That's one. Try, again."

"I don't know."

He shook his head. "Wrong, again. That's two. Try again."

Hamlin didn't seem to be getting any more perturbed than he already was. But still, she was terrified that a third repeat of her answer might bring about severe consequences.

Apprehensively. "I don't know." She was almost in tears.

He shook his head, appearing disappointed. "I thought that you were more intelligent, than that. Think." He put a finger to his head.

"I don't know. I don't know." Tears began to flow.

He reached into the inside breast pocket, of his suit coat. Producing a handkerchief. Tossing it to her. "Wipe your eyes. Don't let your mascara run. And I don't want your eyes to get puffy, so stop crying. What I'm about to tell you is the complete truth."

He walked around the chair, and laid his hands, palms down, on her desk. Looking down at her, he motioned for her to do what he had just told her to do. So she wiped her eyes, and forced herself to stop crying. Looking up at him.

"I am not, I repeat, I am not, going to harm you. So quit your bawling. Not only does it not suit you, but it takes away from your beauty. The redness around your eyes. The repetitive sucking of snot, so that it doesn't run out of your nose, it sickens me. Have a little respect, for yourself. I hate whinners."

He raised his hands near his face, below his nose, making his voice sound shaky. "Oh, please Mr. Hamlin. Please, don't kill me. I have children. I'm expecting a baby. I don't want to die."

He lowered his hands. "It sickens, me. Show some guts." He laughed. "Some guts. Get it? ...It's a pun. Guts. Never mind." He began to pace the room, again. Letting go the question at hand.

He stopped behind the chair, and rest his hands on it. "I'm not yet in my godly state." He changed the subject. "But I soon will be. And with that new power, I'll be able to take the blood of my worshipers at will. Without having to hide and sneak around in the dark of night. I will be unstoppable. Impervious to any tactics used to try and stop me." He strutted, pacing around in front of her.

"I have a little ways to go yet, but I'm strong enough for now. Soon, this shit hole of a world, every man, woman and child, will bow to their new god. Ahh, there's still the question of why the number five, isn't there," he recalled.

She nodded. "Yes." Her voice escaped.

"Well, you've already had your three guesses. But you were wrong, all three times. I guess we'll just have to let it stand." He threatened silence.

No, it couldn't end that way. She knew that his reason, was going to be something frightful and outrageous. But the therapist in her needed to know. She straightened herself, trying to look sturdy again and bit the bullet, so to speak.

"Okay, I'll play along. What, in your twisted mind, made you decide on families of five?"

Hamlin's evil pleasures were weighing on her mind already. She waited for one of his sudden mood swings that would turn him to rage. And that was exactly what she got.

His features turned rock solid and he appeared to be more than just a little pissed off. "You'll play along. What the fuck do you think this is? A fucking, game!"

His stare went right through her. The pressure in her bladder nearly making her piss herself. Her heart was beating so hard and loud she was nearly deafened by it pounding in her ears. And she was sure that Hamlin could hear it as well.

His grimace melted from his features, giving way to a big, wide smile. "Just kidding. But since you had the tenacity to ask, I'll let you in on my little secret." He looked around the room abruptly, as though he was making sure that the office was clear of prying ears.

He looked at her, a bit of a grin on his face. "Why families of five? Well... five just happens to be my favorite number." He pressed a finger to his lips.

"Shhh. Don't tell anybody."

Favorite number? Favorite, number. She just couldn't believe it. This beast, this devil, slaughtered entire families by his favorite number. That wasn't crazy, or psychotic; it was pure evil. One hundred percent. He was as unbalanced as unbalanced could be. But the evil was what drove him. It was this evil that terrified her more than anything else. A mad man she could deal with and treat. But evil. Pure evil. The kind of evil that dwelled inside of Bray Hamlin was soulless and untreatable. The only thing that could alleviate his condition and eliminate this void of darkness would be his death.

He pursed his lips. "Actually, I have to take that back. Five being my favorite number, is only part of the reason why I take families of their size. I need the children," he further confessed.

He paced faster, erratically. Rubbing his cupped hands together. "You see, Nancy. The children are the best source of power. You need your essence to grow. And as you grow the more of your essence you expend, until there is nothing left and you die. But the younger you are the more powerful your essence will be, because you haven't exhausted much yet. I don't care if the mother and father are only in their late thirties, and two of the children are in their early teens or preteens. If that third child is a four year old, or a two year old for example, that child's essence is more powerful than all of the others combined. Because it hasn't exhausted much of it's life yet. It's only just begun. That's why I need the children, you see."

She closed her eyes in a moment of silence, for those who had lost their live's, because of Hamlin's delusions. She felt exhausted, give out. She didn't want to do this anymore. His voice suddenly caught her attention opening her eyes.

"Do you see?" his voice, a bit more stern.

She was terrified, but she just couldn't help herself. She held nothing for him, but disdain. "All that I see, is that you are a fucking lunatic, and you should be shot in the head for your actions." As soon as she finished her sentiments her heart jumped into her throat. He would kill her for sure, now.

But instead he laughed. "That's a good one, I like that. You're very funny."

He sit back in his chair and started staring at her, and it was quite unsettling. She tried not to make eye contact, but her attempts were futile. He was like a bad accident along side the road, you know that you shouldn't look, but you can't help yourself. It was a natural reaction. Curiosity. But curiosity was not all that made her look at him, like a frightened child at an angry parent. She wanted to know where he was in the room. She needed to know where he was. She didn't want him sneaking up on her. But when she looked, she found him sitting across the desk from her. Looking at her, nonthreatening.

"I know what you're thinking," he sang. "You don't like me anymore, do you?" he asked. Just as the calm, before the storm.

She shook her head. "No," she managed.

He raised his shoulders. "That doesn't really matter. You'll still be with me."

"I will not accept the rest of your sessions." As though she had a choice.

He smiled wide. "That's not what I meant. Besides, I don't need to see you professionally anymore. Now that the cats, out of the bag… . Like I actually needed to in the first place. But like I said, that's not what I meant. I mean you are going to be with me. Together, forever. By my side, as I rule this… world."

She tried to scream. To release the bloody murder she held inside. But could only release a soundless breath. What in the hell was he talking about? Her, by his side. That phrase eased her terror just a bit. Because if he wanted her with him, that meant that he wasn't going to kill her. Not now, anyway. But her terror resurfaced, when she thought about what it meant, to be with him.

"Why me? You could take any woman under your wing and keep her by your side. Why me?"

He shrugged. "Why not. You're beautiful, intelligent, sexy, and the only one who in time could ever come close to understanding me… . And of course, you look like you'd be a great lay." He smirked.

Trying desperately not to soil herself, she took a bold stance. "What will you do, when I say no?"

He nearly leapt from his seat and grabbing the letter opener off of her desktop, moved swiftly around the desk. Grabbing a handful of her hair and pulled her head back. Putting the sharpened piece of office equipment to her throat.

"I'm sorry." He was pleasant. "But that's not, an option."

With the letter opener pressed so tightly to her throat. She felt one swallow away from gushing blood down the front of her blouse.

"Mmmm," she tried to speak. Tears rolling down her face.

He released her. Leaving an impression of the blade, across her throat. "How do you like me now?" He placed the letter opener back on her desk. Standing so close beside her, she could feel his body heat. What little of it there was. He was almost ice-like.

She glanced at the opener, but she could feel his eyes watching her. If she went for it, she'd never make it. He was testing her. He wanted to know if she would rise up against him, if the opportunity should present itself. You're damn right she would. But not now. She was never more definite of anything in her life, than at that point. If she went for the opener, she would never make it and it would be the last action of her life. It wasn't much of a test, though. He was standing right there. There's no way anyone would take that chance, especially with him.

"Good choice. Never raise your hand or a weapon against me. It's the best thing, if you want to continue living. And living is something that we will do, together. Forever. Anything we desire will be at our fingertips. I mean anything."

He knelt beside her and turned her toward him, stopping when her knees touched his waist. "You will come to love me. You will come to love wearing the essences of others on your skin. It's a high like no other. I mean, nothing can match the joining of two or more essences together. You can't imagine the ecstasy. It's like nothing you've ever experienced."

He lay a hand on her leg, just above the knee. Then let it slide up to her inner thigh. She tried to close her legs tight, but he managed to slide his hand further up her mid-length skirt. Her body trembled in fear and disgust. But there was a tingling, the likes she hadn't felt for months on end.

She kept tightening her legs together, but could not stop his hand from closing in on its objective. The very source of the tingling. She grasped the edge of the desk with both hands and closed her eyes. He was almost there. She was already trying not to wet herself and she didn't think that she could take his advancements.

He began rubbing her shoulder with his free hand. He could feel her trembling. Then his hand moved to her neck and once again, the massaging began. She took quick, shallow breaths so not to give him the satisfaction of a moan. But her bottom lip quivered when he reached her panties, and forced three fingers inside her underwear. Then inside her. She gasped and opened her eyes, taking another look at the letter opener. A good long, look.

He forced his fingers deep inside of her, again and again. Shame fell over her. She was loosening her legs. A moan slipped past her lips. She glanced over at him, reminding herself of what he was. Her legs squeezed tight again. But he was already inside.

"What you're feeling, is nothing compared to how it feels to wear another's essence. There's really no way I can explain it. You just have to experience it all for yourself." He was silent for a moment while his fingers thrust deeply inside of her, again and again. His thumb starting its work on her clitoris.

"Imagine what you're feeling now and multiply it by one thousand. It sends shockwaves of pure ecstasy down to your very soul." His fingers ran deep and quick.

There was a full wetness now. Not just a drop but a full wetness lubricating his fingers, as he eased them out and forced them back in, repeatedly. Deeper and deeper. Faster and faster.

She let slip a moan, giving him notice of her pleasure. Motivating him to continue laying her with his fingers, faster and deeper. She felt herself moving with him, letting herself go. Another moan, and deeper he went. She was nearing the end.

"One thousand times, what you feel right now. To your soul. It lasts for hours and hours. And then," he suddenly pulled his hand out from between her legs, "and then it's gone."

It stopped. Her pleasure. It just, stopped. She was almost there. She hadn't felt anything for months. But she was almost there and it was going to be explosive. But he stopped.

She opened her eyes and looked at him. Those three fingers he had used on her were in his mouth. He pulled them out and licked in between each one, giving her a dirty smile.

He stood from his kneeling position beside her. Then walked his way back around to the front of the desk where he sat in the chair once again.

"Anything else I can explain, to make your transition any easier?" he asked her, so casually.

She was still breathing hard, and her excitement was fading very slowly. Causing her to stutter when she spoke.

"S… So what d… does all of that mean? I have to experience it for myself? Do you actually think that I'm going to come with you, on one of your massacres? You may have gotten me excited, Bray. But that had nothing to do with the thought of wearing someone's blood.

"You forced yourself on me. And being in the predicament that I'm in, I had to accept it. But there is no way in hell that you can get me to come with you, on one of your hunts." She tried desperately to sound as stout as possible, wet panties and all.

Hamlin laughed. Just not in the cartoonish villian sort of way. "Well, there are other options."

"Like what?"

"What do you think?"

Her counterfeit stoutness had been challenged. But she no longer wanted to give him the satisfaction of seeing her fear. She clasped her hands together so that they wouldn't shake and laid them on her desk.

She raised her shoulders. "I don't know. You're the lunatic. What are you going to do to me?"

"Lunatic. I thought I was psychotic."

"There are many words for what you are, take your pick." She remained steady, even though the crotch of her panties was sticking to her and getting cold.

He touched a hand to his chin, thinking. Then a pleasant look overcame him. "How about you just call me a god," he said, his features were hard, his voice low, yet intense.

His statement, shook her. Her eyes giving away her sheer terror, while a numbing sensation streaked up from her toes and came to rest at the center of her chest.

"How about, Mr. Hamlin." She remained chiseled.

He sit up straight in his chair, his face blank of expression. "That's a good one. Real nice." He toyed with her, but only for a second. "How about I call you, dead."

She took a deep, cleansing breath. Holding back her tears of helplessness. He had finally threatened her life, straight forward. He had said earlier that he was not going to harm her. But, she thought, she may have pushed him just a bit to far, this time. She tried to shrug it off as hollow words. But she suddenly went cold. The kind of cold that overcomes you when you're sure that your blood has stopped flowing, and there you are, semi-dead. Just waiting to be finished off.

"Enough of all this name calling. Let's get straight to the shit. As I see it, you only have two choices, here. Number one, you die. Right here, right now."

He watched as the color drained from her face. She was as pale as the dead. And he did notice her trembling. It was a wonder that he couldn't smell the shit, he had just scared out of her.

"Hold on, now. Don't you go choosing, just yet," he began, in his best game show hosts, voice. "You've still got one choice left." He held his hands just out in front of him. "I know, I know. What could possibly top choice number one? But there is a choice number two. Would you like to continue? Okay.

"Well, here it is." He returned to his frigid and course nature. "You come and be mine and only mine. You'll close your practice and move into my home, where you will make yourself available to me twenty-four hours a day. And you give me what I want, when I want it, with no complaining.

"So if I fuck you too hard, or eat you raw, or even hold you too tight, when we sleep, I don't want to hear a fucking word, because I'm telling you right now it comes with the territory. Then, once my ascension is complete, we can start on you. But you don't need to be godly, so it won't take as many families before you're powerful enough to rule by my side. Then, the world is ours." He sat back in his chair, appearing quite content.

"You have to come with me, now. No pussyfooting around. Let's go," he pressed. "Oh, and if at any time you try to turn me in to the police, and your good friend, Morrow, I'll hang you up by your feet. Skin you alive with sandpaper. Let you set for a few days, so that you can think about what's coming next. Then I'll shower you with buckets of salt. Listen to you scream for a day or so. And unless you die from shock, I'll gut you like a fish, slowly. From your pussy to your sternum, so that you can watch your organs fall past your eyes on their way to the floor."

He could tell that she was terrified, almost to the point of losing consciousness. But yet, she was able to speak. "How do I know that you won't hurt me, if I go with you?"

He stared at her expressionlessly. "You don't. I don't have to promise you anything. I'm just saying it's so. Believe me, or not. You have to make your choice, now. Number one or number two? You don't have a lot of time. Tick, tock. Doctor."

Her mind raced. What should, she do? If she didn't go with him, right now, he would kill her. If she did, he would own her. Either way, he seemed to be getting the better end of the deal. She had to try some way to stop the killing. Maybe if she went with him she could gain his trust and turn his dark side, dorment. Then eventually she could inform the police of his identity and where-a-bouts. And put an end to the Stalker, once and for all.

"Tick, tock."

What she had was a good plan, but it meant being his in every sense of the word, until she could gain his trust. There had to be something else, she could do.

"Tick, tock."

"Just a minute, please." She paused, visibly upset. "Look, either way you look at it, you win. You get your blood… er, essence, with or without me.

What kind of compromise, is that?"

He leaned forward, closer to her desk. "There isn't any compromise. We're not making a deal here, doctor. You accept one or the other of the choices that I have laid out for you. You take it, or you leave it. Live, or die."

Her knees were knocking together. "But what about closing my office? I just can't walk away. There are things that must be done. I have to refer all of my patients to other psychologists. There's my lease that needs to be taken care of. I'll have to sell my home. There really is so much to do." She tried desperately to stall and buy time.

Hamlin shook his head. "What is it with women. You have to make every thing so complicated. Here's what you do. You get on the phone right now and call your landlord. Buy out the rest of your lease on this place. I'll sell your house for you, through one of my real estate agencies. Under an assumed name, of course. And fuck all of the rest of it.

"As for your patients. Let the fucking psychos run rampant in the sewers, for all I care. Fuck 'em." he stood and leaned on her desk, on the knuckles of his fists. "You're running out of time, Nancy. My session is almost over. Then all bets are off."

She glanced at her watch. Only three minutes remained in his session. Her breath almost left her. She had three minutes to decide her own fate. Three minutes to decide whether she would live past those minutes, or become a bloodied corpse there in her own office.

"You've got two minutes," he pressured her.

"Wait!" she breathed heavy. "Can I please have more time? It's not fair. When you walked in here today, you knew exactly what was going to happen. You held all the cards and you knew it. Whereas I was only given three minutes. And I didn't even know that until just now."

She stared up at him, her eyes so wide and imploring.

He looked at her. She was trying to find a piece of his heart that was not tainted by his willingness to do whatever necessary to achieve his godliness. But he almost laughed in her face, and would have, if he didn't want her so badly. There was even a momentary thought, however fleeting, of playing a solo game of tick tac toe with the letter opener, on her forehead. But he let it pass.

"I'll tell you what I'll do. I'll give you until tomorrow morning to think about it. No longer. And I don't give second chances. We'll meet at Venice beach, just before dawn. All of the bums will be on the boardwalk, but the beach will be clear. I'll be able to see you from quite a long distance, from all directions. If you're not there alone, you can count on me paying you a visit, after hours. You can be sure of that. I love making house calls." He wasn't really worried about her turning him in. He held an ace up his sleeve that he had yet to play. He was just trying to keep her in line.

She was frozen to her seat, terrified. Yet she felt a bit at ease. Just a bit. She had the time she needed now to work out a plan for his capture or death, however it played out. If they did capture him, he might prove invaluable as a test subject. She might even be able to write a paper on the breakdown of the human mind, as well as a scientific study into the apparent soullessness and pure evil he exhibited.

She deterred from her previous diagnosis of only to end him. Maybe there was a way inside of Bray Hamlin's head. Maybe he could be learned from. One thing was for certain: As soon as he left her office, she was calling Morrow so that the police could set up a stakeout, outside his home and take him down, once he arrived.

"Thank you, Bray," she said, her voice unsettled. "Tomorrow would be great. And I can assure you that the police will not be involved. I don't want to die."

"I really hope that you're not fucking with me. I really do. For your sake. For your sake." His repetition was more of a promise than a statement, or a threat. "But anyway, I've got some business to take care of tonight." He pepped up. Almost happy. "Family number ten."

He walked behind his chair and leaned on it. Webb suddenly stood. She couldn't let him kill again. Yet, she needed to earn his trust. She had a deal for him, if only he would accept it. If he needed her as much as she thought he did, he would accept it.

"No. I mean, please, for the night. No killing," she pleaded.

"I didn't agree to that. You're lucky that I'm giving you the extra time that you've asked for. I'm not going to barter with you. This family is next. I need their essences. I haven't cured myself in a while. I want their essences."

His tone told her that it was not going to be an easy task to keep him from killing, tonight.

"I've been watching them for weeks. A nice, sweet family of five. Mom, dad, two teenage girls and the cutest little one-year-old you've ever seen." He reflected, "They're the best, you know. The young, remember? The younger they are, the more powerful their essence. One year old is about as powerful as you can get. Unless, of course, you get your hands on a new born."

She cringed at the thought of the baby's slaughter, and the rest of it's family's demise as well. It couldn't happen. She had to try to stop him. Outsmart him.

"Please, Bray. I'll sleep a lot better if I know that no one is going to die tonight. Especially the baby," she begged. "Please, give me a night of peace of mind. And I'll be more than willing to cooperate without any further resistance."

"I expect that cooperation anyway. I don't need to make deals."

"I know you're God. You're the Devil. Whatever you want to call yourself. Just please, please don't kill anyone tonight. I won't call the police. You know that. Help me trust you and I'll be more at peace being with you. Don't you want me to be at the same level of peace that you are when we come together?" She reached out to his sense of pity, if he had any in that black heart of his.

When he answered, he was calm. The same chilling calm he had exhibited before. Voice, and features. "First of all. I never said that I was God. And as for the Devil, he's just a pussy."

Her heart jumped hard, in her chest. Nearly taking her breath away.

"I said I would be a god. And I am very close to my ascension, as it is."

"So you don't need to kill tonight. Like you said, you're almost as powerful as you need to be right now. There is no one even close to your power. No one can threaten your safety, you're much too potent." She gazed at him with saddened eyes. "Would you do it for me? Leave the Stalker at home, just for tonight. Or however long it's possible. Just for me."

He grinned. Coming off as being smart to her deception. "Fine. I will grant this final request just for you. But just so you know, if you try to fuck me, one day soon I'll be wearing your blood."

She looked at him with terror in her eyes. "I would never go against you. I know the extent of your power. And I know that the police wouldn't be any match for your wits, or power. I would only be committing suicide."

She was sly. But unfortunately for her, he was slyer. He smiled. "Okay then, we have a deal. But you just keep one thing in mind. I know that you're only saying what I want to hear. But then again, you may be honest with your words. But let me tell you, you are exactly right when it comes to my power. No one can help you. Not the police, the FBI, no one. Because I am the infinite. And any attempt to capture or kill me would be futile. I really hope that you understand that. That's what I need from you, you know. Not just your soft, sweet smelling company. But I need you to understand. Don't dismiss that. Because that will be the biggest factor in our relationship, that will keep you alive. I can get pussy anywhere. But your understanding is what separates you from the rest.

"And that is nothing more than a very fine line between you and the next psychologist. As long as you possess that understanding, you will always be on my Christmas card list. But without it, you're just another dead piece of ass." He turned around and walked toward the office door. But she stopped him.

"So you won't kill tonight, right?"

"Yes, Nancy. The world is safe, tonight. I'll see you at the beach, just before dawn. 5:00 a.m. And remember: Be there alone, or be dead. I can smell a cop, from a mile away. You have a good night, now." He opened the door and left her in the office alone, with her chilling thoughts.

Though her heart was still pounding and she shook like a leaf in a hurricane, Nancy Webb practically fell back into her chair, allowing her body to go completely limp. She made it. She had actually outwitted the Stalker. After his capture, she would be sitting pretty on her way to writing a directional thesis on his specific psychosis. Which could help millions. And capture countless others killers. A paper that might even dispute Hamlin's very human being. Proving him a devil in the flesh.

She sat up straight and was about to reach for the phone to call lieutenant Morrow. When the door to her office re-opened and Hamlin re-entered the room. She quickly withdrew her hand.

"Bray, was there something else?" she shook again, her heart in her throat.

"Yes, there is. I almost forgot." He walked up to her desk and dropped a ring on it. Then reached into his pocket and produced a lunch bag of hair, tossing it on the desk as well.

Webb picked up the ring. It was a diamond angel, in a gold setting. She picked up the bag of hair, checking it over. It was raven black, with bloodied roots. She knew who the ring belonged to. And even the hair looked familiar.

"Brooke," she managed.

"Yes, Brooke. I have her. I've had her since last Friday. She's all right, for now. Not a scratch on her… . Well except for the bruised jaw. Do you know she can actually talk a mile a minute. Oh, and the hair. I couldn't find my scissors so I had to rip that lock right out of her head. But like I said, she's just fine. As long as you forget about making that phone call, you were about to make to Morrow. Oh, and I'm not stupid enough to keep her at my place. So you might as well forget about any police intervention. Or she's dead."

He smiled. "Sleep tight. See you at 5:00 a.m."

He left her alone in her office, again. She felt physically ill. She was going to have to go with him now, or her good friend Brooke May was to be killed. She dropped the ring and the hair on the desk. She was trembling uncontrollably. Even harder than before. She was his. There was no way around it now. It was checkmate, and she was on the losing end of the board. She collapsed on her desk, and cried. Cried like someone who had nothing else left to live for. Her life was hers no more.

CHAPTER SIXTEEN

1:35 a.m.

Bray Hamlin had promised Nancy Webb that he would not kill on the evening of his third and final session. But then again, she had promised him that she would not call the police and turn him in. But no matter how quickly she withdrew her hand from the phone, when he had re-entered her office, he saw it. He caught her. Negating on a deal that they had agreed to only moments before.

She not only did not keep their agreement, but she screwed the deal, all together. So now another innocent group of worshipers would supply him with their essences tonight. All because she couldn't keep their agreement.

Standing near a first floor window, he began to disrobe in the darkness. He knew that Webb was only telling him what he wanted to hear. So, so did he. He actually had no intentions of not taking the family tonight. He was just going to turn it on her, and let her believe that their sacrifices were on her head.

He checked the windowpane for any signs of an alarm system. And there, at the top of the pane. Visible through the window, were two wires. Half of the time in the suburbs, there were no alarms at all. But every time he had reached out to touch someone in a better neighborhood, there was the alarm. No problem, though. He reached down to the ground and pulled some tin foil and a paper clip from his pants pocket.

All of his wealthy worshipers thought that they were so safe because they didn't live in the suburbs, where a little more than ninety-nine percent of the Stalker's worshipers resided. They had their alarm systems and of course their rent-a-cop patrols. But their essences could be had in the seconds it took him to bypass the alarm. Which he had just done. He bent down again and retrieved the small, metal wedge from his pants pocket and slowly, so not to be heard, forced the window open. They did not know it at the time, but the Fosters were about to become yet another stepping stone in his ascension.

He pulled on his surgical gloves. Keeping a hold of the wedge this time, he slithered inside, bringing it with him. His eyes were already adjusted to the dark, so he was able to make out the features of the living room right away. After setting the wedge on the coffee table, he found his way to the kitchen, only to be interrupted by the sound of shoeless feet walking down the hall behind him.

Inside the kitchen the Stalker hid around the corner of the doorway. Taking a peek down the hall he made out the rather large figure of the man of the house, Mr. Foster.

He was obviously on a late night run to the refrigerator and was totally oblivious to the danger so close at hand. Nor did he know that this midnight raid was going to be his last. Hamlin readied himself to the side of the doorway and waited. He would have to take Foster quickly, and quietly. So not to disturb the rest of the sleeping household.

Foster was yawning when he stepped into the kitchen doorway. Hamlin cleared the corner and threw a high side-kick to the midnight raider's throat, crushing his windpipe. With nothing more than a gasp, Foster grabbed his throat with both hands, as he dropped to his knees fighting for air. Hamlin watched Foster for a few seconds, enjoying the floor show. But he knew that time was precious and he still had the rest of the family to ready, before he could begin the ritual.

He stepped forward and threw another kick. A front-kick. Straight to Foster's nose, shoving the bone into his brain, killing him instantly. He looked Foster over for a minute. He sure was an ugly fucker. How could such an ugly bastard keep such a beautiful wife. Money helped. And it was very likely that he had an enormous cock. But he wasn't about to check. He shrugged it off. At least it was one less body to have to carry down the stairs. Which would cut the time of preparation down considerably.

Leaving Foster's body where it lay until later, he ransacked the kitchen drawers and found the biggest knife he had yet to work with. A six-inch wooden handle. With at least a twelve-inch stainless steel blade. It was going to be a good night. He left the kitchen and walked to the stairs. Ascending the staircase he uncovered a squeaky stair or two along the way. But they were nothing to worry about because he was moving slowly, which made their creaking almost noiseless.

Coming to the first door, he opened it and looked inside. It was one of the Foster's teenage girls. She was beautiful, like her mother. And what a body. It seemed such a shame to sacrifice such fine pussy without fucking it bloody first. But he needed her essence for the ritual, and there was no time to fuck around.

He moved further inside the room right up to her bedside. She appeared to be sixteen to eighteen years of age. Staring down at her, he couldn't help but get wood. But that kind of tension only powered his desire to complete his ascension. He laid his hand gently on her forehead as he raised the knife above her. After one last glimpse at her beauty, he drove the blade down into the base of her throat and twisted it. Opening the wound wide. Her eyes opened for only a split second, making contact with his. Then she expired, without a sound.

Hamlin pulled the blade from the girl's throat and walked back out into the hallway, moving on to a second door. He opened it to a slight squeak, but the sleeping beauty that rest there did not stir. He walked to her bedside, stepping over a pair of bedroom slippers that lay in the middle of the floor. Judging by the size of them, they belonged to Mr. Foster. Who, while in such a rush to fill his face had left them behind.

He gazed down at Mom Foster. The bed covers lay down below her knees. He got a good look at her body. She was even more fabulous than her daughter. All that she wore was a pair of high hip panties and a pull over shirt, which had been cut off to reveal her entire midriff. She was not only beautiful, but her body, as he had noticed before, was a chiseled work of art. The curvature of her lower back led his eyes to her tight, firm ass. So beautiful. With magnificently sculptured thighs. Her body showing absolutely no signs of her having had three children. She was fabulously maintained. A goddess.

It was going to be a damn shame to have to gut her like a fish and tear out her organs, so that her blood may pool in her stomach. She was lying on her stomach so he reached down and slid his hand underneath her chin and pulled up, arcing her back. Her skin was so warm and soft. Which only added to his favor for her. Lifting her body partially off the bed he pinned her mouth shut. She began to struggle just as the twelve inch blade pierced the small of her back. Straight through her, and into the mattress.

Her muffled screams did not leave the room. And she was not dead yet. He jerked the blade out of her, then shoved it back in, again perforating both her and the mattress. Her body suddenly went limp and she wasn't trying to scream anymore. But he shoved the blade through her once more. Just to be sure.

He left the beautiful, bloodied body of Mrs. Foster where she lay and casually made his way to the next room. It belonged to the other teenage daughter. She was between fourteen and sixteen. But unlike her sister, she didn't have her mother's body. Her chest was almost as flat as a board and she was just a little thick in the middle.

He hurried into the room. He had more plans for tonight, so there was no more time to waste. The instant he reached her bedside he swung the knife down fiercely, piercing her through the heart. She made no sound and never woke up. An easy kill. He stared down at her for a moment. She appeared so peaceful, so calm. But inside of her he knew that there was more to her than that. Inside, where her life essence brewed. Even in her death, she was powerful. But soon that power would be his and he would step up to another plateau in his ascension. One step closer to godliness.

Moving further down the hall he came to another door, swinging it open. It was just the bathroom. He looked down the darkened hall, there was only one more door left. This room would belong to the one year old. As he approached the door he could feel the power of the child's essence. It drew him toward her. He couldn't stop now, even if he wanted to. But he didn't want to. He swung the door open and his cock got hard all over again. Her power was immense. He trembled, excited in her presence. The excitement was almost too much to bear. The power of her essence was right there for him to take. And take it he would.

Stepping inside her room he slowly moved to her crib. Picking her up, oh so gently. Not even having to put the knife down. He carried her to her pint size bath tub. She would bleed out quickly and he didn't want to let one drop get away. He laid her in the tub easy, where she remained asleep. He lifted her head up and placed the blade under the back of her neck, then took her by the forehead and pushed down on her, while pulling up on the blade. She had just started to fidget, but only flinched for a second or two.

After the deed was done, Hamlin held the infant's head in his hands, allowing it drain from the neck into the bathtub. After the head was bled dry, the Stalker set it on the changing table and opened it's eyes. Turning it to look out the bedroom door, then picked up the tub and carried it downstairs, setting it on the coffee table then cleared one of the living room walls for his alter to himself.

He chuckled at the thought that the baby's head would really freak out the cops. He'd get Morrow to puke, sooner or later. The FBI should get a kick out of it, too.

One by one he carried his worshipers down the stairs to join their ugly fucking father and husband. And what was left of their sisters and daughters. Dropping them off in the living room, he scoured the kitchen for a bucket, finding one in a small closet there.

Rejoining his faithful in the living room, he meticulously cut each of their stomachs open with a surgeon-like precision. Then, with all of the grace of a trash collector, he ripped out all of their organs and tossed them into a corner behind him, to his right. Hollowing them out, like fleshy canoes, he held each of their bodies over the bucket. Gathering their blood. Their essences.

Setting the bucket near the wall he had cleared. He positioned each of their bodies into their prayer like settings. Just as he had done all of those times before.

There he stood, before his worshipers. Raising the bucket over his head. He doused himself with their blood, then dropped the bucket. He fell to his knees, joining his adorned followers on the floor. Shaking intensely, vigorously. From the ever growing potency of his impending godliness. He remained there for nearly twenty minutes, trembling like a junky in need of a fix. But he already had what he wanted.

He slowly rose, wiping the blood away from his eyes. Then turned and faced the wall behind him. Scripting his name in the Foster's collective dark red essence. With his ritual now complete he retrieved the metal wedge from the coffee table and left his worshipers behind. But instead of going upstairs to shower the blood from his body. He crossed to the opposite side of the house. Stopping for but a second in the foyer to disarm the alarm system. Then proceeded on to open a second window, leaving bloody, gloved hand prints on the window and it's sill. He departed the Foster's home the same type of way he had entered. Disappearing into the darkness outside.

Touching bloodied foot on the plush green lawn, cloaked by the darkness, he snuck his way over to the Foster's neighbors' home. Outside the window he had chose as his point of entry, he found the telephone junction box. Ripping out the wires, he killed the phone lines to and from the house. Again he bypassed the home's alarm system, prying the window open and slithered inside, directly into the living room. So he gathered.

Dawn was still a ways off, and he didn't want to wait any longer to involve his queen into his affairs.

CHAPTER SEVENTEEN

Nancy Webb lay awake in her bed staring up at the ceiling, listening to the crickets chirping in unison, outside her bedroom window. It was a little after 3:00 a.m. But she definitely was not sleeping tonight. She had less than two hours before she had to meet Bray Hamlin on the beach. Her life, as she knew it, was over. But perhaps something good could still come of it all. Maybe she could keep Hamlin from ever killing again. It was a slim possibility, but a possibility none-the-less. Maybe she would even get the chance to turn him in, somewhere along the line. But her fate, as of now, was sealed.

She was not only going to have to share his home with him, but his bed as well. She broke out into a cold sweat, trembling underneath the sheets. She could only imagine what his twisted mind was capable of in the bedroom. She started to cry. Would it really be worth her freedom to only *possibly* stop the killing? And what about Brooke May? A dear friend, but more than likely already dead, she thought.

Hamlin had said that she was fine. Unharmed. But what would happen to her after she was his? And he didn't need Brooke anymore. She wondered if she should just go to the police, right now. But what if Brooke was all right? And he just planned to use Brooke and herself in his little three ways that he was so fond of. If she went to the police and they failed to catch him, then May would die. Hopefully, quickly. But if they did manage to capture him and May was still lived, she would eventually perish. Because Hamlin would surely not tell them where she was. And without food and water, she was as good as dead. And it would be a slow, lingering death.

Her insides felt as though they were jumping. Switching from their own rightful places into each others settings. She was queasy. She hadn't had any dinner, but her stomach threatened to tear out its own lining just to relieve itself. She rolled on to her side, hanging her head over the side of the bed. Then came the dry heaves. Three minutes of constant, unbearable contractions.

She looked up at the clock. She had less than an hour and a half now. She felt as though her heart was going to explode. Sweat ran off her nose and dripped from her face. With the tears of her crying in the mix, she could no longer distinguish between the two fluids. She knew right then that she had to make a decision. Give herself to Hamlin and possibly save May's life, while trying to stop the killing by offering herself up as a sexual alternative. Or turn Hamlin in and pray that the police would catch him and stop the massacre, while just assuming that May was already dead.

Hamlin had promised that she was alive, but then again, could she actually take the word of the most sick and deviant mind she had ever encountered. The mind of a man, who could arguably be the most feared serial killer in history. She had made a deal with the Devil, and now couldn't think of anyway out. Apparently she wasn't as brilliant as everyone thought she was. Actually, she was an idiot. She had played a dangerous game with the Stalker, against what had been a stacked deck. A deck that Bray Hamlin was dealing from. Yes, he held all of the cards and it was a game that she just couldn't win. He was a master player, and she was but a naive beginner.

Now she was stuck between a rock and a hard place. Hamlin wanted her as his companion. She should have called Morrow immediately after he had left her office. Even though he said that May was alive and well, he just couldn't be trusted. If she had she would be in protective custody right now. But instead, she was at home in the darkness, alone. Awaiting the hangman, of sorts.

With the wind sparsely howling past her window, she came to the conclusion that her intelligence was not a mighty as Morrow's gun. Or Hamlin's blade. She couldn't stop the killings on her own. She knew that now. So it was time to do what she believed to be the right thing. Something she should have done hours ago. She sit up in her bed, swung her legs over the side and grabbed the phone. But putting it up to her ear, she found no dial tone. It was dead.

A sudden thumping sound came from downstairs. She swung her head around to look at the door. It was closed. So whatever had produced the sound made a big enough ruckus to not only be heard on the home's second floor, but to be heard through a solid wood door as well. And that meant people. But she had an alarm system. How could someone have gotten in? She wiped away her tears, and the sweat from her brow. She was already more than shaken from her thoughts of Bray Hamlin. But now, even more chills swept over her body.

She was frozen. Her mind, unable to process the excessive threat. She just sit there in her sweat-drenched night shirt. Motionless. Her wet hair sticking to her face. Then suddenly, something in her mind just snapped. She was no longer willing to be the victim. She was going to do something about this new threat. Then she would go straight to the police and turn Hamlin in.

She slid out of bed and made it to the closet. Opening the sliding door, she dug her way to the back where she found her old baseball bat, from her softball days in college. The thought crossed her mind to just stay put and maybe they would just take what they wanted and go away. But then again, she remembered the brutal death of Betty Pierce. Killed, in her own bedroom. More than likely, they were going to want the goodies that lay tucked away up stairs. So she had to make up her mind, quickly: To go downstairs, with the element of surprise on her side, or stay put and let them come to her, knowing all too well that she would be in her room.

She gripped the bat tight. And in a second, she made her choice. She would go to them with the element of surprise on her side. She only hoped that there weren't too many of them for her to handle. Opening the bedroom door, she stepped foot outside into the hallway. It was very dark, but she could see clearly that it was empty. With her knees just about knocking, she reached the top of the staircase and listened carefully, but there was not a sound to be heard. Maybe they'd already gone.

Whether they had or not was a moot point. She still had to go downstairs to at least run to a neighbor's house to call the police. Not only for the burglary, but for the Stalker as well. Yes, she had made up her mind. She would not chance crossing paths with multiple burglars and get herself killed. She would just go for the front door and run to the safety of a neighboring home, and call the police from there.

Stair by stair, she crept down to the ground floor. At the bottom she listened carefully, but heard nothing. She snuck across the foyer, toward the door. But again, a thumping noise coming from the living room, directly at her right, stopped her in her tracks. She tiptoed to the doorway of the room, peeking inside. Though her eyes were adjusted to the dark, she could not see anything. The living room was a deeper level of darkness, with the drapes drawn so that not even the glow of the street lights may penetrate. It was pitch black.

Cautiously, she stepped inside the doorway. Just one step. There was not a sound to be heard. Except for the pounding of her heart, in her ears. The bat shook in her hands. If the intruders were still in the house, this is where they were. She couldn't see anyone, but then again, she could not be seen either. So she might still have the element of surprise on her side.

She took a half step back out of the room, looking toward the front door. She might still be able to make it out. But there she was. A fifty, fifty chance on getting the drop on whoever had broken into her haven. She really needed to contact the police, the Stalker must still be caught. But if the intruder got to her, before she could make it out of the house, she could forget about Hamlin's capture. She might even forget about the rest of her life. She had to get him or them, before they got her.

After a moment she stepped back into the living room, walking further inside. She knew that there was a lamp a few steps deeper into the room. But did she really want to turn it on? The light would totally give her away. What if this intruder had a gun. No, she couldn't turn on the light. She would have to search the room, in the pitch black. She felt physically ill. There was suddenly too much excitement in her life, after an eight month lull.

She wasn't really sure what she was afraid of. There might not be any one there at all. The wind was blowing up a bit, outside. The noise she heard could have been a tree branch, being blown into the side of the house. Her mind had been totally fixated on the Stalker. That was enough to spook anyone, all on it's own. Add in the thumping noise from the tree, and you have a paranoid delusion. The phone being out was likely due to the wind as well. Yes, a downed line that's what it was. She was scaring the hell out of herself for nothing. She was being childish. She would just turn on the light and show herself that there was no one there. Get dressed, and go to the police. The Stalker still had to be stopped.

Allowing her body to loosen up she took two more steps into the room and reached for the lamp that set on an end table, next to the sofa.

"Don't turn on the light." A stern, familiar voice came out of the blackness around her.

She froze in her tracks. Her heart once again, in her throat. She wondered. "Bray?"

"In the flesh."

Chills swept up and down her spine. A breathlessness, settling in her chest. Barely being able to stand. "W… what are you doing here? I thought I had un… until just before d… dawn."

"I just thought that we could do it early. There's only just over an hour left. So, have you packed yet? Are you ready to become, Mrs. Bray Hamlin? Not officially, of course. Say, why don't you looe that bat, you make me nervous. The couch is right in front of you, why don't you toss it there. I mean, I'm sure that you know where your couch is. But like I said, toss the bat." His tone was telling, not asking. Yet it was soft, and calm.

Her mind was racing. If she threw the bat away, she would be opening herself completely to a man that had admitted to killing forty-five people for their blood, to make himself immortal. Who was she kidding, really? She wouldn't have a chance against Hamlin with or without the bat. He obviously didn't want her dead, or she would be already. He had simply come for her early. Her scrambled thoughts could no longer guide her. She just stood there, in a daze.

"I said, toss the bat."

He frightened her back into the now, where she nearly dropped the bat entirely. She looked around abruptly, in the pitch black. But there was no getting her eyes used to it. She couldn't even see the bat in her hands. But somehow, Hamlin could see her. The Stalker could see. He could see her, but she couldn't see, him.

"Toss it."

She could tell by his voice that she was starting to raise his ire, by not doing what she was told.

"Okay," she agreed.

She tossed the bat out in front of her, but did not hear it hit the floor. So it had to have landed squarely on the sofa.

"There, it's gone. Can I turn on the light, now? It's not a fair deal that you can see me, but I can't see you." She started to reach out for the lamp.

"I said, no light. What don't you understand about that phrase? I can see you and that's all that matters. What is it with you and 'deals'?" there was silence only for a second, but it felt like an eternity. Then his voice once again, came out of the darkness.

"You never answered my question."

She swallowed, hard. "Which one was that?"

"Are you packed? Are you ready for our meeting on the beach?"

"No. I was trying to get some sleep. I was going to get up early and pack. I just needed some rest," she told him a bit breathlessly.

"Just trying to get some sleep, huh. With the way you're breathing, it sounds to me like you were running wind sprints. Just a little exercise, to maintain that beautiful body?" He was calm and controlled.

"No, I was just scared. I thought that I had burglars in the house. I was afraid of what might happen. Can I turn on the light, please?"

He could hear the sheer terror in her voice. She was almost hyperventilating.

"Well, now you know it's only me, so you can calm down. And no. No lights. Not just, yet. If you ask me again…" he let his threat trail off.

"Well, what do you want? I mean, you break in here a little after 3:30 in the morning, just to ask me if I'm already packed? I agreed to meet you at the beach. No police, and ready to disappear. What more do you want from me?" she was still scared, but becoming more defiant.

"I didn't trust you, I thought that you might have gone to the police. I didn't even expect you to be here. I expected you to be in police protective custody by now." He was actually surprised.

"Well, here I am. I wouldn't leave Brooke to die. There are no police here. So why are you still here?" her voice was now unshaken. Having regained her forged steadiness.

"Okay now, I know that you've been through a lot tonight. But don't you *ever* speak that way to me again."

"I'm sorry." She reverted back to her cowardly ways. Leaving her stoutness behind. Terror once again, shaking her voice.

She looked all around in the darkness that surrounded her, but she couldn't see anything in the pitch black. Even when Hamlin spoke, she couldn't tell where in the room he was. It seemed as though he were drifting through the darkness, like a phantom shadow.

Her legs were shaking, but the house was not cold, no. She had tried to put on a show of force, but she had fallen short. She was becoming more and more terrified, by the moment. Since he had stopped speaking after his little threat. But it had only been about a minute. And she nearly leapt out of her skin, when he spoke again.

"So, are you ready to go with me? Or do you still want to meet at the beach?" as if he didn't know.

"I'd like to meet you at the beach, if it's okay. I still have to pack and get myself ready. You know, take a quick shower, put on some makeup, do my hair." She tried to buy time.

"You wouldn't be trying to stonewall me now, would you?"

"No. I would never try to mislead you, Bray. I enjoy living, very much. I just need time to get ready, is all," she said, still shaken.

She looked over the blackness, trying to hone in on his voice. But she could still not detect him.

He sounded pleased. "I guess I never should have doubted you. Maybe I shouldn't have sacrificed that family tonight, after all. But I really didn't think that you were going to go along with our little deal. Oh, well. I needed their essences, anyway. I guess I'll have to start trusting you, huh." He chuckled, devilishly.

A sinking feeling hit the pit of her stomach as tears began running down her face. She was shocked and her voice cracked when she spoke. "You were planning on killing them all along, weren't you? You never had any intention, of keeping your word. You bastard!" she cried.

"Nancy, Nancy. You poor girl. You're never supposed to take the word of a psychopath as the gospel. He will only rip your heart out. Literally."

She wiped the tears from her eyes. "So does that mean you're going to kill me now?"

"No, that part I meant. I do want you, Nancy. I need you. Your body, your beauty and your understanding. That is what I need the most. You must, understand me." He sounded almost as if he were pleading.

"I could never understand you. There is nothing to understand. You're just a lunatic. A mad man. I just wish you were dead!" her blood boiled. And her stoutness this time, was quite real.

"Watch what you say, you're treading on thin ice. You must understand me." His voice came from an undistinguished point, in the darkness around her. Sounding perturbed.

"No, you're not upset because I sacrificed one of my many flocks tonight. You're just pissed off because I showed you that you're not as fucking smart as you thought you were. The great intuitiveness of renowned psychologist, Nancy Webb, was not worthy enough to match wits with me," he spouted, with great pride.

"Match wits. Understand you. What is it that you want from me, exactly? I can diagnose you to a certain degree, but I could never really understand you. You love what you do; I can't understand that.

"You think that wearing your victims blood can raise you to a higher plain, but you're wrong. That's what I understand. Your mind is not right. That's what I understand. You're a perverse, blood thirsty, fiend. That's what I understand." Her voice was still shaking, but she called it as she saw it.

A bit of a laugh came from out of the darkness. "So you do understand. You wanted inside of my mind, doctor. Well there it is, all laid out for you in living color." He paused only briefly. Before quoting, from one of his favorite songs. Melodically.

"Welcome to my nightmare. I think you're gonna like it. I think you're gonna feel, that you belong." His unsettling laugh, followed. Then suddenly, stopped. "Welcome, my mind is wide open to you. But have you learned? Have you? I think, so." An eerie moment of silence, followed. Then: "Turn on the light, Nancy. Turn it on, now."

Her knees suddenly felt like they might buckle. She broke out into a cold sweat. Now that he wanted the lights on, she wasn't so sure anymore that she wanted to see him at that point. Tears continued to run down her face.

"Bray, why don't you just go home and I'll see you in just over an hour," she lied this time. This time, as soon as he was gone, so was she. Directly to the police station. And directly to Morrow.

"Whoa, whoa. Get a hold of yourself. What, are you on one of those emotional rollercoasters? First you're scared, then you're pissed. And now it sounds like you're crying like a baby. Get a hold of yourself, woman. Then, turn on the light, like I told you to." He didn't sound very comforting.

"Please, just let me see you later," she pleaded.

"No. We can talk, now. I said, turn on the fucking light." He scared her with the power of his voice.

She hesitated, terrified.

"Now! Turn it on, now!"

She jumped, then reached out a trembling hand and turned the lamp on.

There stood Hamlin behind the lamp, directly in front of her. Nude, and covered from head to toe, in blood. Wide eyed, with a fiendish look on his face. The blood just beginning to coagulate and dry on his skin. He had been wearing it for a while.

Webb laid down a series of ear splitting screams, while trying to back away from him as fast as she could. But she slipped and fell into a shallow puddle of blood on the carpet. The blood spat high on her thigh and hip, her hand dipping into it. A scream lodged in her throat, as she stared down at her blood drenched hand.

Hamlin moved around the end table and stood in front of her. Letting himself all hang out.

"Sorry about the carpet. I stood in one place, too long." He knelt down with her. "Do you feel the essence of the blood? It's powerful, isn't it. Coursing through your body, like an electric charge. Expanding your mind and emblazoning your soul."

She stared at him in horror. Her glassy eyes, reflecting his image. Her mouth hanging open in a silent scream, as she shook uncontrollably.

"You feel it, don't you. Of course you do. You and I are one, right now." His fingers left blood streaks down both of her cheeks. Then a single stripe across her forehead, and one down her nose.

She closed her legs tight, as he ran both of his hands up the outsides of her thighs. Stopping when he reached the bottom of her short nighty.

"You're trembling. Excited? I bet you're wet, aren't you? Shall I feel for myself?" he slid one of his hands further up her night shirt. Forcing his fingers between her legs, caressing her firmly on the outside of her panties.

She gasped and tried to close her legs tighter. Trying to stop his advancements. "Stop! I'm not, like you! There is no one on this fucking earth that is like you! You fucking insane bastard!" she blurted out. Impulsive and angry, while trying to wriggle away.

Her mind raced out of control. Fear, animosity and shame hit her relentlessly, in wave after wave. His touch was becoming arousing.

He pulled his hand away, displeased. "I guess you're right; you're not like me. I've basically told you my life story. I've allowed you into my mind. Yet you refuse to understand.

"Like you said. You think that I'm just a fucking lunatic." He suddenly went calm. "But I don't believe you. I'm sure that you do understand me and that's the only reason why you're still breathing. And I'm not the lunatic you think I am. My approaching immortality will prove that to you. Because with every drop of blood that I wear, I do come closer and closer to my ascension. My godliness. I'm almost there. You can still come with me, if you just let yourself, understand." He stood.

He appeared more compromising. "I'll give you one last chance. Believe in me. Come with me. I do need you, Nancy. More than you will ever know." He appeared desperate. "You know what they say. It's lonely, at the top."

It was disturbing the way that he stood there, naked and covered in blood. His composure that of a priest on communion day. "Become one, with me."

She went to wipe the blood from her face, but he grabbed her wrist and stopped her.

"Leave it. Feel the essence, as it empowers your soul." He released her and backed away. "Feel it," he urged, calm yet animated.

She stared down at the blood, on her hands and legs. She could feel it drying on her face, as her heart pounded heavy. She felt frivolous, still trembling, uncontrollably. Her mind muddled and frozen. Absent of lucid thought.

Hamlin opened the drapes of the window he had entered through. It was still open. He slid one leg outside, straddling the sill. Looking back at her.

"You know, you may live in a very fine neighborhood, with security patrols and all that. But you really should invest in a better alarm system. Any wacko from right off the street could just climb right on in here. Then, where would you be? Although, Betty Pierce had a damn good one. And it didn't help her out much, at all… I'm still going to give you that one last chance to live. I'll see you in an hour and a half. 5:30. I'll give you the extra thirty minutes, so you can clean up a little first. Oh, and don't forget. Brooke is waiting to see you, again. But if you don't show up, consider yourself and Brooke pieces of my ascension." he slipped out the window and disappeared into the darkness.

Nancy Webb's stare was locked on all of the blood. She had never seen so much. It was everywhere. On her hands and legs. She was sitting in it. It seeped down the wall from the window sill. Hamlin's bloody footprints were everywhere. There was blood on everything he had touched. Everywhere he stood.

Suddenly her hushed shock became hysterical screams. She leapt to her feet and bolted up the stairs. Rushing into the bathroom, she ripped the shower curtain off of it's rings and stepped inside the tub, turning on the water. The down pour washed away her tears, the blood going with them. But the soothing warm water could not alleviate the mental anguish Hamlin had just bestowed upon her.

She cried for the innocent lives that Hamlin had taken in his insane plight for immortality. She cried out of fear for her own life and the life of Brooke May. Which she was certain had already been extinguished by now. She had hoped to stop Hamlin's killing, somehow. But he had reneged on his agreement, not to kill his tenth family that very night. So it was certain that he would never stop. No matter what she might do in his favor. So it was off to the police.

She may not be able to stop Hamlin's massacre of the families of Los Angeles, but Josh Morrow, could. And she hoped that he would only do it with a bullet. Even if they did not capture Hamlin right away, she would much rather remain under twenty-four hour guard, as long as it would take to end his reign of terror, than to forever remain in the grasp of the unpredictable Stalker.

CHAPTER EIGHTEEN

Uniformed sergeant Jeremy Webster led a fatigued Josh Morrow through a hopping squad room, toward one of the precinct's interrogation rooms.

"When did she get here?"

The sergeant glanced at his watch. "About five minutes ago. 4:10 a.m., or so."

"What does she want? Did she say?"

"No she didn't, sir. But she appears to be quite upset. Her hair and clothes are damp, but it isn't raining outside. So wherever she came from, she was in a big hurry to get here."

Webster opened the door to the interrogation room and let Morrow step inside.

"Thank you, sergeant. I'll take it from here."

Webster closed the door, leaving them alone.

Nancy Webb sit at a table at the center of the room. Even though the air conditioning to that section of the station was on the fritz, she was shaking like a leaf in the windstorm.

Morrow stood across the table from her. "Why are you wet, doctor?"

She rocked herself, in the stationary chair. "I needed to get out of the house, quickly." Her voice was shaking.

"Why did you have to leave your home, so quickly? What's going on?"

"I didn't know if he was still around. I had to get out of there, fast." She appeared to be in shock, staring off into space.

Morrow walked around the table and removed his suit coat, draping it over her shoulders. "Who, was still around? Who are you talking about? Were you burglarized? Did someone harm you?"

"I didn't tell right away, because he had Brooke, my assistant. But I don't think that there's much of a chance that she's still alive." She continued to rock. "I thought that I could keep him from killing anymore. I thought that we had a deal… ." She let her sentence trail off, while staring at the wall in front of her.

"Who? Who are you talking about? You've got to give me more. Who are you talking about?"

Morrow knew that she was in a state of shock, and needed to warm up. But he just wanted one answer, first.

"Who, are you talking about?" his voice was soothing. "You know who, who is?"

She looked at him with a fear in her eyes. The likes he had never seen before.

"The Stalker."

Morrow knew that he wasn't going to get much more out of her, until she was warmed up and dried off. So he had one of his female officers take Webb into the locker room to dry her off and clothe her in some departmental sweats. While he called special agent Scott Ross down to the station house.

Ross had just left the lab and was heading home when Morrow called him on his cell phone. He was only a few minutes out and hurried back. He walked in to Morrow's office, only a second after the female officer led Webb, wrapped in a blanket, back into the lieutenant's berth, where a hot cup of coffee awaited her.

With Webb warm and dry now, and sitting across the desk from Morrow, with her senses about her, they began again with the question of who it was that they were looking for.

"All right. Special agent Ross is here. Now, who is he? Are you exactly sure that this man is the Stalker? How did you find out? How did he let it slip? What happened, tonight?" Morrow seemed to disorient her with his many questions.

She sipped her coffee, while staring at him, strangely. So he calmed himself and eased back into his chair.

"I'm sorry. Too much, at one time. Just let it go, as it comes."

"Really all we need, is a name. We can take it from there, but only if you're sure about him," Ross urged, from his chair, beside her.

She set her cup on Morrow's desk, closing the blanket more tightly around herself.

"He's been a patient of mine for the past three weeks. But he only just revealed himself to me this past week. Yesterday, actually. We had a session together, yesterday." She sipped at her coffee again, then replaced the cup on Morrow's desk.

Morrow gave her a friendly smile. A supportive smile. "What has this man done to lead you to believe that he's the Stalker?"

"He told me, yesterday," she repeated.

"Did he give you any specifics? What exactly, did he say?"

She shook her head. She was dead tired and her was mind obscured. "He didn't actually come out and say, 'I'm the Stalker.' He was just a bit more subtle than that. He just insinuated that that was who he was at first."

"At first. What did he do, then?" Ross asked.

"He didn't do, anything." She left out his advancements on her. "He told me about the crime scenes. In exact detail. How the bodies are positioned. He knew everything. He even told me why."

"You know, I don't give a rats ass why he's doing it anymore. Do you have a name, or don't you?" Ross pressed.

"He kills families of five. Because five, is his favorite number." Webb stared coldly, at the special agent. "But you don't care why families of five are being butchered."

Ross rubbed his chin. "I didn't mean it like that. I meant… ."

"I was right about what he does with their blood," Webb cut him off. "He thinks that by wearing his victims blood, he can take their life essences, their strength, and add it to his own. Until he becomes immortal. And right now, he believes that he is almost a god."

"Look, I was just thinking that we could get him into custody first. And then worry about why he does it," Ross explained, apologetically.

"I'm sorry. I'm just very tired and upset right now. He broke into my house tonight. I don't know how he got past my alarm system, but we were right on about why he never leaves any evidence behind. Except for a few hairs here and there. Not only does he wear surgical gloves, but he also kills in the nude. He was just covered in blood."

"So why did he pick you to tell all of this too?" Ross wondered.

"I don't know. He must have heard about my involvement in the case. Which shouldn't have been very hard. It's been all over the news. But what I don't understand is, why he waited so long to come to me. Well, he is very patient. He watches his victims for weeks on end. I think he likes to take his time with things. All things. But I was booked up for more than two years. That's why he killed one of my patients and took her sessions. If the case file that you have on the murder of Betty Pierce is still open, you can close it now. It was him. He came to me, to toy with me. To fool me, and he did. I never had a clue... ." She appeared distant. "He wants me to understand him."

"What?" Morrow asked.

"He kept saying, that he needed me to understand."

"Understand, what?" Ross joined in.

She paused. "His mind, I guess. His thoughts. His reasoning toward his immortality. It's like he needs someone else to believe in him, too. Or it won't happen." She shook her head, wearily. "I don't know."

"Okay," Ross began, conceding to Webb's chain of investigative interpretations. "Now that we know why he does what he does, can we finally, get down to a name? We need to pick this guy up, and quick. Before he tries to leave the city. Or worse, the state. What's his name?"

They could see it in her eyes that she was terrified. Too terrified to answer the question. She closed her eyes for only a moment, drawing in a deep breath.

"He is extremely wealthy. What if you don't capture him right away? He could hide away, for years. And knowing him the way that I do, it is entirely possible that he would do just that. Then when I'm not longer under police, or federal protection, he'll come back and kill me." She was petrified.

"He won't get away. I promise you. This is the Stalker we're talking about. We're gonna hit this fucker with an army. He will not get away," Ross guaranteed.

"He has a lot of friends who are high officials in state, local and federal authorities. He knows a lot of people." She continued to fear.

Morrow looked her deep in the eyes. He had a name in mind. And he feared that she had the same name, in her's. But it was his duty to capture the Stalker. No matter who he was.

"I don't care who, his friends are. Or how powerful they might be. No matter who he is, publicly. He's still the Stalker and there are no amount of friends in the world that can save his ass." His features softened. "Who is he, Nancy?"

Her eyes fluttered, wearily. "Hamlin. Bray Hamlin. It's Bray Hamlin."

God damn it! Morrow sat back in his chair. Hamlin was the name on his mind all right. He was hoping that she wasn't going to say it, but she had, and now it was time to deal with it. To reach out and grab the Stalker, Hamlin. He shot a glance at Ross, who looked just as uncomfortable as he felt.

This was not good. Bray Hamlin, the name that was synonymous with the one good thing in L.A. that could always be counted on to help the less fortunate. His donations to many charities, not only in the state of California, but nation wide, were always notoriously large in sum. He had even paid for a new wing on the Los Angeles Memorial Hospital, which bore his name.

He was a symbol of all that was good and pure. He was a saint. Especially to the people of Los Angeles and the state of California. Not to mention that he was very good friends with all of Morrow's superiors. The chief and commissioner of the L.A.P.D., the mayor, the governor and several judges, most of them federal. And upheld strong standings, within the community.

He was their buddy. He had had countless lunches and dinners with them and their families. Not only was he always welcome in their homes, but he was a trusted friend. Godfather to some of their children. Yes, getting an arrest warrant for Bray Hamlin was going to be tough. But proof was proof. Webb's eye witness to his bloodied, nude body, should be enough proof to get the warrants they were going to need for his arrest.

"Bray Hamlin." Morrow echoed. "I knew you were going to say that."

"Yes. Bray Hamlin." She swallowed, hard. "Where's your army, now?" She looked helpless. Terrified.

A feeling of impotence came over Morrow. Again, he looked at Ross. "Maybe you ought to get the warrant." He passed the buck.

"Why me?"

"You're the one with all of the federal connections. I mean, you're a Fed."

"And?"

"Well, you would have more of an influence with them than I would."

"Not true."

"You're both afraid to even call for a warrant, and you're going to protect me." Webb seemed to be on the verge of losing it.

"No, no." Ross raised a hand to calm her. "I do live next door to federal justice Ramsey. My family and I have had several picnics, with him and his family. I suppose I could call him." He sounded unsure.

"You suppose," Morrow wondered.

"I can call him," Ross corrected himself, "I will call him."

Morrow slid the phone across the desk and set it in front of him. "Call him."

Ross glanced over at Webb. She was sitting quietly in somewhat of a daze. Staring straight forward at nothing in particular. He was going to ask her one more time, if she was absolutely sure that it was Hamlin. But instead he just picked up the phone and dialed. Waiting for a response and after several rings, the tired voice of federal justice, Walter Ramsey, picked up on the other end.

"Hello."

"Judge Ramsey. It's Scott Ross. Are you awake enough to have a talk with me?"

Ramsey sat up in bed and turned on the lamp at his bedside. Putting on his glasses he looked at the alarm clock.

"It's 4:52 a.m. What could you possibly want at this hour?"

"Well, sir. We've caught a break in the Stalker case, and we could really use arrest and search warrants, A.S.A.P."

"Damn, good. What's the bastard's, name?" Ramsey joined in, enthusiastically.

"Well, sir… ."

"What's the man's name? No name, no warrants. Speak up, Scott. Who is he?"

"Um, Bray Hamlin, Walter. It's Bray Hamlin."

"What! You can't be serious. This is just a joke, right? That man is saintly. What type of evidence, do you have?"

"Well, we have sort of an eye witness, so to speak."

"So to speak. Who is this witness, and what did they see, exactly?" Ramsey sounded doubtful.

"It's Doctor Nancy Webb. The psychologist helping the police to profile him. Well, apparently he became a patient of hers and slowly revealed to her that he is the Stalker," Ross explained. Or at least, he tried.

"He told her he was. That's all that you have. I'm going to need a lot more proof than just, 'he told me so.'"

"I understand that, Walter. And I think that this next bit of information will be just that."

"It had better be."

"He broke into her house, tonight. She said that he was nude and covered in blood. And that he knows exact details of the crime scenes. That only we and the Stalker know. If that doesn't make her an eye witness, I don't know what will. Can you get us the warrants?"

"I want to talk to this, Doctor Webb. I need to hear this from her," Ramsey insisted, refusing to believe.

"I'm afraid that's not possible, Walter. She's pretty much been out of it, since she got here. And I'm afraid that she is still that way," Ross told him. "We need those warrants. It's all you, Walter. I know that the two of you have been close friends, even since before, his parents died. And I know that in the city's eyes he's a saint. But Bray Hamlin is the Stalker, without a doubt. Like I said, it's all you, Walter. We need those warrants."

"God damn it!" Ramsey accidently woke his wife.

"What's the matter, honey?"

"It's nothing to concern yourself with. Go ahead and go back to sleep."

He returned to his call. "Goddamn it, Scott. I just can't believe it. He's Beth's godfather, for Christ's sake. My daughter's godfather. He's been in my house a thousand times, and around my children." Ramsey nearly exploding with outrage.

His wife lay by his side, listening. But only heard one side of the conversation. She had no idea what was at stake.

"All right, then," Ramsey spoke up. "Meet me at my office in twenty minutes. And may God help us if you don't get him tonight. He knows who we are. Where we live. Including you." There was an intense pause. "I don't want that hanging over my head. I'd never get another decent nights sleep again."

"Don't worry. In that instance we have more than enough people to protect you."

"Oh yeah? What about the rest of his former friends? In the police, government, and judicial systems. Can you protect all of us, Scott?"

"Let's just make sure that it doesn't come to that. The quicker we get those warrants, the faster we can haul him in." Ross held a confident tone.

But that tone didn't settle Ramsey much. "Before we go, I have one request. I want a few agents stationed at my house, until you bring him in."

Ross thought that Ramsey's request was rather selfish, but if it got them the warrants quicker, why not?

"Absolutely. I'll send them right away. By the time we meet at your office, they'll be there and in place."

"Good enough. I'll see you in twenty minutes." Ramsey hung up the phone.

"What's going on, Walter? What's so urgent that you have to go to the office, at this hour for?" Mrs. Ramsey wondered.

"They've found out the identity of the Stalker. They just need some warrants, to take him down. That was Scott Ross on the phone. I'll be gone for about an hour or so. You go on back to sleep." He pulled on his pants.

"Bray, is the Stalker?" she said in disbelief.

Ramsey slid on his jacket, now completely dressed. He looked at her. "How did you know I was talking about Bray Hamlin?"

"You mentioned that he was Beth's godfather. I know who Beth's godfather is. My God. Bray? Are they certain?"

He nodded. "I know that it's hard to believe. It was hard for me too, but they have proof. I know you love him like a son, but he's our man. Now don't worry. The FBI will be here, real soon. Besides, he doesn't even know that they're coming. Go on back to sleep, there's no need to worry. I'll lock up good and tight, when I leave." He kissed her and left.

Mrs. Ramsey lay there alone in bed. Completely shocked by the events unfolding before her. A deep foreboding building up inside of her. Her husband was right. Bray Hamlin was like a son to her. And as a mother would, she just couldn't believe that her son was capable of these allegations that he was a stone cold killer. The worst in U.S. history. Go back to sleep, indeed.

Walter Ramsey left his wife and two teenage girls alone in their home. After locking the front door tight, he got into his car and sped off. He still couldn't believe that Bray Hamlin, was the Stalker. Talk about a shock to the system. Hamlin was a valued and close family friend. It was a living nightmare. The godfather to one of his children was apparently the most feared and sought after serial killer in Los Angeles' history.

Special agent Scott Ross hung up the phone. "I've got to go meet judge Ramsey, at his office. It'll take him about twenty minutes to get there."

"Price, the task force, and I will meet you at Hamlin's place." Morrow noticed Price's entrance into the squad room.

Federal agent Bicket, was right behind Price. Both had cups of coffee in their hands. And both looked like they had just been awakened from a short nap, after a long, hard day.

"Okay," Ross agreed. "Just be sure to let agent Bicket know where we're going."

Morrow motioned over the feeb's shoulder. "Why don't you tell him."

Ross looked over his shoulder. "Never mind. I'll just take him with me. We'll meet you there, as soon as possible," he told Morrow, leaving him alone in the office and picked up his partner on the way out.

Jonathan Price watched after the feebs, for a moment. Then joined Morrow and Webb in the lieutenant's office. He looked bewildered. "What in the hell, is going on? I got a call, telling me to get my ass in here, but they wouldn't say why."

"That's because I wouldn't tell them. I didn't want any blabber mouth, leaking information to the press. We've got a fix on the Stalker. We know who, and where he is. Doctor Webb came to us with the information, just a while ago," Morrow told him.

Price looked down at Webb, who was still seated in front of Morrow's desk. Staring off into space.

"Who is he, doctor?"

Morrow led Price outside his office. "She's been like that on and off, ever since she got here. But she did tell us who he is. He was at her house, tonight. Scared the shit out of her."

"So who is he?"

Morrow paused, then. "Keep your voice down… . It's Bray Hamlin."

"What?" Price whispered.

"That's right. I'm calling in a tactical team. Then we're all going to meet Ross and Bicket, at Hamlin's mansion. Do me a favor and get sergeant Webster to come in here and sit with Webb. Tell him he's to stay with her until we get back."

"You got it."

Morrow headed back into his office to phone the tactical team, while Price searched the squad room for sergeant Webster.

Morrow made a call to lieutenant Tom Decker, leader of one of the best units of the L.A. Tactical Assault Teams. A call in which Decker promised to have his team ready to take the target down just as soon as all of his men made it in from their homes, and they could reach the suspect's home.

Price re-entered Morrow's office with the very bulky sergeant Webster, right behind him.

"Are we ready?"

"Yeah. Why don't you go get the car, I'll be right there." Morrow waved for Webster to come further inside.

"Look. All that I want you to do is sit at my desk and answer the phone if it rings. But your main objective is to watch over Doctor Webb. Make sure that she's comfortable."

Morrow went and helped Webb to her feet and guided her to the sofa, where he sit her down.

"You lay down for a while and get some rest. I've already got eight black and whites, thirty-two officers, headed to Hamlin's place, right now. I'm about to join Price and head out there myself. We even have a tactical team that will be joining us as well. He won't get away, Nancy."

She couldn't find solace in the sincerity of his voice. Because she knew better. It was not going to be that easy to capture the Stalker.

"You're going to have to kill him, you know. There's no way he'll be taken alive. He thinks that he's so close to being a god that he is impervious to any physical attack on his being. I can promise you that he will never see the inside of a courtroom."

She paused, appearing a bit dazed. "You're going to have to put him down. He will see to that. Be very careful, Josh. Because he's got nothing to lose." She was drowsy.

Morrow laid her on the sofa, giving her a throw pillow for under her head. Then covered her with the blanket she had been wrapped in.

"Josh," she grabbed his arm. "I was suppose to meet him at Venice Beach, at 5:30 a.m. He's just disturbed enough to think that I might still show up. What time is it?"

Morrow looked at his watch. "It's 5:12 a.m. I don't think he'll be there."

"It doesn't matter. I won't be there. So if you guys miss him. I'm as good as dead." She was scared and disoriented.

"Don't worry." He stroked her hair. "You've got nothing to worry about. There's almost a full squad room out there, and sergeant Webster is in here with you. You're going to be fine," he promised. "I have to go now. When I get back, Hamlin will either be behind bars or dead. Either way, you've got nothing to worry about."

He smiled at her as she closed her eyes. She was exhausted and couldn't help but to fade off to sleep. He was about to close the biggest case of his career and put the Stalker out of their misery once and for all. In one way or another.

Morrow left the station house and joined Price outside, where he was waiting in the car.

"Is Webb all right?"

"She'll be fine, once we get this bastard. Let's go."

Price drove out of the parking lot and heading toward Beverly Hills. "I take it that we have the national guard, coming with us."

"Damn near."

5:37 a.m. Jonathan Price guided the unmarked sedan through the deserted streets of Beverly Hills. In the darkness just before the dawn. They were about to take down the most elusive killer he and Morrow had ever sought.

Doctor Webb had been right on about the Stalker's fetish for wearing the blood of his victims, so Morrow had told him. The psycho fuck actually thought that he could become immortal by doing so.

But for reasons still a bit cloudy to Morrow, the psycho revealed his identity to Webb, in hopes that she would understand him. What the fuck was that all about?

Turning himself in to Webb, Morrow thought, made the Stalker, Hamlin, a lot bolder than he had first anticipated. The ballsy bastard actually took up sessions with the very same psychologist that was profiling him for the police. Which either made him very fucking stupid, or even more psychotic than even he could control. Or just arrogant enough to believe himself incapable of capture. It was a slap in the face, really.

But none of that mattered now. Their forces were gathering, and were nearly ready to take the psycho down. They were just waiting for the tactical team and the feebs, with the warrants. The arrest of the Stalker was going to be a feather in the caps of one and all. Even though no one really figured him out. Instead, he had confessed himself to Nancy Webb.

Webb did nearly have him profiled, dead to rights. But it still took Hamlin's confession to end the manhunt. The front page of the afternoon newspaper, and the top story of both the radio and television news were going to shake the social world to its very foundation. Once they found out that their king was a psychopathic, serial killer.

Four black and whites set to the side of the road. Dark, and waiting. Price pulled to the side of the road in front of them, just a few yards away from the opening of Hamlin's gated driveway. Now they just had to wait for the feebs to bring the warrants. And the tactical assault team to show. Then, they could roll.

Shortly after their arrival, a dark gray sedan parked behind the four marked units across the driveway from Morrow and Price's position. It was the Feds with the warrants.

Special agent Scott Ross left the sedan and jogged past the driveway to Morrow's car and Climbed into the back seat. "We've got the warrants for Hamlin's arrest, To search the grounds around the house, and to search the house. Are you ready to go?"

Morrow shook his head. "We're still waiting for the tactical team."

"Why? We've already got eight black and whites. Four men to a car. Then there's us. I think that we have enough fire power to collect one man. Who's likely sleeping in the first place," Ross objected to Morrow's precautions.

"Look. I've got twelve black and whites cruising around the neighborhood. On both sides, and behind the house. But we're still going to wait, for the tactical team. I don't want to rush in there, without the proper back up." Morrow shifted himself in his seat.

"Webb told me that she was suppose to meet him at the beach, at 5:30. Well, she didn't show up. So he knows that something is up. So he's either not here, or he's set up some traps and is waiting for us. So we're sitting tight, until the tactical team shows up."

"Fine. But they had better get here, soon. I'm not waiting the rest of the night. Jesus, it's almost daylight, now." The Fed was displeased.

The feeb left Morrow's car and returned to his own, rejoining his partner.

"Are we going in?" Bicket wondered.

Ross shook his head. "Not yet. Morrow want's to wait."

"Wait for what?"

"The tactical team. They should be here, real soon. At least, they'd better be."

CHAPTER NINETEEN

5:52 a.m.

With the reddish orange crescent of the sun peeking out over the horizon, the tactical team's van showed up and parked beside Morrow's car. Morrow leaned over Price, and spoke through the driver's window to lieutenant Tom Decker, who had emerged from the vehicles cab.

Decker was the leader of Able Team, one of the finest tactical teams, Los Angeles had to offer. He and Morrow spoke for less than a minute, then Decker climbed back into the van's front cabin.

The van then sped off, executing half of a U-turn, ramming the front gate and sped up the driveway toward Hamlin's mansion. Price turned on his headlights and followed the van up the driveway. Ross and Bicket followed the four black and whites that were behind Morrow and Price, with four more marked units, behind them.

As they drew closer, the majesty of Hamlin's three story mansion came into full view. There were lights on in the first and second floors. The first floor was the one that was the most lit. The second, had only two rooms with lights on. Maybe he was there, after all. But it didn't seem that he was asleep.

"All uniforms surround the house, and keep your eyes open. We don't want him sliding out a window," Morrow ordered over a hand-held radio.

He drew his gun, as they came closer to the mansion. "And remember, this guy thinks he's immortal or damn close to it. So be ready for anything. He's nuttier than a fruit cake." He lowered the radio, only to raise it quickly back up to his mouth. "One other thing. He's probably expecting us, so watch out for booby-traps."

The tactical squad used a battering ram to blast open the front doors, then entered Hamlin's estate one by one. Flanking one another with automatic rifles at the ready, they discovered immediately that the huge, open foyer was clear. The squad began breaking off and searching by twos, filtering throughout the mansion. Some moving up to the second floor, with Price and Bicket joining the crew. While Morrow and Ross concentrated their efforts on the ground floor.

The mansion was so immense that even with their night vision goggles on, any number of the tactical squad could have gotten lost in the maze of adjoining rooms, had the lights not been left on.

Backing up a member of the tactical squad during the search of what might have been an entertainment/living room. Where in the far right hand corner set a poker table and a pool table set off to the left. Both far away from the living room type setting. Morrow got the all clear sign, and led the way back out into the foyer where they met a second member of the tactical squad.

"Why don't the two of you go find the basement, and when you do, get a couple of others to help you check it out," Morrow told them.

Hidden beneath a black cloth face mask and a black helmet, the squad member he had just backed up in the room across the foyer, gave him a thumbs up then took off to look for the basement. The other, a clone of the first, followed him without a sound.

Morrow didn't like what was transpiring. His hand radio was on, but the only air traffic was that of the task force members, telling him that each room was clear. A hollowed feeling in his chest was telling him that they had missed Hamlin. Not that he had gotten away, but that after leaving Webb's home he had never come back to his own. He likely had other homes throughout the city and state. And as Webb had suggested he might, he was probably going to go into hiding in one of them. To disappear from their radar, at least long enough until he was ready to come for her.

Detective Price returned from the second floor and joined Morrow in the foyer, confirming his dreaded thoughts. "We can't find him, anywhere. I don't think he's here. We've hit every room on the second floor, but there's no sign of him. They're starting to search the third floor now, but I've got to tell you, it doesn't look good."

FBI special agent Scott Ross, appeared out of the room to the right of the foyer and joined Morrow and Price.

"This is bullshit, he's not here. God damn it, if Webb had only come to us sooner... ."

"Doctor Webb," Morrow cut him off. "Was in fear for the life of her secretary, as well as a damn good friend of her's. She was trying to think of another way for us to get to Hamlin, without tipping him off that she had already done so."

"A friend. She was worried about the life of one friend, when there are entire families at stake. Yeah, that's a fair trade." Ross was more than just a little pissed off.

"Hey, hold on." Price stepped in. "We're all here for the same reason, and it's not to judge whether Doctor Webb came to us too late, or that she put the life of a friend ahead of what could become dozens of families, but to find Hamlin and either put him away or in the ground. So why don't we do that and stop fighting among ourselves."

Morrow rubbed the back of his neck. "Yeah, okay. Let's not get excited. This is a very big place, with a lot of room to cover. So let's just take it easy. Just because we haven't found him yet, doesn't mean that we're not going to. He owns this place. He knows it like the back of his hand and I'm sure that we're just not looking where he is. But we will." He looked at Price. "Call in a few K-9 units and get about half of the men from outside, to come in here and help the search."

Price made the calls Morrow had ordered and within a minute, sixteen uniformed officers stormed inside the mansion. Price ordered many of them to join the upstairs search. Then the rest were to join the rank and file of the downstairs crew. Then, after the call came back from the dispatcher that the K-9 units were on the way, he rejoined Morrow and agent Ross at the center of the foyer.

"You've found absolutely nothing, upstairs?" Morrow asked his partner.

"No, nothing. But the uniforms have already joined the search, and the K-9's are on the way."

"How many?" Ross asked.

"Three."

"Look," Morrow began, talking to Price. "I want you to start the upstairs search, again. Don't just check the rooms, but look for any hidden doors or passageways. He could have installed them himself. He's a very intelligent man. He could be anywhere."

"Got it." Price started to walk away, but turned and came back. "Oh, one other thing. The upstairs is very dirty."

"Dirty as in, someone hasn't dusted today, or what?" Ross asked.

"No, dirty like the top two floors haven't had anybody living up there for years. Thick dust, dirt crusted. Some of the rooms are completely empty, and some are just full of junk. Box's, old furniture. Shit like that."

Price ran a hand back through his hair. "The only two clean rooms on the second floor, are the ones that had lights on when we got here. One is the master bedroom and the other a bathroom. I guess he's not one for having a clean house."

"Well it's as clean as a whistle, down here," Ross jumped in.

"So he only keeps the rooms that people might see cleaned up." Morrow stated out the obvious.

"Yeah, sounds like a lonely man," Ross observed.

Morrow looked at him, somewhat surprised. "Sounds like a secluded psycho, to me. What, do you feel sorry for this guy?"

"Hell no. I'm just saying that he might actually have a lonely life. I could give a rats ass, but that's all I was saying," Ross clarified.

"The fucker's a billionaire. He has everything a man could want, probably more. But instead of getting a real life, he slips away off into his own little world and starts killing families because he likes marinating his balls in other peoples' blood. All the while, believing that he's becoming a god. This fucker is gone. He needs to be put in the ground. Not understood or felt sorry for." Morrow burned.

"Those are my exact sentiments," Ross agreed. "So why don't we stop talking about putting him in the ground. Find the fucker, and put him in the ground."

Morrow agreed, with a bit of a nod. "Price, get back upstairs and tell everyone to do it all over again. Check every nook and cranny. If he's here, I want him found."

Price bolted off, without word, taking the stairs quickly to the second floor.

"And no one stops until I tell them to! Make sure you get the attic, too." Morrow continued to bark out orders, even after Price had disappeared up the stairs.

The lieutenant holstered his gun, yawning, his hands on his waist. "Sorry about that, I haven't had much sleep lately. This bastard has been tormenting me for two months."

"No problem, I've lost a bit of sleep myself. Although, you do have the hours on me."

They were quiet just long enough to hear the voices of three of the many officers in the house, checking in with the disappointing news that the rooms that they had searched were all clear. They both lowered their heads a bit out of frustration. Then, the call came.

"Morrow, this is Decker. Where are you?"

"In the foyer. Hey, I sent a few of your men to find the basement. Do you know where they are?"

"They're with me, in the basement. I think you'd better come down here. I've got something you won't want to see, but you really need to take a look at it," Decker told him.

"Okay, we're on our way. Where exactly is the basement?"

"You see the staircase, right in front of you?"

"Yes, and?"

"Take a walk down the hallway right beside it, to its left. Then take another left. Then half way down that hall, take a right. Then halfway down that hall, there will be one of my men standing next to a doorway. That's the basement. Hurry."

"We're on our way."

Agent Bicket came down the stairs, fresh from helping to search the second floor. He had heard the call from Decker and joined Morrow and Ross in their hustle down to the basement. Passing Decker's officer at the doorway they took a steep set of stairs down, until they came out of a doorway that was flush the wall. Leaving the basement as one clear, gigantic room.

"This is bigger than my fucking house!" Ross exclaimed.

A huge space in one of the corners was being used as a weight room. So coroner Harold Minor had been correct in his assumption that the Stalker was a weight lifter.

"He has a nicer gym than our station house does," Morrow mumbled.

In the corner opposite the weight room, set a martial arts dojo. Swords, sai, kendo sticks and shurikens, just to name a few, covered the two walls that bordered it.

A heavy weight punching bag hung a few feet away from this area. It was in seriously bad condition. They could see where Hamlin had punched and kicked holes in it, but had repaired them instead of getting a new bag. He wasn't just being cheap. He was more than likely keeping the bag to remind himself of his ever growing power, or so Morrow guessed.

Either way, it was a familiar sight to Morrow. Causing a recall of memories, best left in the past.

Over on the far side of the basement, is where they saw lieutenant Decker. They went to join him, but he met them halfway. A morbid look about him.

"What's up?" Morrow asked.

"You're not going to believe this. It looks like our boy was very active long before becoming the Stalker. Check this out."

Decker led them to another corner area where the floor was covered with gymnastics mats. As they got closer they could see that these mats were covered with darkened, encrusted blood stains. But there was only the slightest bit of odor of decay to be sensed. There was a small shelf on the far wall that held cans of air freshener Hamlin must have been using to keep the smell to a minimum. So it appeared that not even the Stalker liked the smell of long time decaying blood.

"Right here." Decker pointed to one of the walls that bordered the mats.

Taped to that wall were driver's licenses. Licenses, with bloodied fingerprints all over them.

"He must have brought them here one by one, over the years and fought them to the death. God only knows, where their bodies are," Decker wondered, aloud.

Morrow stared at the wall. Entranced by the evil that had taken place there. There must have been two or three hundred licenses on that wall, he figured. He had always known that the Stalker was the biggest psycho he had ever known of. But this took the cake.

Breaking away from his concentrated stare at the wall. Ross looked to Bicket. "Get a methane probe out here, and when it gets here start with the backyard. If there are any bodies buried out there, we'll find them."

"That's probably the best place to start," Morrow agreed, still staring blankly at the wall of licenses.

Decker agreed, "Yeah, it's worth a shot. I personally don't think that he would be that stupid. He own's a metal refinery somewhere in Los Angeles. He could have just taken them out there at night, and dumped them into a melting pot. There wouldn't even be a cell particle left."

"But either way, I'll bet we solve a lot of missing persons cases once we start getting these names into the computer." Morrow's eyes were still glued to the wall, at this alter of death. Where it appeared that the Stalker had been hard at work over the years, honing his skills before making his public debut.

"Let's get a photographer down here and get some pictures of this place, so we can start taking these licenses down," Morrow ordered. "And let's get an A.P.B. out on Bray Hamlin."

***

Bray Hamlin slowly drove by the entrance of the driveway that led up to his home. There were red and blue lights, flashing everywhere. He could see from the road that up near the mansion there were uniformed police, everywhere. Just as he had thought she might. Webb was weak and could not accept the power of the essence, and had involved the police. She could not accept his need for her. His willingness to share his immortal rule over the world, unopposed by man or God. Now, for her inability to understand, her time as his doctor was over. And her time on this Earth was short.

Luckily he had been cruising the area around the beach waiting for her to show, but did not want to sit still while doing so. Then 5:30 a.m. came and went, and she did not show. So he cruised a little longer, before coming home. And rightfully so, he knew that the authorities would be there.

If he had been at home when the police came for him, he may have been caught unprepared. Normally he wouldn't worry, but he knew that there was still some mortality left within him. His ascension was not yet complete. He was mightier than any man, but God was still one up on him and he knew that the old fellow would be on their side.

He drove on past the driveway along the neighborhood street. He counted several police units in his neighborhood. But none of them gave him more than a passing glance. It didn't really matter that the police had taken his home, and were now traipsing around throughout the place. It didn't matter that in a few of hours his bank accounts would be frozen. Because he had a Swiss bank account with a little more than ten billion dollars in it. Another beautiful home in Bel Aire. And a new Corvette. All under an assumed name. If he had not been prepared for this scenario, he would not have visited Webb in the first place. They should have figured on that, dumb asses. They just couldn't keep up with him. His intelligence was far greater and nearer to perfection, than any man could ever hope to be. And once his ascension was complete, his foresight would be unequaled. Even by God.

Once his ascension was complete, he would no longer be hindered by his physical self, but instead would be unleashed by his heightened spiritual stamina. But for now, he had been up all night and was tired. It was time to go home, to Bel Aire. And get some much needed rest.

He would wait until the death of Nancy Webb, before beginning his new life as Mark Logan. He knew an excellent plastic surgeon that could help him in that respect, if he had not yet reached his godly plateau. The surgeon was a dear old family friend with very tight lips, for the right amount of money. Actually, he wouldn't have to pay him a cent. Why waste the money when he could just give this family friend a little surgery of his own. Cutting his face off and putting it back on inside out, before cutting his throat would do. True, he was an old family friend. But one that he could barely tolerate.

But as he had previously thought, before making any whole sale changes, he was going to give Webb at least a few weeks to get used to her round-the-clock guard. Then, whether he was still mortal or not, once she felt safe, her worst nightmare would come from out of the darkness, and wear her blood. It was not going to be a quick death, no. He would bleed her slowly, so that she might watch him steal her essence, her life force a little at a time. All the while making her wear the organs of those who thought that they could protect her from his wrath.

He would possibly finish his ascension before he would strike, or maybe his final rising would wait until Webb's blood soaked his skin. And no matter who was on duty, be it the police or the FBI, when he came for her, a literal blood bath was going to ensue.

***

7:33 a.m.

Josh Morrow walked through the crowded squad room toward his office. He had bad news for Nancy Webb. The task force had not found Bray Hamlin. He was not where they had hoped he would be, and had slipped through their fingers and vanished. Though they had an A.P.B. out on him, it was not likely that they would find him any time soon. Like she had pointed out earlier, he was very wealthy and would more than likely hide out in a new home, either somewhere else or in town. Or he may even hide out in another state all together, until the coast was clearer and then come for her.

How could he tell her, a woman he had come to know and respect, and even have a secret yearning for, that her life as it were, was over? No longer would she be able to go to her office and treat her many patients, her life's work. Or even go for a simple walk around the block of her highly secured neighborhood in Beverly Hills, where she had lived only a mere eight blocks from Hamlin, the Stalker himself. But she was going to become a prisoner in a preselected safe house until either Hamlin was found, or had disappeared for good.

He entered his office and motioned for the bulky sergeant Webster to leave. Webster removed himself from Morrow's office, and the lieutenant closed the door behind him. Webb immediately sat up from her prone position on the sofa. She was still a bit groggy, but was anxious to here the news of Hamlin's downfall. He smiled at her. Not a meaningful smile, but more of an attempt to prepare her for the bad news she was about to receive. And she knew the difference.

Her face grew painful and scared. She began shaking her head trying to convince Morrow that what he was about to tell her, was not the truth. Tears began to run down her face as Morrow sat down beside her and took her in his arms, holding her in an attempt to take away her pain. She cried almost hysterically and he didn't want to say the words, but he had to tell her, even though she already knew the truth.

"I'm sorry, Nancy, but he wasn't there. We searched his mansion four times, he just wasn't there. There is an A.P.B. out for him, and every cop in the state is looking for him, not to mention the FBI. Hopefully he's left the state and is someone else's problem now. But until we know that he's either gone for good, or he comes for you, we're going to put you in a safe house, until whatever happens, happens. You'll be under twenty-four hour guard. We're going to work something out with the FBI, where we will split time in watching over you." He raised her head to look into her eyes, gently wiping her tears away while stroking her hair and beaming a comforting, warm smile.

She felt warm and safe in his grasp. For a few fleeting seconds all of her fears had left her. Hamlin did not exist. Her life was not in danger of being extinguished, and all was well. She had totally forgotten about her life threatening situation, so warm in his arms. Until Morrow spoke of it again.

He stared deep into her eyes. "I promise you that as long as I'm breathing, Hamlin won't get anywhere near you. I'll put him down, by any means necessary." He smiled to comfort her. "I can't lose you now, that is, if you don't want to be lost."

Apparently her earlier flirtations hadn't gone completely unnoticed. She smiled back at him, terribly uncomfortable. Both terror and admiration in her eyes.

"Don't let him get me, Josh." Her voice was shaking. "No matter how long he stays out of sight. No matter how long he refrains from coming for me. I betrayed him, and he will not be satisfied until he's wearing my blood. He will come. Don't let anyone convince you otherwise. And when he does, he will kill anyone who stands in his way." There was terror in her voice.

Morrow caressed her face. "I won't let anything happen to you, Nancy. I promise you that. If and when he comes for you, I'll be there. And I will stop him. I vow that to you, right now. He will get to you over my dead body."

She leaned in and kissed him lightly and he obliged, kissing her back. Then they slowly pulled away from one another.

"I don't want to be lost," she answered his earlier calling. "And I don't want to leave my home. I don't want him to take that from me. I don't want to be holed up in some safe house that he can just follow us to. He is watching, I know he is. Please Josh, don't let him drive me from my home," she implored.

He stroked her hair. "Okay. It's not a spectacular idea. But it shouldn't be that big of a deal. You'll still have your twenty-four hour guard and an alarm system."

She nodded. "I'm going to have a new one installed immediately."

"Then I see no problem with letting you stay in your own home. It won't make it anymore difficult to protect you. I'll tell the brass the same thing. I don't think that they'll mind. Hamlin more than likely wouldn't expect you to be there, anyways. That is, if he's still in town."

"Thank you, Josh." She appeared to be a bit more relaxed. As relaxed as she could be, with the Stalker out for her blood.

"Don't thank me, now. Save that for once we've got him. Dead, or alive."

***

With three weeks time having now past since Nancy Webb had handed Bray Hamlin over to the authorities, she remained in hiding. They had told her that they had an army that was going to take Hamlin down. They told her that she had absolutely nothing to fear. But they were wrong. Their army did not catch Hamlin. Instead, he had slipped away into the night, leaving her life in peril. She had been placed under the 24 hour guard of four-man teams. Two of the team members would remain inside the house with her, and the other two would park outside in front of the house in an unmarked car. The FBI and L.A.P.D. were splitting time in protecting their only witness that could link Hamlin to the murders. But ever since the night that the Stalker had disappeared, the police and the FBI began wondering if Hamlin might have fled the country, or at least the state. Was he actually insane enough to come for her? Or were his threats no more than empty words? Just a failed attempt to keep her from going to the authorities. Maybe he was just going to pick things up where he left off, in another place, at another time. But the big question on Webb's mind was: Was Brooke May actually alive when she turned on Hamlin? Or was his promise of her being alive just as shallow as his promise not to kill the tenth family on the night in question?

Those questions remained unanswered to the authorities. But as for Hamlin coming for her, Webb knew that he would indeed come sooner or later. He was coming. She knew that his disappearance was but a trick to lower her protector's defenses. He was out there all right. Watching, waiting and when he felt that the time was right, he would come for her. And she believed that there wasn't anything or anyone that could stop him. With the exception, possibly, of Josh Morrow. But if by some chance Morrow could not put an end to Hamlin, as he had promised he would, all that she could do was wait for that night to come. Yes, night. He would come at night. Cloaked under the cover of darkness, just as he had always done before. She could only hope that when it came time for her to feel the steel of the Stalker's blade, he would make it a quick death. Just as she hoped it had been for Brooke May. Though he had promised her otherwise.

No one understood him like her. Even then, she understood very little. He was a tough read for her to make. All that she knew for sure was that he was deluded enough to attack an army, just for the chance to boast about the kills he had made afterward. So it didn't really matter how many guards she may have at any one time. Which was the four that she had now. They would not stop him of course. She knew that to him, no matter how spread out they might be. Including her, all that Bray Hamlin was going to see would be five fresh worshipers for the Stalker to add to his total.

CHAPTER TWENTY

Josh Morrow showed a great personal interest in her case. There was something between them. Nothing they had talked about, but it was there. An unspoken bond between protector and protected. Unfelt by her toward any of her other bodyguards. There was a definite connection between them. She could tell by the kiss they had shared weeks ago, and by look in his eyes. The eyes were the windows to the soul, and she was a good judge of souls. She had been right about Bray Hamlin. She hadn't figured him exactly as the Stalker, but she knew that there was danger there.

Morrow's true feelings for her shone through his eyes bright and clear. He had definitely caught on to her flirtation after all, the last time she had visited his office, before she came in with the news about Hamlin. She was by far not the only thing on his mind and most definitely, not the first thing. That honor went to the Stalker.

He was not allowing his feelings for her, however deep they might be, to take away from his better instincts to protect her. But every now and then he would drop his guard and she could see his true, softer self, beneath his tough exterior. Many times he had sit up with her in the night, talking. Sometimes, from dusk until dawn. Especially on those nights when her anxieties grew too strong for her to sleep. Most nights though, they would stay up for several hours past midnight, just for one another's company.

She knew that his many self-appointed shifts inside her home were because of his feelings for her, and her safety. And that he was not just using her as bait. He just figured that in the house would be the best place to be, in the event of an attack. That way he could take Hamlin down, and make sure that it was done right. Then she wouldn't have to disappear, and they could share a life together. He truly cared. He was there for Hamlin, had the Stalker enough luck to get inside. He did want first crack at him, but as of her foresight for being the affection of the lieutenant's desires. She wasn't just being full of herself. When someone reveals to you their most embarrassing moment in all of it's unpleasantness, voluntarily. Such as, while at eighteen years old in the early part of 1972, Vietnam, he had soiled himself during his very first fire fight. And also took the blame, with no reason given, for his not-so-recent divorce. While at the same time, wanting to know all about her. He cared.

So did she. Actually, she couldn't wait for the night to come. Sleeping in during the day so that she could stay awake for most of, or all of the night. Just so that she could sit up with him. But on just a few occasions he did not show, but apologized for his absence on the next go round. And even though the ever present danger of the Stalker loomed above them, when together, it was like they were teenagers again. The accidental touching, and the laughing harder at one another's jokes than necessary. It was high school, all over again.

They were free spirits around one another, with not much held back. She felt more comfortable with Morrow than she ever had during her entire five year, failed marriage. She let go of all her inhibitions. From embarrassing childhood moments, to losing her virginity on prom night. To her own divorce, which was messy and definitely not her fault. She liked that he knew these things, she was comfortable with it. Just as she was with him. Morrow was there for her in a big way, as she tried to be there for him in the late night hours. Trying to ease his restless mind that took him away from her, at times. Thoughts of his past, perhaps. But he was not as outgoing with his darker times, as she was. Albeit those times for her were not very dark.

Usually she could relax peacefully, knowing that Morrow and his crew were around in the night. Making sure that the shadows didn't jump out at her. Which most of the time, allowed her serenity in the darkness.

***

Now twenty-nine days into the manhunt for Bray Hamlin. A hunt that continually turned up goose eggs. The FBI and the L.A.P.D. upper brass had decided to continue the manhunt, but were calling off Webb's twenty-four hour guard and handing her over to the U.S. Marshal service, for entrance into the witness protection program, until Hamlin was found and she could testify at his criminal proceedings.

***

Morrow parked his unmarked cruiser in the driveway of Nancy Webb's home. As he walked up to the front door he looked over the darkened streets of the Beverly Hills neighborhood. He knocked, as Jonathan Price left the car, replacing his cell phone into his jacket pocket.

"So what does the wife think about this being our last night on guard duty?" Morrow asked.

"She's elated. She want's Mr. Johnson home at night," he cracked a lusty grin.

"We're still going to be spear heading the manhunt, but I know what you mean. I'll be able to go home and hopefully get some sleep at night. Look, why don't you and Mr. Johnson go tell the feebs across the street that play time is over. We've got her until the Marshals come and get her in the morning. Take the car," he tossed Price the keys, "take their place and give your wife an obscene phone call. Then every now and then, make a perimeter sweep. No less than four or five times."

"You got it, boss. I'm on the phone, now." Price took the unmarked unit and parked it behind the Feds unmarked car, across the street.

As the front door to Webb's house was being unlocked, Morrow took a good lookout over the street, as far as he could see, but saw nothing suspicious. None of the vehicles parked along side the road seemed out of place. Except for the fact that they were parked in the road. Most of the vehicles in the wealthy neighborhoods were parked in the home's driveway or garage. But there were only a few. Visitors, most likely. Nothing out of the ordinary. But as far as he knew, Hamlin was still out there and he was on a death watch. Just waiting for the right moment to strike. But he was optimistic. Maybe they would get lucky and Hamlin would stalk for blood, in another country all together. Or at least, another state. Preferably, as far away as possible. Maybe the East Coast. He just didn't want anymore of the fucking psycho's dirty work on his hands.

The front door opened behind him. He turned to face the feeb, one of two inside the house. "Shit, it's about time. I knocked five minutes ago. What in the hell took you so long?"

"Just being cautious, I couldn't see your face. Then I saw Price and I figured it was you. And it wasn't five minutes. It was more like two."

"Whatever." Morrow followed him inside and closed the door behind them. He followed him all the way into the living room, where the other Fed was pulling on his jacket.

"Where's Webb?" Morrow spoke up directly.

"Take it easy, man. She's in the kitchen, making dinner," the second agent told him. "Man it's gonna be great getting off of this gig. Let the Marshals worry about it now."

"You got that right," his partner agreed.

"Well, nice knowin' ya,." the second feeb told Morrow, insincerely, as he and his partner left.

Morrow let them out, then locked the door up tight behind them. Then quickly joined Webb in the kitchen. He knew that after tonight she was going to disappear into the federal witness protection program, at least until Bray Hamlin was caught. But if Hamlin was never caught, she would be out of his life for good. She would exist only in another place, under another identity. Hopefully, never to be found by the Stalker. That being the only solace that he could gather from their situation.

Morrow looked her over, he could see the side of her face. She didn't really appear to be too upset about the whole mess. Hell, she probably felt safer already, knowing that she was now going to be protected by the Marshals. They were better suited for the task. It was one of the things that they did, and they did it well. Yeah, she had to feel safer knowing that she was going to have the Marshals watching her back. Not that he and his crew, nor the FBI, were inept. It was just that the Marshals could do it better. He really didn't want her to go. She was the best thing that had ever happened to him since before his wife left him, so long ago. And he knew that the feeling was mutual, not just because of the kiss they had shared a month ago. But their time that they had spent together felt like a series of dates. A series of dates that had gone very well. Yeah, she was interested all right. She was as interested in him, as he was in her. They had become too close to one another, for there not to be something there.

"Hello." He let her know that he was there, so not to scare the life out of her.

She turned around to find him tearing a piece off of a loaf of French bread. "Hey, Mister. That's for dinner. You and Price are going to have dinner with me, right?"

"Well, I am. I'm making him sit out in the car, and make dirty phone calls to his wife."

She smiled, warm. "We'll have to take something out to him."

"Don't bother. His wife made him a meatloaf sandwich, it's his favorite. You couldn't drag him away from it."

"Okay, then. I guess it's just you and me." She smiled warmly.

"What are we having?"

"Spaghetti. If you'll help me set the table, we can eat."

"Okay."

She wasn't showing it, but he knew that the move from the protection of the police and the FBI made the whole situation even more frightening. She was going to be taken to a safe house in another state, and even though she would be under their expert guard. She would still have to look over her shoulder until Hamlin was found. Whenever, if ever, he was found. It had to be tough. She would have no contact with either her family or friends. That was the rule. Although she would from time to time, be able to slip a letter to her loved ones through the Marshals themselves. It wouldn't of course, have any post markings on it. And she would be warned heavily not to mention anything about her where-a-bouts. She would, more or less, be cut off from the rest of the world as she now knew it.

"So did the Marshal's representative tell you where they are going to take you? And if they did, don't tell me," he said.

She shook her head, as she swallowed the wine that accompanied their meal. "They didn't say. All that I was told me was to pack for cooler weather."

They sit down to dinner together, but neither spoke a word during that time. There were moments of brief eye contact but again, not a word was said. Their mutual attraction was clearly known. But known as well was that this would be their last dinner together, maybe forever if Hamlin wasn't found. Then Webb truly would never be safe. And in that scenario, they would never be together. They knew this, and accepted it at face value. So their future together all hinged on a mad man's dedication, to either continuing to fuel his ascension, possibly else where, or backing up his threat to come for her blood.

After dinner they each took a glass of wine into the living room. Sitting together on the sofa, Webb relaxing and Morrow letting down his guard.

"So, why are there only two of you tonight?"

He tried to come off as innocent. "Well, brass has been bitching about all of the overtime that they've been paying out this month. So I thought I'd give them a break. Only Price is getting paid, for tonight. I'm here, voluntarily… it's just that this is our last night together. I mean, I thought that we could do this, just the two of us." He grit his teeth. "I mean, Price and I could handle this one last night together, just the two of us. Since Hamlin hasn't shown himself for a month. I thought we… ."

"Did you want to be alone with me? Because I would like that, very much. I mean, we can really get to know one another. Then when Hamlin is caught, and I can resume my life again… ." She shied away for a moment, but figured what the hell was she being so timid for? She liked him, and she was positive that he liked her too. So to hell with it. She was just going to say it. "And I would really like it if you were a part of it."

He smiled. "All right, you got me. There are only two of us tonight, because I do want to be alone with you before you go. But in a getting to know, sort of way. I wasn't thinking that I'd get lucky."

"Sure," she teased.

They laughed. Not a hearty laugh. More of a whispery, under their breath laugh. It was all finally said and done.

Webb looked into his eyes and spoke in a more sultry voice. "Maybe if you play your cards right." She smiled, seductively.

She caught Morrow off guard. But once he realized that she wasn't kidding, he put his wine glass on the coffee table and sat back on the comfortable sofa. They looked at each other for a moment, then leaned in toward one another and lightly kissed. Then the kiss became deeper and more heated. But in a last second move, before possibly heading to the bedroom, Morrow slowly pulled away and sit back. He may have been letting his guard down, but it could not be totally lowered.

He smiled, a bit nervous. "Sorry."

She smiled back. "That's okay. Would you like another glass of wine?"

"No. No, thank you. I still have half a glass." He looked around the room for a minute. He was a bit rusty with his civilian articulation skills. Then, from out of nowhere: "Tell me something about yourself. I know that we've talked a lot over this past month. But I mean, something that no one else knows."

CHAPTER TWENTY-ONE

"Something no one else knows." She crossed her legs, stretching an arm across the back of the sofa.

"Truthfully, there is nothing about me that at least one person doesn't already know. I guess the one thing that I would like to keep as quiet as possible would be something that only my old study buddy in college, Nathan, knows.

"We were cramming for finals, and neither one of us had really studied, for anything. Any class. We were a little bit too busy going to parties and getting drunk. You know, being stupid. Then we finally realized that it was nearly time for finals. We only had like four days to prepare for everything, so we went on a four day cram session. The only way we could pull it off was by taking speed.

"Well," she looked shameful but continued, "when the tests were all over, Nathan stopped cold turkey. But for the better part of the next three months, I was hooked. It was like I couldn't get through the day without it. But when Nathan found out he immediately put me through a one man intervention, and got me clean. Now I just drink a cup of coffee or two, to give me that little boost. To help me through the day. But I don't drink on weekends."

She leaned forward and picked up her wine glass off of the coffee table. "What about you? Anything I should know?"

Morrow downed the rest of his wine, then stood up and paced a little. "Do you remember when I told you about my last title fight?"

She nodded. "Yes, of course."

"Well, after that fight I started having these nightmares. Nightly. I just couldn't sleep. Here's something that we have in common, sort of. My doctor gave me sedatives to help me sleep, and I was drinking a lot at the time. I just started mixing the two. My doctor, who is a friend from Vietnam, he was a medic, then." He sat down, again.

"Well, he got into a pretty hairy situation. His platoon was under heavy fire, and he was hit. While retreating, the remainder of his platoon left him for dead. Well, my platoon came in from a flanking position to cover their retreat. We were under heavy fire. Machine gun, mortar, grenades." He leaned back into the soft sofa cushions, appearing somewhat uncomfortable.

"We started retreating ourselves. Most of the platoon was already gone. The Cong were coming through the trees, just up ahead. And that's when I heard him. Just barely, over all the noise. Then I saw him, so I grabbed him and flung him over my shoulder and got the hell out of there."

His head now hung down a bit. "He knew that I was having a problem with the sedatives. So whenever I came back for a refill he tried to talk some sense into me. But then I'd just remind him of Nam." He paused, staring at the glass top coffee table.

"It killed him to have to owe his life to someone, and have the power to let that person destroy himself. I was really bad off. I was slowly killing myself. It wasn't the booze, I could handle that. But my wife couldn't take it anymore so she divorced me, a year or so later. A short while after that, Kevin, my doctor friend, finally got it through my thick skull that he was not going to allow me to keep using Nam as an excuse. He finally got me cleaned up, but my wife wouldn't come back to me, though. Then about four months later I realized that not working was just aggravating my recovery. I had a law degree from Berkeley that I got after coming home from the war. I joined the L.A.P.D."

She moved down the length of the sofa and sat next to him. She laid a hand on his shoulder, massaging it softly.

"I guess we do have something in common. Does it feel better now, knowing that someone else knows about that turbulent time in your life."

He raised his shoulders. "Yeah, I guess so."

"You guess so. Come on, doesn't it feel good to get that off your chest? I know I feel better."

He released a cleansing breath. "Yeah, it does feel better. Like a giant weight being lifted off my shoulders." He looked deep into her eyes, while she sat so close.

"Thank you. Until now, only Kevin and my ex-wife knew about that. Now it's like it's just out there, no more secrets, take it or leave it. Thank you for that." He smiled into the face of an angel.

***

A mere block away from Webb's home. There, camouflaged in the darkness, sat a black Corvette, its engine silent and cooled off. It had been there for a while and Bray Hamlin, Los Angeles' most wanted man, sat behind the wheel. He had been scouting out Webb and her bodyguards for two weeks now. He had every movement they made timed to the second. And every night, every move was like a well oiled machine. From the time that the Feds arrived, until the time that the police relieved them at dusk. He could afford to sit out in the open in broad daylight if he liked, because the windows of the Vette were polarized. Unable to be seen through.

Many times he had been sitting down the street and not only watched the shift changes, but watched Webb take little strolls around her yard. He knew that she was teasing him. Tempting him to come and get her, with her four armed guards at the ready. At the time his existing mortality had kept him from doing so, but he had cured himself last night and was nearly at the peak of his ascension. All he would need now to push him over the top would be Webb's and her bodyguards' essences, and he would be a god.

He noticed that Morrow had arrived early tonight, and his partner was the only guard left outside the house. Price was his name, so he believed. The detective had already made one perimeter check tonight, and he knew that there were more to come. In that instance he would be waiting for him, with bated breath. Since Price was the only outside guard, that left the middle aged, former kick-boxing champion Morrow left on guard inside. He scratched his chin, an evil grin crossing his lips. Not only was he going to kill Webb tonight. But he was going to take Price out as well. Then Morrow was going to give him a shot at his undefeated title, he had left behind so long ago.

He didn't know why four federal agents had been replaced by two police detectives, and he didn't really care. Because as soon as detective Price went on his second perimeter sweep, his impromptu plan, would be set in motion. Then the last little bit of mortality left within him would be gone. Then the world would bow down to their new lord and master, and cringe at his feet. Begging for their sweet merciful death.

***

"You know," Webb sat back, relaxing on the sofa next to Morrow. "You never told me much about your last title fight. Does what happened, still torment you? Even now, after you've kicked the sedatives?"

He stared at the coffee table, again. "If by torment you mean sweaty nightmares more nights than not, then yeah, I would say that I'm still tormented."

She lay her hand on his leg. "You know, if you tell someone exactly what happened, those nightmares may let up."

"I don't need to tell anyone what happened, because there were thousands of people there, watching. But that still doesn't make it any easier to sleep." He shook his head a bit.

"I wasn't there. Would you tell me, please?" she massaged his thigh.

"Okay. I don't see what good it'll do, but I'll tell you. But you're going to have to stop that." He looked down at her hand. "Otherwise, I won't be able to think, with all of the blood rushing away from my brain. If you get my meaning." He smiled, big and wide.

She pulled her hand away from his leg and set it on her lap. She too, smiling. Embarrassed. "Sorry."

His smile slowly faded away, until his features were somber. His thoughts racing backward in time. It was so clear to him he could almost hear the crowd cheering.

"Actually, the fight was like any other fight, up until the eighth round. I had knocked him down three times, by then. But the three knock down rule was not in effect for that match, though it was a title fight. But the judges do look at that. I mean it does factor in when it comes down to the judges awarding points and in the final decision. Unless there's a knock out.

"He was bloodied up and looked a bit wobbly." He paused, rubbing his hands together.

"Did you express any concerns to the referee?"

"No. I had no concerns. My fights were always a bit one-sided. It was nothing new," he told her, trying not to sound conceited.

"So how did it happen, if he wasn't that badly injured? How did he die?"

"Well, come the eighth round he knew that he was going to have to knock me out to win the title, because of the three knock downs he had sustained already." He stopped. Appearing disobliged to continue.

"Please, don't stop now. You can rid yourself of this torturous guilt, once and for all. Just finish telling me what happened. Please, Josh. I am trying to help you. But I can't if you won't talk to me," she implored.

CHAPTER TWENTY-TWO

"Well," he broke his silence. "He started attacking me with everything he had. At first, I only defended. Blocking what I could, but he was landing too many blows and he was hurting me. So I mounted the offensive, and fought my way off the ropes. Once we were at the center of the ring, I figured that I would end the fight then and there. I threw a spinning heel kick." He stopped again.

"Just a little more," Webb urged, holding his hand.

It took a minute, but he continued. "The heel of my foot hit him in the right temple, hard. He hit the mat, like a bag of rocks. His only movements were these sickening twitches. After a minute or two, even those stopped." He stared off, captured in the memory.

"The fight doctor jumped into the ring immediately, but when he turned him over to check his pupils, we all noticed that his eyes were rolled up inside his head. When his twitching stopped, he was dead. Though the doctor said that he was likely dead, before he even hit the mat."

He looked at her. Closing his hand, around hers. "That's what I see, about nineteen nights out of each month. The twitching. The whiteness of his eyes. All because I didn't want to lose some damn belt."

"Did you mean to kill him?"

"What! No. No, I didn't. What kind of a question, is that?" he pulled away, but was stopped by the arm of the sofa.

"A question that you have been asking yourself for the past fifteen years. And now that you've just answered it. It's likely that those nightmares will leave you. Not all at once, but they will fade little by little, until the guilt of what happened no longer haunts you at all. You know that you didn't enter that ring with the sole purpose of killing that man on your mind. You entered that ring to fight, not only for a belt but for money. It was your job to be in that ring. It was his job, too. Both of you knew that there was danger involved, every time you stepped into that ring. You took that chance, and so did he. It could just as easily have been you, down on that mat."

She let go of his hand and draped her arm across his shoulders. "It wasn't just some trivial belt you were fighting over. It was your livelihood. It was an accident, Josh. It's been fifteen years, you just have to let it go. Let the guilt go. It was an accident." She turned his head to look him in the eyes. "Let it go, Josh. You have to forgive yourself, before the healing process can begin. You've already admitted that it was not your fault, that's half the battle right there. Now you have to forgive yourself. Accidents happen every day, and a lot of those accidents result in death. There's no way that you can change the past, you can only live in the now. It wasn't then, nor is it now, your fault. Just leave it behind, you have to leave it behind."

She could tell that he was still brooding over the fight, so she tried a new angle. "You've killed before, in Vietnam. Were you able to release those killings?"

"A lot of guys couldn't, but yes I let them go. But those were a faceless enemy, who were trying to kill me. I did what I had to do to get out of there alive. But I wasn't standing three feet in front of them. They weren't someone that I knew. I knew him, Nancy. When we weren't in the ring, we were friends. Not the closest of friends, but I knew him. We used to work out together. And just to keep that God damned belt, I had to kill him. Sure, not on purpose, but I killed him just the same. I stood no more than five feet away, and I watched him die."

She leaned in and held him. And with her mouth next to his ear, she whispered. "It was a mistake, an accident. You're forgiven. I'm sure that even he would forgive you, if he could. I know I do. I forgive you, Josh. I forgive you."

At 10:02 p.m. Jonathan Price left the comfort of the Ford Taurus, that set across the street from Webb's home. In the morning there were going to be U.S. Marshals crawling all over the place. And after their extraction of Doctor Webb, he and Morrow would continue the manhunt for Bray Hamlin. But his would not likely be the only case that they would be assigned. They would now have to take on more responsibility, since the Stalker's trail had gone so cold.

He switched on his flashlight as he entered the darkness that engulfed the side and backyard of the home. He took care to watch the trees and shrubbery that bordered the yard to his far left, which placed him directly in between them and the house. With his hand on his gun he moved on, searching every possible opening in the foliage where a body might fit, in an attempt to hide from the light. He even shined the light up into the tree tops. Hamlin could be anywhere and he wasn't taking any chances.

Moving into the back yard he could barely see a thing. It was much darker than the first time he swept the perimeter, the moon being only a slit in the sky. His flashlight lit up the dark only a few feet in front of him where it was then swallowed up by the pitch blackness, leaving him almost blind. He loosened his tie and unbuttoned the top button of his shirt. It was warm. Sometimes the night could be cool, but not tonight. He was worried. If something were to happen, he would be going one on one with the Stalker. Not something that he relished. Even though Hamlin hadn't been heard from in a month, he was still quite wary of his situation. Sure he had a gun, but Hamlin was a sneaky bastard and one hell of a fighter. So he had gathered, from all of the drivers licences the psycho had collected over the years. Over two hundred people he had beaten in hand to hand combat. Undefeated, to the death.

Even with all of that in mind, he was still on the job and that meant taking risks. And he was taking one hell of a risk being on outside guard, alone. Though his flashlight wasn't helping him to see much, he stepped deeper into the backyard, moving on to check out the southern tree line.

***

Cloaked in black clothing, Bray Hamlin stepped up to the same living room window that he had used to enter Webb's house the first time he had come to visit her at home. Looking in from the outside, he noticed Webb and Morrow on the couch, holding one another. Bitch! She was supposed to be his, but she was settling for some old has-been instead. Yes, he was going to kill her slowly, right after he saw just what Morrow was made of.

He looked past them, out through the doorway into the foyer. He could see half of the front door from his vantage point. The half that had the control terminal to Webb's new alarm system on it. His eyes lit up, as an evil grin crossed his lips. The light on the terminal was green. Morrow had forgotten to re-engage the system, after letting the Feds out. He was probably in too much of a hurry to see lover girl to remember to push a few buttons. He wasn't going to have to use his alarm bypassing skills tonight, after all. It was going to be like shooting fish in a barrel. Now all that he had to do was take Price out of the picture, and let the games begin.

***

Jonathan Price walked through the darkness of the home's backyard. With his tension easing up some toward the end of his second perimeter sweep, he took his hand away from his gun and covered it with his jacket. He would likely only have to make three more rounds, before the Marshals got there. Then he could go home and spend the next few days with his wife. A small leave of absence he was sure that Morrow would sign off on. A leave of absence during which he would lay around, like a bum sleeping on the boardwalk. And wished that he had become a doctor, like his mother had wanted.

From out of the darkness behind him, a silent running Bray Hamlin leapt into the air and threw a massive side-kick to his spine. A sickening crack, heard only by Price and his attacker, pre-empted his body falling lifelessly to the ground. His back, broken.

Hamlin knelt down to his side, looking him in the face. Though he lay there motionless, his eyes were still open. He wasn't dead, yet. Paralyzed, but not dead. And he could still speak.

"Man, that sounded painful. How does it feel? Oh I forgot, you can't feel anything." Hamlin laughed.

"Fuck you, you insane prick," Price spat, breathlessly. "I may be fucked, but Morrow is going to kick your fucking ass. You're going down tonight, cocksucker."

"Oh, but Morrow doesn't even know that I'm here yet. But I have plans for a title fight for later on, so he'll get his chance. But for now, let's just keep that on the down low."

"The down low, huh."

Even though his back was broken and he was totally paralyzed, Price still felt the pain of his injury. There was a sharp stabbing pain like a skewer had been lodged in his back, and it was becoming harder and harder to breath. His sight was growing dim. So if he was going to do something he'd better do it now, before it was too late.

"So you've got a little surprise match, set up between you and Josh. Only he doesn't know it yet, huh?" his breath was fading, fast.

Hamlin nodded. "Yep."

"I don't think that it's going to be as much of a surprise, as you think it will be."

"Why is that?"

At the top of his lungs, Price tried to warn of Hamlin's presence. "Josh, he's here! Hamlin is h... ."

Hamlin cupped his hand over Price's mouth, holding it shut. Then pinched his nose shut, cutting off his air supply. The only way that the Stalker could tell if Price was struggling or not, was to look into his frantic eyes. He did so for about thirty seconds, before nonchalantly looking around, while slowly suffocating a paralyzed Jonathan Price. He kept his head on a swivel, while calmly making sure that none of Webb's neighbors heard a thing. And when no one so much as turned on their back porch light, he believed that the coast was clear after five minutes of cutting off Price's air supply. Then left the dead detective and made his way toward the back door of Webb's home.

***

Morrow and Webb eased back away from each other, so that Morrow could answer his cell phone. He pulled it out of his inside jacket pocket.

"This is Morrow... What?... When?...God damn it... No, that's not necessary, we'll be fine. The Marshals will be here at 5:00 a.m.... Yeah, thanks for the heads up. Good bye." He put the phone back into his pocket.

He stood, and Webb stood with him, moving to the center of the room. Morrow was quite disturbed by the phone call he had just received, and she didn't like his sudden agitated state.

"What is it? What's wrong?"

He paused, staring at her, looking undecided as to whether he wanted to let her in on the subject of the call or not.

"Hamlin is still here, he never left the city, or the state as we had hoped, when he didn't turn up. I mean, it's been a month for Christ's sake."

"Are you sure? How do you know?" she sounded on the edge of terror.

When Hamlin had not shown himself for so long, every ones' tensions had slowly eased up. But now he was back and their anxieties were returning, ten fold. Morrow knew that he had to get back on the job. He was there to guard Webb, not to play tonsil hockey with her. No more of this touchy-feely crap. He was a cop. Webb's bodyguard. It was time that he started acting like it.

"They found another family a little while ago. They've only been dead since last night. He's still here."

"Now he must think that he is even stronger. That could provoke an attack," she warned.

"They wanted to know if we wanted any backup. I told them no. I mean, with the alarm to warn us if he tries to get in, and Price just outside, I didn't deem it necessary for back up. But if it would make you feel better, I can call them b… ."

She placed a finger to his lips. "No. I don't need anyone else. You two are just fine." She looked at her watch. "It's after 10:30 p.m. now. The Marshals will be here at 5:00 a.m. I think we're safe."

She stepped forward and kissed him, softly. But he eased her back away from him.

"I can't, not now. I really need to be sharp."

"Okay." She sounded disappointed. "When, then? I'm going to disappear tomorrow. Who knows how long I'll be gone. Will you wait until Hamlin is found? Can you wait for me?"

"You're damn right, I'll be here. With bells on. No clothes, but bells."

They shared a half-hearted laugh.

Webb stepped back. "Hey, how about some coffee."

"Sure, I could use a cup."

"I'll be right back." She turned away, heading for the kitchen.

"I'd better give Price the heads up." He picked up a hand radio off of the coffee table. "Price, it's Morrow." There was nothing but static. "Price this is Morrow, come in." Static. "Put the phone down, and stop talking dirty to your wife." Nothing in return.

Morrow spoke softly, to himself. "God damn it. He better not have left his radio in the car again."

He moved to the bay window and opened the drapes, taking a look outside. He saw the Taurus. It appeared to be empty but he was not alarmed. Price was probably on another perimeter sweep, and he was notorious for leaving his radio behind in the car, whenever on foot. He'd give him a few more minutes to finish the sweep, then he was going out after him. If Hamlin was still around, Price needed to know about it. Because the sneaky bastard could be anywhere out there. Just hiding away in the darkness, waiting for an opportunity.

CHAPTER TWENTY-THREE

Bray Hamlin snuck up to the back door of Webb's Beverly Hills home. He picked the dead bolt lock with ease, but upon opening the door he found that it only opened three inches, before the chain lock stopped it. His final cure was coming tonight and even though he would only have the essences of three people instead of five, meant nothing. He was about to push the envelope and free himself from his mortal bonds tonight. Then, come the morning, the whole world would know of his potency. And this simple chain was not going to stop him now.

Hamlin placed his shoulder to the door and leaned in on it, settling his weight behind it. Slowly increasing the pressure until little by little, he forced the screws right out of the door jam. Freeing the base of the chain lock from the jam, soundlessly. Opening the door wide he walked right into the laundry room at the very back of the house. Unheard and unannounced. Peeking through the inner doorway into the kitchen, he saw Nancy Webb standing with her back to him, waiting on the coffee she was brewing. Behind her on the table set a coffee cake. Next to that cake set an eight-inch bladed butcher knife. He waited and watched the action in the kitchen, for only a few seconds. Making positive that Morrow was not going to join her and ruin his entrance, but the scene remained the same. Morrow was no where in sight, and Webb still stood with her back to him. The setting was perfect.

He moved swiftly, entering the kitchen without a sound. Taking the knife from the table he snuck up behind Webb, grabbing her in one arm while both of his hands moved into position. One covering her mouth, and the other holding the blade of the knife to her throat.

"Welcome to my nightmare," he whispered in her ear.

Webb seized up. Every muscle in her body tightening to the likes of rigor mortis. She knew that voice, even though it was only a whisper. It was Bray Hamlin. The insane serial killer that she had broken her promise to. A promise to never tell the authorities who he was. And he held a very sharp knife to her throat.

With her personal guard having been cut in half, albeit Josh Morrow, who was armed, and a world class martial artist, was in the house but didn't know of Hamlin's presence. Armed, and ready to kill. She could only imagine where detective Price was, and how he had met his fate.

Her legs wobbled beneath her, as her breath quickened. Short breaths that threatened hyperventilation. Her body quaking, rigorously. She had never been quite so terrified before. Except maybe when Hamlin had broken into her house the first time. She was desperately trying to fight off passing out.

"Guess what I've got for you." He pressed the blade tighter to her throat. Drawing minimal blood, from the small pressure cut. "Do you remember the time, when I told you not to turn me in to the police? But you did, anyway. Do you remember what I said that I would do to you?" He sounded nostalgic, yet hard.

"Only now, I get to do three of you. Oh yeah, Price is already dead. Laying out in the backyard. He actually went out with some balls. But that's enough about him. Let's talk about you. You never did really feel safe, did you? No, I didn't think so. That's because you knew that I was coming eventually, and you've always know that there is no one that can stop me. Not even lover boy, in the living room." He spoke softly, so not to alert Morrow.

Her mind raced trying to think of some way out, but all that she could think of besides the Stalker holding a knife to her throat, was Morrow in the other room. But Hamlin already knew about him, and didn't seem to be too worried about it.

"I'm going to gut you and take your blood. Morrow's, too. Then Price's," he told her. When he spoke again he sounded sincerely sorrowed. "It's too bad that you couldn't see things my way. I would have treated you like a queen. Of course you would have been a queen. Ruling by my side. Your every want and need, your every desire, brought to you on a silver platter."

"We could have been a universal one. We could have ruled our worshipers stringently, together. It's a pity that you chose to die instead. Such a pity."

Webb began nodding only so slightly, so not to cut her throat further.

Speaking beneath his hand. Now appearing to accept his offering, unconditionally. To be his. To accept his company and rule. She didn't want any further blood shed, or death. Especially if it were on account of her. She just wanted Bray Hamlin to leave. Preferably without her, but that didn't seem to be in the cards she had been dealt. So she would go with him to avoid a clash between the Stalker and Morrow. A clash that could only end in death for one of them.

"Oh, now you want to go with me. Well I'm sorry doctor, but that offer has been rescinded. You had your chance and you blew it. You blew it, hard." He paused, while glancing down the hallway toward the living room. It was clear.

He guided her back away from the stove, and the steaming hot pot of coffee. Facing her down the hallway.

"Now it's time to go and see what lover is doing. Let's go. Move very slowly."

He guided her from behind. Leading her directly to the living room doorway, and crept inside where Morrow stood with his back to them. A portable police radio in his hand. They moved a little further inside, then Hamlin cleared his throat, announcing their presence. Which started Morrow turning in their direction.

"There's something wrong. I'm going to have to go out and look for Price." He froze, staring into the soulless eyes of the Stalker, the Devil himself.

"I'm sorry, but detective Price is no longer with us. He's lying dead in the backyard, waiting for the two of you," Hamlin told him, casually.

The Stalker stood wide open behind Webb. He didn't even try to conceal himself, giving Morrow a clear shot. But the lieutenant knew that he was just baiting him. If he went for his gun, Hamlin would cut Webb's throat. He didn't like it, but it was time to negotiate with this psychotic devil of a man.

"What do I have to do, to get that knife away from her throat?"

Hamlin shrugged a bit, a lighthearted look overcoming his usually chiseled features. "Oh, I don't know. Maybe stand on one foot and squawk like a chicken."

"Don't fuck with me, Hamlin. What do you want me to do?"

"Don't be so, rambunctious." Hamlin continued to play, "Oh, I've got it. Drop your pants and recite Mary had a little Lamb, and give the doc here a little, and I do mean little, thrill before you both die. Or maybe you can give us a striptease, while singing 'It's raining men.'"

The Stalker appeared to think for only a moment. "Ooh! How about, you take your fucking gun and you toss it toward that wall, off to your left. And I don't mean some fucking, o'lay toss either. I want you to pretend that you're pitching pennies, and see just how close you can get that fucker to that wall."

There was a cold savageness in Hamlin's eyes now. His voice, a deeply pitched fury. Yet he remained the picture of calm.

"All right, don't get happy." Morrow reached for his gun.

"Hold on there, champ." Hamlin stopped him. "Reach in there with your left hand. Using only your index finger, and thumb. Pull it out by the handle, and then throw it away. And no fucking around," the crazed billionaire ordered.

Hamlin portrayed a calmness the likes Morrow had never seen before. He was calmer than a new born baby in slumber. But his eyes told the real story. He was the figure of Death in disguise.

As for Nancy Webb, just as Hamlin held an unhumanly calm, Webb was as terrified as a child trapped in a nightmare in the endless dark of night. And the helplessness in her eyes made his heartache. But he couldn't do anything, except follow Hamlin's orders. Bray Hamlin, a notorious serial killer responsible for the deaths of hundreds, held her hostage with a knife blade to her throat. And he was about to get rid of his gun. Things were not looking up. He just hoped that Webb didn't make any sudden moves out of fear that would cost her her life.

Staring into Hamlin's crazed eyes, Morrow did as he was told. He slowly removed his .9mm from his shoulder holster, with the two fingers specified, and tossed it across the room. Where it landed very near, the far wall.

"What now?"

"Now, you can get rid of your back up," Hamlin instructed, intuitively.

"I don't carry a back up. Why don't you ease up on that knife?" Morrow bartered.

"Don't give me that shit! Any cop worth his weight in doughnuts carries a back up gun. Lift up your pant legs and show me. If you're lying, I'll cut her throat, right now!" he didn't sound very calm, anymore.

"Why don't you ease up on that knife, first. Then I'll do what you want." The knife against Webb's throat was making him nervous.

"Fuck easing up on the knife! Show me your fucking sock's! Who's in the driver's seat here, motherfucker! I'll cut her fucking head off, right now. You don't bargin with me. You don't have any options. Show me!" Hamlin exploded.

"Okay. Okay." He raised his pant legs and exposed his socks. No gun, just socks. "There, I'm unarmed. You can see that. So why don't you ease up on that knife a little, huh."

Hamlin eased up and lowered the blade to the base of Webb's throat, where he held it loosely. Removing his other hand from her mouth, he wrapped his right arm around her waist and took hold of her left hand.

"There you go. Now can't we all just get along?" He was lighthearted again.

"Okay, now that's better. What is it that I can do for you? What is it that you want?"

Hamlin continued to have his fun at the expense of their terror. "I want to end world hunger. To have peace in the Middle East. And finally, I want Gilligan to get off of that fucking island. Oh wait, he did." His eyes suddenly widened, exposing his blackened soul and glistening rage. "I want the blood from both of you fuckers, that's what I want, dick."

"How can I stop you?" Morrow wondered aloud.

"You know, I'm glad you asked that question," Hamlin began, casually. "I'll tell you what I'm gonna do. Instead of just cutting her throat and shoving this knife up your ass, being the kind hearted man, that I am, I'm going to give you both a chance. And it all rides on your shoulders."

"What kind of chance?"

An evil grin crossed Hamlin's lips. "I know what you used to be, Mr. former heavy weight kick-boxing champion. That is, until you lost your nerve after fighting the greatest fight of your career. I like to know who's pursuing me. What exactly was your record? Wins and losses."

"Eighty-one and five," Morrow obliged.

"Is that right? My personal wins and losses are just a bit better than yours. You see, I'm two hundred and twenty-seven wins, and no losses," Hamlin boasted. "I trust that you found the driver's licenses, on my basement wall?"

Morrow nodded. "Yes, we found them."

"You mean that you were telling me the truth?" Webb's very shaky voice, joined in.

"For the most part, yes. I just never told you that when they lost, they died. Don't get me wrong, they fought valiantly for the most part. That is, until they finally realized that it was to the death." He reflected back, a glistening of gratification in his steel, cold eyes.

"They were all good fighters, though. Like I told you, Doc. They were kick-boxers, karate fighters and sometimes just big, mean motherfuckers."

"What does all of that have to do with us?" Morrow asked. Though he already had a damn good idea of where Hamlin was going, with all of his talk of fighting.

"I'll get to that a little later. Right now I'd like to know just how hard I made it for you to catch me? I made it hard, I know. I probably gave you fits, didn't I? I can only imagine what it must have been like for you." Hamlin grinned, smugly. "It must have been like trying to find a member of the Hells Angels, in a gay bar. Or a real set of tits in Hollywood. Or coming across an Italian war hero."

Morrow nodded somewhat. "Yeah okay, I get it. A needle in a hay stack."

"What?"

"That's enough! I'm getting tired of your fucking games. Just tell me what in the hell you want." Morrow was pissed.

The smile faded from the Stalker's face. It was apparent that he was finally ready to be totally serious. Something that they were likely going to regret.

"You retired the heavy weight champion of the world. Now I may not be a heavy weight. Actually, I'm probably a bit smaller than you all thought."

The six foot tall Morrow did notice from across the room that Hamlin was a bit smaller than they had thought. "Yeah, we were expecting a five-ten, body builder. But I guess I'll have to settle for you."

Hamlin's face became chiseled with rage, his eyes shooting daggers. "I want a shot at the title," he began, disturbingly calm. "You and me, a fight to the death. Right here, right now. If you win, you save your new lover. I die and you stop the Stalker. But when I win, you both die and I wear your blood. What'da ya say?" he proposed, spiritedly.

"Do you get to keep the knife?"

"No, it's going to be hand to hand, just the way that God intended it to be. I want a fair shot at the title." He paused, digging into his bag of appropriately timed zingers. "And believe me when I say I'm going to hit you harder than Teddy Kennedy does a bottle of vodka."

"What about Doctor Webb?"

"Oh, don't worry about her. She'll be right here, watching you die. All the while knowing that she's next. But before we get this on, I have a little message for the good doctor, from Brooke. That's right, Nancy. She was still alive when you turned me in. So until I could come for you, now, I took her slowly. Skinning her alive six inches at a time, for days. I did half her body, before I finally decided to just put her out of my misery."

Webb cried for her friend. She had killed her. She never held the blade, but she took her life just the same when she turned Hamlin in. Giving her up for dead.

"Don't worry, Nancy. I finished her off in a good way. She was such a sex kitten, I got her good, just the way she liked it. I fucked her to death with nine inches of razor sharp, stainless steel. I've never heard a woman scream so loud. And trust me, I've penetrated some pretty tight orifices in my time. But damn... . Did you know that she was a screamer?" he appeared to be entranced by the reminder of his conquest. That, and he was just being a prick.

"And do you know what was strange? The younger the better, right? She was in her twenties, but her essence was very powerful. It must have been because she was such a vibrant soul. That you caused to be extinguished."

Webb continued to cry and began shaking. Her captor having to hold her up, because of her legs buckling beneath her.

"Oh come on now, don't be such a baby. You knew that she was dead. You just didn't know when she died. Buck up, because I have a message for you, from her. Her last words, really. Lets see, what were they exactly? Oh yeah, that's right. She wanted me to tell you, 'Aahhhh!'" he screamed in her ear at the top of his lungs, laughing afterward.

Morrow had had enough. He took a step forward, but Hamlin pressed the blade against Webb's throat again

"Not so fast. We're going to do this on my start, not yours."

Morrow raised his shoulders. "So when do we start?"

Hamlin spun Webb out to his right, like twirling a dance partner. Then shot out a side-kick to her back, sending her to the floor screaming in agony. He stuck the knife into the door jam a good two inches deep, then faced Morrow again.

"How about right now, you old pussy."

They moved in on one another, amongst the living room furniture. It was just like two fights in a ring, but there were no ropes to limit the fighting ground. The fight itself would be no holds barred, and to the death. The last man with a pulse, wins.

Morrow threw a spinning heel kick toward Hamlin's head, but the Stalker ducked out of the way and moved in quickly, punching Morrow in the stomach. Following it with a ridge-hand to the shoulder, fracturing Morrow's collarbone. The former champion backed away swiftly, then attacked right back with a front kick to Hamlin's chest, as the Stalker moved in on him, sending him staggering him back. Morrow moved in on his adversary, hitting him in the nose with a left jab. The Stalker's head snapped back, as blood seeped from his nostrils. But even with watery eyes, Hamlin wasted no time in retaliating. A spinning back kick to Morrow's chest sent him floating backward, where he crashed hard to the floor.

Again, Hamlin wasted no time in moving in on his opponent. He lifted Morrow to his feet and hit him with a right cross. Then spun into a left back fist, ending the flurry with a front-kick to his stomach. Dropping Morrow to the floor, again. Morrow was quick to regain his feet, as Hamlin closed on him. They met in front of the sofa and coffee table, where Morrow thrust a spinning back kick to the Stalker's chest. Driving him back, but he did not go down.

Instead, Hamlin's eyes widened with a fierce intensity. A devilish smile crossing his lips. "Yeah, lets go! Show me what you've got left, old man!"

By the arm of her lounge chair, Nancy Webb pulled herself up from the floor, to her knees. Which wasn't an easy task being that her arms and legs were very weak, and shaking because of the kick to her back, courtesy of Bray Hamlin. Her back was rigid and inflamed with fiery, stabbing pain. Continuing to use the chair's arm, she was finally able to raise herself to her feet. But with her legs barely beneath her, she wavered unsteady. She kept her feet by clinging to the chair. Watching the fight for a moment she repeatedly straightened herself, only to be forced to bow over again because of the stiffening pain. After several minutes she was finally able to stand up somewhat straight, using the arm of the chair as a crutch to keep herself from falling back into the prone position.

From her vantage point it appeared that Bray Hamlin was landing more blows. He was much faster than Morrow, but the lieutenant seemed to be holding his own against the Stalker. They were both bleeding from the nose and mouth. Hamlin's jaw was heavily bruised, more than likely from a kick. And Morrow's left eye was black and blue, and almost completely swollen shut.

She looked across the room for Morrow's gun, where she found it laying some fifteen feet away. Now all that she had to do was reach it, which wouldn't have been any problem had Hamlin not assaulted her with a kick to the back. But, as it was, her legs were very unstable beneath her, and her back was on fire with agonizing pain and stiffness.

Grabbing each piece of furniture as she came to it, she helped herself along, moving as though her legs were paralyzed. More or less dragging them behind her at times. Each piece of furniture served as a stepping stone toward her objective, Morrow's gun. But she quickly ran out of furniture and fell to the floor, dragging herself along with terribly weakened arms. Her legs almost useless. Inching her way toward what might possibly be her only means of salvation.

Her crawl was frenzied, but slow moving. She knew that she had to reach the gun, before the fight was over. Because her defender was being beaten to the punch on a regular basis now, so she saw over her shoulder. He was still a great fighter, but over a decade older than the thirty-eight-year-old Hamlin. To old to even suggest that he might have a chance against the Stalker. Hamlin even appeared to be toying with him at times. Out fighting the ex-champ with his blazing speed and maneuvers, beyond Morrow's comprehension. She hated to think of it, but Morrow was out of his league against Hamlin. And she had a terrible feeling, more of an aching in her heart really, that told her that Hamlin was going to be the victor in this match between them. A match to the death.

Morrow threw a painful right cross, his broken collarbone in flames. But Hamlin was quick to block it and retaliated with a right hand to Morrow's kidney, then an immediate straight out punch to the ex-champ's chest. Hitting him squarely in the breast-bone. Morrow clenched his chest with both hands, agonizing, while the Stalker readied himself for another strike, unfazed by the pain in his fist.

Hamlin stepped forward and threw two punches, one immediately after the other. Morrow dodged the first and blocked the second, then sent the Stalker staggering with a front-kick to the chest. But again Hamlin did not go down, instead he just stood there his face animated with beaming insanity, ready for more. Morrow moved in on him slowly, looking for a hole in his defenses. That's when the Stalker's hands dropped low just above the waist, as though he were anticipating a low blow to his stomach or legs. Leaving himself wide open for a chest or head shot, and Morrow wasted no time in exploiting this weakness. He spun quickly, throwing a spinning heel kick toward the Stalker's jaw, but Hamlin was only baiting him and was more than ready for the kick. He quickly side stepped and blocked Morrow's kick with his forearms and caught his leg on the way down, cradling it in one arm while wrapping his free arm around Morrow's waist, lifting him up chest high before throwing him down on the hard wood and glass top coffee table, splintering the wood and shattering the glass.

Hamlin was enraptured. He wrestled Morrow to his feet and spun him around twice before letting him go, flinging him across the room where he hit the wall next to the fireplace, with bone shaking force. Knocking the wind out of him, and inflaming his back, fiery and numb. Where he slid down the wall to rest on the floor in agony.

The Stalker hustled back to the knife and pulled it from the door jam, he was tired of playing around with such an inferior opponent. "Enough fucking around. This game is over."

Hamlin took long strides to cross the room, rushing to claim his latest victim. Morrow moved slowly, but as fast as he could to regain his feet. His back being rigid with obvious broken ribs, but as soon as he stood Hamlin was there and he had not a second to defend himself, before the Stalker shoved the blade deep into his abdomen. Morrow grunted loud, in the most pain he had ever experienced in his life. He could feel the cold steel inside of him, cutting through his organs. Knowing at that moment that he was not only going to die, but he was going to be leaving Nancy Webb to fend for herself, against Hamlin's obvious intentions to kill her and wear her blood.

Hamlin grabbed him under the chin and raised his head to look him squarely in the eyes, twisting the blade, just to see the look of complete anguish on Morrow's face. The blood from the wound increased from a steady trickle to a near stream, as the ex-champ tried to hold his stomach closed to keep his organs from spilling out onto the floor.

Hamlin had a euphoric look in his eyes. "Now introducing, the new, heavy weight champion of the world."

Morrow's blood doused Hamlin's ungloved hand, animating the Stalker into an almost orgasmic state. He stared into Morrow's drooping eyes.

"Do you feel it? Do you feel your life essence withdrawing from your body? Tell me, what does it feel like? To die, I mean. You see, I'll never know that experience myself. Tell me."

Blood began seeping from Morrow's mouth much more than before, and he spit it in Hamlin's face. "Fuck you."

But the Stalker only seemed to enjoy it, the blood on his skin and made no attempt to wipe it off. "No, fuck you." He suddenly yanked the blade out of Morrow's body and allowed him to slump to the floor.

CHAPTER TWENTY-FOUR

Hamlin had seen Webb trying to scurry away while he battled Morrow, but when he turned to see where it was that she was trying to escape to, that's when the first shot hit him. The .9mm slug tore into his shoulder. His body jerked from the impact, but he felt no pain. His ascension must have been completed with the essences of the family he had taken, the night before. In his mind he was immortal, unable to be killed by some piss ant little gun. But her treachery swung him from splendor to a disturbed fury in mere seconds.

"What in the hell do you think you're doing? You can't kill me, Nancy. I am complete. I am a god. All that you've managed to do is ruin a five hundred dollar shirt. Now give me that gun." He took a step.

With her legs barely able to hold her own weight, she wavered while her weakened arms struggled to keep the gun trained on him. She fired two more shots, the first striking Hamlin in the upper chest and the second shattering a lamp behind him. He looked down at the wound in his chest, sticking his pinky finger in it, sizing up the damage that would heal itself almost immediately. He looked back at Webb, even more disturbed than before.

"Kill him." Morrow spoke up, very weak.

Hamlin pointed the knife at him. "You, shut the fuck up. Why don't you just die already."

He turned his attention back to Webb. "That's a sixteen shot .9mm you're holding. Fifteen in the clip, and one in the breech. That's not enough. Trust me, there can never be enough. Drop it right now and I'll kill you quick. But shoot me again, and it will take days," the Stalker promised.

"Shoot him," Morrow told her.

Hamlin took two steps and Webb fired three more times, all three slugs hitting him in the chest. He grimaced somewhat then took two more steps, as blood began to seep from his mouth in a steady trickle. The front of his black shirt noticeably wet.

"That's it, I'm going to skin you alive, just like Brooke," he said, with pure fury.

The mentioning of May's name didn't bode well with Webb, but she was still scared shitless and the searing pain in her back left her legs unsteady and shaky beneath her. But she was able to stay her ground and pull the trigger four more times. The first two slugs missed the mark completely. The third lodged itself in Hamlin's right thigh, the force of the slug nearly sweeping his leg out from under him, but he managed to keep his feet. The forth slug embedded its self into his stomach, but he kept coming undaunted.

It was unbelievable. Her greatest fear involving the Stalker case was that Hamlin, in his own mind, would be in such a state of belief of his immortality it would become genuine, and no amount of lead would put him down; he would continue his assault either until he bled out or she struck enough vital organs to drop him. So if she had to get away from him, she was dead. She could barely stand, much less run away.

Hamlin kept his stride and slowly gained ground on her. With blood spilling out over his bottom lip covering his chin and soaking his shirt, drizzling to the floor. He still kept coming. His body was swaying a bit, with his legs starting to shake with every step. His eyes continually trying to roll up inside his head, but he kept coming.

"You just couldn't understand, could you? I wanted you to be mine. We could have lived together forever, immortal. But you had to fuck it up, you had to turn me in. You just couldn't understand and now, now I wouldn't have you if you begged me. And believe me, when your skin starts to peel from your body, you will beg. You'll beg for death. Don't worry though, I'll be sure to make certain that you're still alive when I gut you."

He kept walking slowly but steadily, a wheezing sound venting from a punctured lung. Webb closed one eye and tried to sight on his heart. She pulled the trigger, but the slug hit him in the lower pectoral region. He smiled at her his teeth bloody, as he breathed short, rapid, wheezing breaths. Webb pulled the trigger and held it down for no more than a second, but the automatic fired three shots. Two of which struck Hamlin in the chest. Bloody bubbles of air began accompanying the spillage from his mouth, but he still would not stop. He would not go down. His physical strength and his maddened mind would not allow him to fall. She had only two more shots and then he would be on her. He was too close as it was already, with the bloodied butcher knife still clutched tightly in his hand.

Her legs nearly gave out under her own weight, but she managed to keep her feet and took aim once more. He was almost on top of her now. She squeezed the trigger and a single shot found it's way to Hamlin's heart. He stopped in his tracks, but only for a moment, a glassy-eyed stare about him. He was covered in blood, only this time it was his own. Miraculously, he took two more steps toward her. He was no more than three feet or so away now, raising the bloodied knife.

"You can't... kill me. The Stalker...is all... powerful." He breathed shallow breaths, the wheezing from his punctured lung becoming more and more apparent. "Your essence...will be... mine. Your life... is over." Blood poured from his mouth, dousing the floor where he stood. He was as pale as death itself but he stepped forward one more time, the knife raised to strike.

Nancy Webb extended her weakened arm, the barrel of the .9mm no more than one inch from Hamlin's forehead. With her fear having subsided completely, a great animosity took her over as though she were possessed.

"You need me to understand you, to believe in you so that you can believe that you are what you want to be. Well I don't believe in the boogieman, so stalk this."

She pulled the trigger.

The slug tore through Hamlin's skull, leaving a hole the size of a child's fist in the back of his head. He stood there for a moment longer before his eyes rolled up inside his head, the knife falling to the floor, where he soon joined it, hitting the floor like a bag of rocks where he lay in a pool of his own blood. Poetically ironic.

Webb dropped the gun and began to cry, her body quaking. She took shaky baby steps around Hamlin's body as she headed across the room toward a slumped over Josh Morrow. Stopping along the way to pick up the phone and dial 911. With an immediate answer on the other end of the line, she told them only what was necessary.

"We need help. Lieutenant Morrow is down, the Stalker is dead. Come quickly, please." She dropped the receiver with the dispatcher still on the line.

She gradually made her way over to Morrow and agonizingly lowered herself to her knees the muscles in her back, rigid and stiff like a board burning like a wild fire. She could tell that he was still alive, barely. She touched his face lightly and lifted his head to look him in the eyes.

"I've called for help, they'll be here soon," she spoke softly so not to allow her voice to quake.

"There's no need." He choked up blood. "We both know that I'm not going to make it to any hospital, it's too late. It was too late when he first stuck me." He looked down at his wound.

She followed his gaze and there she saw his hands holding his insides back from spilling out on to the floor.

She cried. "I'm sorry that I couldn't get to the gun in time. I could have stopped him."

"You did stop him. This isn't your fault, you know that." He coughed up more blood. "He was just better than me." His eyes began to droop.

"No Josh, hold on. Don't leave me."

"Don't worry about me, Nancy. You made me see that my guilt was not just. It wasn't my fault that my opponent died, it was an accident. I won't be taking that guilt with me. Thank you for that. I've accepted that it wasn't my fault. Now you have to do the same." His eyelids lowered and his breaths grew shorter. He grimaced and coughed, spewing up blood.

"You even helped yourself. Now you don't have to leave your life behind. And you've saved countless lives. You bagged the Stalker." He closed his eyes and exhaled his last breath, laying dead in her arms.

She heard the sounds of sirens closing in, fast. Help was coming, but they were much too late. She held Morrow, cradling him in her arms, rocking back and forth, crying. She held him, uncaring of the sight of his organs spilled out over the floor.

When the police arrived on the scene they had to kick in the door to gain entrance into her home. But once inside, no one even attempted to remove her, because no one wanted to get that close to the carnage. So she continued to hold him and rock him like an infant. She held him and would not let go, not until the coroner arrived and separated them. She started to scream and shake hysterically, once Morrow was pulled from her grasp. An EMT had to give her a sedative before she could be removed and transported to the hospital.

Only after the crime scene pictures were taken and the chalk outlines were drawn were Morrow and his remains scooped up into a body bag and carried out to the coroner's vehicle, with Bray Hamlin being carried out right behind him. Detective Price was found in the backyard where the Stalker had let him lay, and was taken away as well.

***

Nancy Webb was restless during her week long stay at L.A. Memorial Hospital. She awoke every night in a cold sweat, reliving the terror of that night only a short time ago.

Though the media couldn't wait to get an interview with her about her near death at the hands of the Stalker, and the actual history of her connection to the most feared serial killer ever known in the City of Angeles, she wasn't seeing anyone but the police and the FBI about the whole of the events that left two police officers and one psychopath dead. As far as she was concerned, the authorities could tell the tale of the Stalker to the prying media. All that she wanted to do was heal her physical wounds and try to repair her fractured psyche. But with dreams of the Stalker haunting her nights and the mad mans' imposed will influencing her mind-set during the light of day, his grotesque and perverse thoughts, mixing with her own, her mind took its time in ridding itself of these visions and psychotic sentiments.

But the one good thing that had come out of all that had transpired that night, was that Bray Hamlin could no longer hurt her or anyone else. He could no longer take the innocent lives of anymore families. He no longer held the City of Angeles hostage within his reign of terror. The Stalker was dead and gone and hopefully, by the grace of God, burning in hell where he belonged. And she prayed that there would never be another one like him again.

EPILOGUE

Now, two years after the Stalker had been laid to rest, high in the mountains of Boulder Colorado, Nancy Webb had retired from her practice and sought the seclusion of these mountains, far and away from the disturbed and emotional distressed sea of humanity, known as the City of Angels. And the world in general.

In this new peaceful and serene setting, she had the time now to truly exorcize what demons from her association with the Stalker that she had left haunting her psyche. Then there was her short infatuation with, and the death of, Josh Morrow. And the physical and mental trauma caused by Bray Hamlin were still taking their own sweet time to heal. Her nightmares of that night two years ago used to haunt her dreams constantly. And at times she could still feel the presence of the Stalker. Mostly at night, when her mind was more susceptible to his madness. Her days however were easier. Painting, bird watching and long walks through the wooded terrain around her cabin, with her dog and only companion, a gigantic Rottweiler aptly named Moose.

Moose gave her comfort. She felt safe with him. Just as she had felt with Josh Morrow, before that illusion was shattered by the evil of Bray Hamlin. But if in some way Moose were taken away from the safety equation, she had a .38 revolver that sometimes rested in her bedroom night stand, but usually it was in a holster on her hip, as it was now while she sat on the cabin's front porch, in her rocking chair where she relaxed with Moose by her side.

She wore it everywhere that she went, with the exception of town. So when she went for supplies she relied solely upon Moose. She liked to believe that she wasn't being paranoid, but she knew different. She had a gun and a huge dog to protect her. But to protect her from what? She lived high in the mountainous region, at least fifty miles to the nearest point of civilization. She kept telling herself that there was nothing to be afraid of anymore, but her doors and windows were always locked up tight when the night came. She slept with her revolver unholstered and lying on the night stand beside her bedside, always within reach. And with Moose never far away.

She was still probing her own psyche even now, years after the incident was over. She counseled herself on a daily, and sometimes nightly, basis. Trying to once and for all rid herself of the Stalker's psychotic visions of grandeur and relieve herself of the entire occurrence. But Hamlin's evil had laid down roots deep in her mind, more than she had thought. The psychosis of his mind stuck inside of hers, not wanting to let go.

Unfortunately for her, ridding herself of Bray Hamlin meant the possibility of forgetting Josh Morrow and the short time that they had spent together. It hurt her terribly, having to come to terms with the notion that a man that she had come to care for was dead and buried because of her. It pained her soul. But Morrow had told her, just before he died, that it was her turn now to forgive herself for something that was not her fault. And she was slowly coming to grips with it all. Trying to accept the loss and the terror and lay it to rest once and for all. Her mind as well as her life, were slowly coming back to her and were nearly hers once again.

***

Guiding his Jeep four wheel drive over the rocky, dirt roads of the mountainous terrain, further and further back into the deep woods, detective sergeant William Hollosey of the Denver police department searched for the cabin of the renowned psychologist, Nancy Webb. He remembered the Stalker case of two years ago, in Los Angeles. He also remembered that it was Webb who had profiled him for the police and ultimately brought him to justice. He knew that she had retired and moved into these mountains, after her deadly confrontation with the psychotic Bray Hamlin. According to Webb's realtor he was on the right track. Now he just needed to keep his eyes open for the hidden entrance to the driveway to her cabin.

Hollosey was hoping that Webb would come out of retirement, just long enough to give him an accurate profile of a killer that was just as audacious and insane as the Stalker once was.

The newspaper and television reporters were calling him the Decapitator, for obvious reasons. He was slippery and cautious and had killed five young women up to this point. And it was just his dumb luck to have drawn the assignment, just a little under a month ago. He had no leads, no suspects and no witnesses. He had passed on the police psychiatrist's profile of the killer, mainly because the guy didn't know what the fuck he was talking about. It was the worst piece of garbage he had ever read. So he decided to solicit a second opinion from the formerly renowned psychologist, Nancy Webb. He had read her profile on the Stalker and found it to be nearly perfect, and hoped that she could do the same for the Decapitator.

He found the entrance to a driveway that he hoped would lead him to the retired Dr. Webb's cabin, here high in the mountains. It was a bit narrow and bumpy as hell, but it was no problem for the Jeep. Soon he saw the tip of an A-frame roof and as he drew closer to the cabin he could see a lovely blonde woman sitting on the deck-like front porch, with a monster of a Rottweiler sitting right beside her. He stopped the Jeep at the end of the driveway, no more than twelve feet away from the porch. Both Webb and the dog watched him as he stretched after leaving the confines of the Jeep. It had been a long ride and he wasn't relishing the return trip, especially without Webb's profile. He closed the Jeep's door and in that instance, Moose stood up. His heart jumped into his throat, but Webb pet Moose and whispered in his ear, and he sat back down.

"Who are you, and what do you want?" she spoke suddenly.

"I'm detective sergeant Hollosey, of the Denver police department. I was wondering if I might have a moment of your time?"

"For what?"

Holosey reached back into the Jeep through the open driver's window, and produced a briefcase. "You really have to ask? It's been all over the news for the past month."

"I don't want anything to do with the news. I don't read the paper, and I don't have a television. It's nothing but bad news, anyway. So I'm afraid I don't know what it is that you're talking about."

He took a few steps closer. "He's not going to attack me, is he?" he motioned toward Moose.

She shook her head. "Only if I tell him to."

"Then may I come closer?"

"Sure."

Hollosey approached the porch, stopping at the bottom of the stairs.

"Can I see some identification?"

"Absolutely." He reached inside his suit coat and produced his badge and photo I.D.

She leaned forward in her chair and looked the I.D. over, then sit back again, petting Moose. "Okay, you're a cop. Now what do you want from me?"

He replaced his I.D. in his pocket. "Well, we have ourselves a serial killer in Denver, and I was wondering if—"

"I don't do that, anymore," she cut him off.

"Can I at least tell you about him?"

She raised her shoulders. "It doesn't matter if you do, or if you don't. Like I said, before. I don't do that, anymore."

"People are dying. Five, so far. Don't you even care?" he wondered, dejected.

She shrugged again. "Not anymore."

"I can't believe that. You've been a caring healer for nearly two decades. You can't just switch it off."

"I didn't just switch it off. It's taken me two long years, and counting. Just let me let go," she told him.

"Can I at least tell you about him? Then you, decide. Please?" Hollosey implored.

She thought it over for a few minutes, then said, "Fine."

Hollosey set his briefcase on the stairs and opened it, removing a single file and started reading from it.

"It started a little under a month ago. All of the victims are young women, in their mid-twenties. It is believed that he kills them, decapitates them and then rapes them. In that order. The decapitation is post mortem, so is the forceable entry of the rape. The rape coming much later than the decapitation. Apparently the sick fuck likes to wait for rigormortis to set in, for a tighter sexual encounter."

He held out some pictures for her to look at, but she refused to take them. So he replaced them back into the briefcase, and continued reading.

"He must keep their heads as souvenirs, because we haven't found one, yet. The coroner says that he bleeds them out, before he does anything else. They all have a small circular wound just below the naval, directly into the stomach. We believe it's a screwdriver."

He shuffled through the pages. "There's an indentation tattoo around the wound of a drainage plate. But the name on the thing is so worn that we have nothing to go on there."

He flipped further through the pages. "We figure it goes something like this. He grabs them from behind and most likely knocks them unconscious. Their hands are then bound behind their backs; that's why there's never any tissue samples under their fingernails, because by the time that the struggling begins they're already bound. And that's the way they're found. Nude, their hands bound behind their backs, and decapitated. In normally quiet areas around the city. Quiet until now, anyways. He drops them along side of the road, usually back in the grass a little. But he doesn't even try to hide them, in any way. He just tosses them there and leaves them.

"He uses a condom when he rapes them. He leaves it laying there, right on the body. But we're shit out of luck with the DNA. sample from the sperm. That is, until we get a suspect to match it with. So far the abductions have been from all over the city. Mostly from low-income housing neighborhoods. So we've found out by the two that we were able to identify by finger prints. Besides that, there's no pattern. Not yet, anyway. The drop off points are also random. Yet they're in the same types of neighborhoods, all over the city." He paused, while staring down at the file.

"He leaves nothing but the sperm-filled condoms, behind. Not one hair. Not one print, foot or finger. In short, this guy's a fucking ghost. So do you think that you can help me?"

Webb began rocking in her chair, shaking her head. "I'm sorry. My heart goes out to the victims and their families, but I just can't help you. I don't do that, anymore," she echoed her earlier sentiments.

Hollosey step foot on the bottom stair. "Look, I know what happened with the Stalker case. But I'm here to tell you your name will not be issued to the press. No one but you and I will ever know about your involvement in this case. This guy won't even know that you exist. Please doctor, help me. Help me save these young women," he implored, his eyes calling out to her.

She sat quietly, staring at him. Petting Moose. An uncertain look about her.

"I know that you're concerned about your safety. But all I can do is promise you that only you and I will ever know of your involvement. That's all I can do, is promise you that. I swear, no one will ever know," he guaranteed.

Again, she said nothing. She just stared at him, and pet Moose. "Give me the files," she spoke suddenly.

Hollosey pulled out a short stack of five files from his briefcase and walked up the porch, handing them over to her. Moose's eyes followed his every move, but he stayed where he sat, beside her.

***

Sergeant Hollosey sat on the porch steps drawing in the dirt with a long stick, while Webb studied the files for a little more than an hour and a half. He had to lean away from Moose every now and then, because the monstrous Rottweiler kept sniffing at his ear. Finally Webb made a move. She handed Hollosey back the files, then returned to her rocking chair.

"You might want to write this down, because I'm only going to say it once. Then I'm going to ask you to leave my property, and never come back again," she forewarned.

Hollosey tossed the files back into his briefcase, and readied pen and paper. "Shoot."

"He is Caucasian, because all of his victims are and serial killers tend to hunt within their own ethnic group. He is young, in his twenties. Twenty to twenty-five years old. He lives alone, definitely in a secluded area. He doesn't want any nosy neighbors poking around. He needs privacy, so that he may execute his chores.

"The drain is likely in the basement of his home, where he can hose down his girls. Washing away their blood, urine and excrement. He wouldn't want a dirty lover, so he must make them presentable. The heads are not just souvenirs. I believe that he takes the heads off before he rapes them so that he doesn't have to face them. But he does keep the heads, as keepsakes, or trophies. Some men make notches in their bedposts, he keeps their heads. He might even set the heads off to the side while he rapes them, so that they can witness what he's doing to them. He probably rapes them several times, there is even evidence that he sodomizes them. He's likely trying to humiliate them.

"He humiliates them like maybe he was, in the past. Not exactly in the same way, mind you. But humiliated, just the same. By his mother, or even an older sister. I don't think that he had brothers, and he definitely never knew his father. There likely never was a male figure in his life. He was never taught to be a man.

"His mother was likely his only authority figure while he was growing up, and she emasculated him. Yet he doesn't do what he does, to get even with her."

"Then what does he do it, for?" Hollosey broke in.

"I was just getting to that… he desires women just like any other man, but he's vastly intimidated. Afraid of them. The intimidation factor is probably caused by his mother's dominance over him. But still, he's not looking to get even. But that is why he takes them by surprise. He's very easily intimidated, and likely not very strong. So he knocks them unconscious, then binds and gags them while they're still out. That way they no longer pose a physical threat to him. The gag, I believe, is applied because their screams may disturb him. He was likely scolded quite often by his mother as a child, and can no longer tolerate that octave, that pitch, of a woman's voice."

She watched Hollosey as he turned his notebook to a clean sheet. Trying to keep up with her.

"He is socially inept. Not only when it comes to women, but society in general. He's a cast off, a loner. He likely drives a van. Something to cart his victims in back and forth from pick up to drop off, without being seen. Right now the abductions appear to be at random, but soon a pattern will form. A circular pattern. His home will be somewhere near the center of that circle."

"How do you figure?"

"He's too afraid to venture off too far from his home. He may have some type of disorder that allows him to collect social security benefits, or some other type of state assistance. He doesn't work, I'm sure of that. As far as the circle goes, I'd say that none of his victims thus far, nor will any future victims be abducted anymore than twenty miles or so, from his home. So you may want to cross reference any owners or renters of any secluded homes, twenty miles in from the existing circle, what there is of it, anyway, with anyone in that area receiving some type of government assistance and who drives a van.

"As for the heads, most serial killers like to take trophies to remind them of their conquest. The same goes with your boy. He likes to feel strong, something that he's not. He keeps the heads to remember the physical dominance he held over his victims. He likes to look at the fear in their eyes, again and again. It empowers him to see this fear that he has instilled in them. They're likely on display at his home, most definitely in the basement."

"So apparently, he's never heard of a fucking camera." Hollosey wrote in his notebook. "But what's the deal with the condoms? Does he just want to be sure that we know that he's raping them, or what? I mean, he's leaving his DNA at every crime scene. If we were to bring him in as a suspect, say from within the circle you mentioned, we've got him. So why leave the condoms behind?"

"I believe that he only uses the condoms to keep from catching a disease. He probably doesn't even think about it in the way of leaving DNA behind. He's just a very timid and frightened man. He just doesn't want to catch anything. He desires physical contact that in no other way would he receive. So leaving the condoms at the crime scene doesn't really concern him. He probably doesn't even realize that he could be implicating himself, if brought in as a suspect. Actually, he probably doesn't even realize that he's begun a pattern around his home. Not realizing that he's setting himself up for a fall. As for why he leaves the condoms at the crime scene, instead of just flushing them down the toilet, I don't know. Maybe it's all a part of his bad boy image. His defiance against women."

She held a long pause, trying to think of anything else that might be of some use to Hollosey's search for the Decapitator. But nothing else came to mind.

"I'm sorry, but that's all that I have for you. Now please, go."

Hollosey nodded with a bit of a smile, as he put away his pen and notebook. Locking up his briefcase he stepped off the stairs and walked over to the Jeep, tossing the briefcase inside. He looked back at Webb. She was sitting as she had been when he had first arrived, a little more than two hours ago. Staring off in to the woods, petting Moose. He had intended on thanking her, but decided against disturbing her any further. Besides, he wasn't even sure that she would acknowledge him any longer. Although she had given him a very detailed profile on the Decapitator, she appeared to be a bit odd to him. But then again, anyone would be after having to face such a once in a lifetime psychopath like the Stalker. So instead he just climbed into the Jeep, turned it around in the clearing in front of the cabin and slowly drove away until he could no longer see Webb's cabin in his rearview mirror.

***

Nancy Webb continued to sit on the porch of her cabin, petting Moose as the sun began its descent. Once the darkness had come and the full blackness of the Colorado mountains had settled in, she moved inside the cabin into the light, away from the night. Away from the blackness of the human heart. The dark, and the unimaginable horrors of the human mind.

Printed in the United States
1463400004B/389

9 781591 292791